Fleur McDonald has lived and worked on farms for much of her life. After growing up in the small town of Orroroo in South Australia, she went jillarooing, eventually co-owning an 8000-acre property in regional Western Australia.

Fleur likes to write about strong women overcoming adversity, drawing inspiration from her own experiences in rural Australia. She has two children, an energetic kelpie and a Jack Russell terrier.

www.fleurmcdonald.com

FLEUR McDONALD
Fool's Gold

ALLEN&UNWIN
SYDNEY・MELBOURNE・AUCKLAND・LONDON

First published in 2018

Allen & Unwin
83 Alexander Street
Crows Nest NSW 2065
Australia
Phone: (61 2) 8425 0100
Email: info@allenandunwin.com
Web: www.allenandunwin.com

 A catalogue record for this book is available from the National Library of Australia

ISBN 978 1 76029 396 3

Set in 12.4/18.2 pt Sabon LT Pro by Bookhouse, Sydney
Printed and bound in Australia by Griffin Press

10 9 8 7 6 5 4 3 2 1

MIX
Paper from
responsible sources
FSC® C009448

The paper in this book is FSC® certified. FSC® promotes environmentally responsible, socially beneficial and economically viable management of the world's forests.

To those who are precious

Prologue

1945

The stars and the cold breeze were the only witnesses to the death.

Perhaps a bird saw the woman throwing the rope over the branch of the thick salmon gum, and maybe a dingo, sniffing along a scent, stopped to watch the woman take the steps to her final breath.

Paddy doubted it though.

It had been weeks since he'd seen a dingo and no doubt even longer since one had passed this way through the thick bush north of Barrabine. Water out here was scarce and wild dogs, like all creatures, stayed within walking distance of a watering point.

Scratching his head in distress, Paddy stood and watched the body swing gently for a few more moments. He'd heard about scenes like this over the years, but had never seen one firsthand. He wished he hadn't come across this one—the whole sight was causing his heart anguish.

Even though there didn't seem to be any witnesses, there had been visitors. What would have been a pool of blood on the ground under the body was now a small hole where the ants had scavenged. The line of moving black was scurrying busily up the tree trunk, across the branches and down the end of the rope for titbits to take back to their queen. A crow had been sitting on the dead woman's shoulder when Paddy had first arrived. The damage the bird had done to her face was indescribable.

Looking away, he surveyed the familiar landscape. Red earth stretched for miles, scattered lumps of ironstone and quartz lying on the surface. Saltbush and bluebush littered the landscape, while salmon gums and gimlet trees rose tall and majestic against the blue sky.

The landscape was harsh; hot and dry. Too hard for some, while others loved it. The land, weather and life had clearly been too tough for this woman. It was pointless to question her decision; there would be many reasons, he knew. He'd heard about them from his friends and their wives—too isolated, too hot, too hard. Paddy understood. Sometimes, when he'd finished shovelling dirt from the depths of the earth without finding any gold, he'd thought life was too hard as well.

He searched the area for any sign of life—a little humpy or camp, the smell of smoke—but the landscape lay quiet, not revealing where she had come from or who had loved her. Barrabine, the closest town, was too far; she wouldn't have walked from there. She would have lived around here somewhere. Somewhere within the vast miles of red dust, little water and no company. With a man gripped by gold fever.

He'd seen it before and knew he would continue seeing the pattern for as long as he travelled through these empty miles.

Still, surely someone had to be missing her. Or perhaps he hadn't been back to camp to realise she was missing yet. What if there were children . . . No, he banished that thought. No mother would have left her children at camp by themselves to do this.

Scratching at his three-day growth and keeping his eyes averted now, he felt agitated and sad, as though he had to do something for her. But what? It was too late to help her. Too late to plead with her not to do this.

Paddy did the only thing he thought right. He took a shovel from his battered old car and began to dig. He'd give her a burial so the dingos couldn't dig her up or the crows peck at her. Or the ants finish eating her. Then he would travel to Barrabine, stopping in at all the little digs along the way, letting people know what he'd found.

The next of kin might be angry he had buried her, but the way he looked at it, he couldn't leave her here like this. If he put her in the ground, at least the family would know where she was. There would be somewhere to come and mourn and remember. He would have to find and tell them. Make sure they knew what had happened to her.

From the treetop a crow watched his effort, the only noise the shovel hitting the hard earth and his grunting. Puffs of red dust rose with each shovelful and his breathing became more laboured.

Finally he was done.

Driving his car close, he stood on the roof and cut the rope and the body fell into the grave he had dug with a thud. He said the only prayer he knew and then started to fill in the grave.

'Heavenly Father, hallowed be Thy name, Thy kingdom come, Thy will be done on earth as it is in heaven . . .'

Casting around for rocks, he couldn't see any big enough, so he got out his handsaw and started to cut wood to lay across the mounded dirt.

Chapter 1

1997

'We're not staying here long, are we?' Melinda asked, her lips curled in disgust.

'For as long as the department wants me to, I guess. Maybe one or two years.' Detective Dave Burrows pushed open the gate of his new house and ignored the hissing sound that came from Melinda as he said, 'or two'.

He'd been told his new partner, Spencer, was going to meet him at the house with the keys, but either they were early or he was running late because there was no sign of him. Maybe there was a key somewhere, so they could get out of the incessant heat.

He ran his fingers along the doorframe. Nothing. He lifted the frayed mat before moving on to the empty pot. Nope, no key.

This hadn't been the welcome to Barrabine he'd been hoping for. He'd wanted his new wife Melinda to love the place as soon as she arrived, for there to be a welcoming committee of . . . well, he didn't care who, just someone to make Melinda feel comfortable and happy. To make a friend straightaway. For the house to be lovely and modern.

Sadly, it was tiny and rundown, with a patch of brown lawn at the front. The fibro dwelling had a small porch, which would keep the northern sun from the doorway, but there weren't any verandahs to keep the house from heating up or to sit on with an evening drink.

The garden was a mixture of stones and dead weeds and was distinctly unappealing.

Like the entrance to the town.

The expansive blue sky had seemed to shimmer as they'd driven seven hours east from Perth and were closer to Barrabine, and the shiny-trunked gums had large pieces of bark hanging from their branches. For a moment Dave had had to squint—the bark looked like a body hanging, swaying in the breeze.

Dave was sure he'd never seen dirt as red as this country. It was the colour of rich copper. Then there was the ground, scattered with little stones glinting in the sun. He'd pointed it out to Melinda, saying it looked like blue metal had been spread across the ground, and bushes and trees grown up through it. She'd shrugged, clearly not impressed.

There'd been no mistaking that they were heading towards a mining town. Piles of dirt which seemed to reach the sky had risen above them, so long they seemed to create a range line. Their bluey-grey dirt didn't seem to match the red on the surface and Dave wondered how deep they had to go down for it to change colour.

Then the shanties had appeared—small tin sheds on the fringes—and Melinda's lips had formed the same thin line that she wore now as she'd crossed her arms.

They'd been only minutes inside town boundaries when Melinda had made mention of the rubbish lying on the road and, yes, he'd had to agree there was a lot. Beer bottles and cans, takeaway chip buckets and plastic containers.

She'd fallen silent as they'd approached the centre of Barrabine and seen a group of Aboriginal people sitting around a campfire, their swags near the fence of a house. The children ran around playing chasey, their feet bare, their smiles wild and delighted, while the adults stared at the passing cars with blank faces.

Following the directions Spencer had given him over the phone, Dave had made a series of turns through wide treeless roads and found their street, driving along slowly until they saw the number 12 on the gate.

Not sure whether to ignore Melinda's gasp at the sight of the house or to follow suit himself, he'd decided to grab her hand and give it a squeeze. The two of them had sat in the car, the air-conditioner blowing, and stared at their new home. It was nothing like they'd imagined.

The heat had stifled them both as they'd got out of the car, and the north wind had howled around the side of the house, slamming the car door shut from under Dave's hand.

'Geez.' He looked at Melinda; her mouth was still a thin, tight line. That was not a good sign.

Nope, the welcome hadn't gone according to plan.

The streets were dusty and everything looked tired and worn and in need of a good clean.

Dave had to admit Melinda had a point—not that she'd made one out loud, but he knew his wife well enough: she didn't like it here.

He supposed he could have asked for a posting to a coastal town. Somewhere there wasn't excitement. Or perhaps he could have asked for a position in Bunbury, where Melinda's parents and two sisters lived. That held less appeal to him than living in Barrabine did for Melinda. Not that he would have told her that.

To Dave, the posting to Barrabine was exactly what he'd wanted—it was a town on the edge, the wild west. There would be excitement, mystery and intrigue here. Everything a newly badged detective looked for. But the main reason for this posting was it would help him get to where he wanted to go: the stock squad, a squad which focused on agricultural areas, solving sheep theft and rural crime. For him, that would be the perfect job.

Melinda moved closer to him just as a voice called out from over the fence.

'Oi, missus!'

Dave saw Melinda freeze and groaned inwardly. It was a welcome of sorts, just not the kind he had envisaged. He put his arm around her and turned with a friendly grin.

'G'day, mate. How are you? Bit warm today.'

'Who you mob?' the curly-haired Aboriginal man wanted to know.

'Looks like we're your new neighbours . . .' He broke off at the sound of a horn and turned in time to a police car pulling up at the kerb.

A short, fat man hauled himself out using the handrail. He had a large smile on his face.

'Dave, my man! You've made good time. Didn't think you'd be here for another half an hour. I was going to open the place up and give it a bit of an air before you got here. Get the air-con on.' He gave his hand a cursory wipe on his shorts and held it out. 'The heat's made itself felt today.'

'We had a smooth run,' Dave answered, taking Spencer's hand and shaking it hard. 'How're you going?'

'Excellent, excellent.' He turned to Melinda. 'You must be the new bride! Congratulations. Welcome to Barrabine.'

'This is Melinda.' Dave turned to introduce her.

She nodded before saying, 'Thanks.'

Dave wanted to cringe. One-word replies were an even worse sign than tight lips. He glanced at her out of the corner of his eye and saw she was swallowing hard. Maybe she was on the verge of tears.

'Come in, come in.' Spencer ushered Melinda towards the house.

'Oi, who you mob?' the Aboriginal man reminded them all he was still waiting for an answer. 'G'day, Mr Spencer.'

'G'day there, Ernie.' Spencer turned and said to Dave, 'Ernie will make a great neighbour. Always keeps an eye on what's going on, don't you, mate? Loves a chat,' he said

9

by way of introduction. 'Ernie, Dave and Melinda Burrows. Our new detective and his missus.'

Dave felt Melinda recoil at the word 'missus'.

'G'day,' Ernie nodded to them both. 'Good neighbours, good neighbours.' He gave a grin, showing a perfectly white and straight set of teeth, and Dave couldn't help but smile back. His cheeriness was infectious.

'Go on with you now, Ernie,' Spencer waved him away. 'Let these good people settle in before you start having a yarn. All right?' He turned back to Dave.

'I don't mind having a yarn,' Dave began but was silenced with a look from Melinda.

Spencer slipped a key in the lock and madly shooed all the flies out of their hiding place in the shade, then threw open the door. 'Now I know this place looks a bit ratty from the outside,' he said, 'but it's nicely renovated inside. Come on in, Mel. You don't mind if I call you that, do you? Have a look at your new home!' He gave another wide smile and gestured as if he were a gameshow host.

'I'm Melinda, not Mel,' she said, walking in front of Spencer and into the house.

Spencer paused. 'Apologies. My mistake. Everyone seems to have nicknames around this place. Melinda it is.'

'Sorry,' Dave said softly to Spencer's back as he followed him inside. 'Long day, and I think it's all a bit of a . . .'

'S'all right, mate.' Spencer stopped and gave him a wink. 'I've been here for a few years. Seen it all before. Barra can be a bit of a shock to anyone, let alone a new bride. Don't worry about it. Gawd, you should've seen Kathy when she first got here. Cried for days. They adjust after a while. Come on, in you go.' He patted Dave's shoulder and turned back to the dimness of the house.

Dave was pleased to see the house was certainly better from the inside. It had the smell of new carpet and paint, and even though the kitchen looked a little tired, it was clean.

Dave watched as Melinda ran her fingertips across the benchtop, then looked at them to see how much dust they had collected. She brushed her hands across her shorts and moved off down the dark passageway. He could feel her eyes everywhere, taking in her new home. What he couldn't see was her reaction.

Spencer continued to talk as if he hadn't noticed Melinda's aloofness or the fact she'd walked out of the room. 'I'm sure you'll feel much better once your furniture gets here, Melinda. Should only be about an hour away. I rang head office to check and they gave the driver a call on the radio. Having familiar things around you always makes a place feel like home. And I guess you've got some nice photos of the wedding to hang on your wall. Pictures always make a house seem homelier too. I know my wife has covered almost every spot. Photos of the kids when they were at school, holiday snaps, landscapes. You name it, it's up there.' He gave a bit of a chuckle. 'Bit of a mad photographer, so she is.'

Dave frowned as Melinda didn't answer. He hoped her rudeness wasn't as obvious to Spencer as it was to him.

Spencer slapped his knee. 'Oh, hell, I forgot. I've got bread, milk, coffee and butter in the car. I'd better grab the bag before the heat gets to them. And Kathy, that's my wife, she's coming over to see you tomorrow, Melinda. She's more than happy to help you unpack and show you around. Local knowledge is good to have when it comes to Barra: where to shop, when the fresh fruit and veg trucks come in, and all of that. Be back in a sec.'

The front door slammed, leaving Dave and Melinda alone.

Dave made his way to what he thought was the main bedroom and stood in the doorway watching as Melinda turned in circles looking at the room. He could see the outline of a dark brown stain on the ceiling, under the new paint, but the walls were a clean, vivid white. Briefly he wondered how long they would stay like that with all the dust around. He hadn't been here ten minutes and the red dust was already over his hands and shoes.

'What do you think?' he asked, then quickly wished he hadn't. Her thoughts probably weren't going to be good ones.

Melinda remained quiet.

'It's comfortable,' Dave said, hoping to get Melinda talking. 'And we don't have to pay rent. We're going to be able to save a heap of money here, honey.'

She nodded and swallowed hard. Realising she was indeed close to tears, Dave went to her and put his arms around her.

'It's okay.'

Melinda rested her head against his chest and muttered something.

'What's that?' He leaned down to hear what she was saying.

'I'm sorry,' she gulped. 'I'm being a cow.'

Dave smiled. 'Look, all of this is new and I know it's a long way from your mum and dad, but you'll settle in quickly. If Kathy is anything like Spencer, she'll be warm and friendly. In a couple of months you'll have new friends and a new job. We'll both have new friends and new jobs.' Dave's tone was earnest, as if he were reminding her he was new here too. 'Spencer said Kathy had a bit of a hard time settling in too—maybe you guys could chat about it.' He hoped those words would bring some kind of comfort.

'I know, I know,' she nodded and Dave felt hot tears on his chest.

'Look, I know Barrabine seems a little . . .' He paused, not wanting to say rough or backward and give her more reasons not to like the place; finally, he settled on '. . . isolated. But we'll both get used to it.'

'What if I can't get a job?'

'I'm sure the hospital couldn't say no to a paediatric nurse as good as you.'

'They can if there aren't any vacancies.'

'We'll work it out, Melinda. I promise.'

❧

'And this, Dave,' Spencer said in a loud voice, 'is Plenty Street. There's always plenty on offer here.'

Dave looked around at the buildings trying to work out what the plenty on offer was. They were plain and without signage.

'They're the brothels of Barrabine,' Spencer explained with a flourish. 'Now, what you need to know is brothels are an important part of Barrabine—single men make up the larger part of the population and there's a need for sex workers here. As a copper, you have to understand the history and why we leave them to their own devices. If they weren't here there'd be trouble, if you get my meaning.' He looked over at Dave and raised his eyebrows. 'There are only five left. Used to be ten. We have a great working relationship with the madams in Barra. They come to the police first if anything goes wrong. Us. The coppers. And we need that. Sometimes they can give us the heads-up if someone is odd or causing trouble, and vice versa.'

That certainly is different to the city, Dave thought.

They drove in silence for a while, Spencer taking quick turns here and there before saying, 'Down here is the jail.' Spencer listed the number of criminals incarcerated; it was more than Dave had expected. 'I had one bloke put away last week. I've been chasing him for years.'

'What'd you get him on?' Dave asked, his eyes running along the razor wire at the top of the fence as they drove slowly by. You'd have to hope no one ever got away because the jail was almost in suburbia. It seemed to go from houses to jail without any land or break in between.

'I'd known for ages he'd been illegally prospecting on mine leases—ones that didn't belong to him—but I'd never managed to get there quick enough to catch him in the act.

'We had a bit of rain last winter and the dirt gets real slippery out here—even after a small amount. Well, Clever

14

Clogs managed to get himself bogged on someone else's lease, with ten ounces of gold in his pocket.' Spencer let out a laugh and his large belly jiggled, touching the steering wheel. 'Of course, he tried the oldest trick in the book: he'd found it elsewhere. Trouble was,' he turned to Dave gleefully, 'I got a search warrant for his GPS and, after a little more research, I managed to come up with a wit who had heard him bragging in the pub the night before, saying he was heading back out to the same spot as the GPS had shown he'd been because he'd clean up out there! He's gone inside for a couple of years. Pretty happy with that result.' Spencer gave a bit of a laugh. 'Now if he'd kept his mouth shut, I doubt I would have been able to get him put inside. I've found that people who've found gold can't help but brag.'

'That's a good thing for the gold squad, I guess. Anyway, well done. Always a great feeling when you get a result like that. Especially if you'd been chasing him for a bit.'

'Dead right, my man, dead right. Proving where gold has been stolen from can be a bit of a problem sometimes. It doesn't come out of the ground with an address or GPS coordinates.'

'Other than gold stealing, what other type of crime is most prevalent here?' Dave asked. Just then he saw a group of young boys with a shopping trolley running down the street. There were two inside the trolley, one pushing it and the others yelling encouragement.

'Look at those little buggers! Kids making their own fun. We don't interfere with that type of thing too much, although they should take the trolley back.' Spencer shrugged. 'We have a lot of break and enters, alcohol-related crimes and DV.' He paused. 'It's the domestic violence that gets me,' he said. 'I hate it when uniforms go out to a job, come back with the perp, lock him up and when we're ready to throw the book at him—or her—then the vic decides they don't want to press charges and the lowlife walks. Trouble is it happens again and again and again. You start to recognise the address when it's called out over the radio and know what's been going on.'

'I get what you mean. When I was in uniform, same thing used to happen. It's awful.'

They drove in silence for a little while and Dave contemplated what he was seeing. The main street had lots of shops, from clothes and sports gear to gift shops. He counted three cafés and made a mental note to ask a few different people which made the best coffee. There weren't very many people out on the street and he guessed the heat was keeping people indoors.

'Usually busier than this,' Spencer said, as if reading his mind. 'But school went back today and the mums will be breathing a sigh of relief at not having to be out in the heat, trying to entertain the kids. Town is always quiet the first week back to school.'

'It's fierce, isn't it? Different heat to Perth. Dry and . . .' He tried to find a word to describe it. 'Like the air wants to crackle. And the flies! They weren't this bad when I lived out in the wheat belt.'

'You'll know what crackling is like then when you see the lightning! Man, some of the thunderstorms that come through, I tell ya . . .' He went on to describe how the clouds would start to build up about three in the afternoon and before long they would turn inky black. 'The first thunder crack always stops the town. Don't reckon I've ever seen lightning split the sky the way it does here. So bright, I tell you. Sometimes it rains and sometimes it doesn't. But, when it does, the drops are about as large as a fifty-cent piece and the air smells so sweet. You know that rain on dry ground smell?' Spencer smacked his lips. 'Mmm, I love it!

'You know, lots of things about Barrabine can take a bit of getting used to, for sure,' Spencer continued. 'But I wouldn't want to live anywhere else now, and Kathy loves it too.'

Dave wanted to ask him how long it had taken Kathy to settle here. To find friends and be happy, but he wasn't sure he wanted his work partner to know that Melinda had cried herself to sleep last night, thinking Dave hadn't heard her. But he had and his heart had hurt the whole time.

'And the kids, what do they do? Why weren't the ones we saw back there in school?'

'Probably playing hooky first day of term. We'll keep an eye on them. As coppers, we work hard at having good relations with the kids in town. Some are more well known that others, as you would know from Perth. We'll head up here,' Spencer said, flicking his blinker on and driving up the winding road to the top of the hill. 'Finders Lookout.' Parking the car under the lone tree, which didn't offer enough shade, he pulled on the park brake and indicated the steel structure with a spiral staircase leading to a platform. 'Too hot to walk to the top, but there's a nice spot around here you can look out over the town. Come on.'

Together they stood, hands in pockets, and surveyed Barrabine. The silver roofs threw off the glare of the midday sun and there was a continual line of cars on the highway. Further out, Dave could see the red scars of the mines, slashed across the earth. There were large, heavy machines moving in the distance. The railway line glinted in the sun but remained empty of carriages.

'What's that noise?' he asked. The hum had been a constant since he'd arrived. He caught a glance of the main street, lined with heritage buildings, and the tall structures, all different heights. Spencer had told him these were mine shaft headframes.

'That's the mines,' Spencer said softly. 'The noise is there all the time. Day and night. They work round the clock to harvest the gold.' He continued to stare straight ahead. 'This is a hard town, Dave. One where fellas would rather put you in the ground than give up where they've found the yellow stuff. Where some blokes would rather take the gold from others than look for it themselves.

'The miners work hard, especially the ones underground. And they play hard too. In a sense, Barrabine is like the last frontier.' He turned and looked at Dave. 'I hope you're prepared.'

Chapter 2

Waiting to greet Dave on his arrival home from his first day at work was a swarm of small black bush flies at the front door. Waving his hands around, he tried to swat away as many of them as he could and then make a dash inside with only a few following him.

'Shit,' he muttered, nearly tripping over a cardboard carton and having to grab the wall to save himself. The lounge was filled with half-unpacked boxes and furniture was pushed up against walls. Loud music was blaring from the stereo.

'Hello?' he called out. 'Melinda?'

'Down here.' Her reply was muffled, as if she had her head deep in a box.

Stepping cautiously around the mess—he was sure they hadn't packed so much when they'd left Perth—he made his way down the passage, looking in each room, curious to see what changes had happened while he'd been at work.

They hadn't lived together before they'd got married—he'd been in a little one-bedroom unit, not far from the police station, with nothing but of bit of cooking gear, a bed, TV and fridge. He'd taken his washing to the laundromat. He liked living minimally; it was part of who he was. Having lived in the shearers' quarters on his father's farm for five years, he'd always managed to fit everything he had into one small room. This house full of furniture and things Melinda said they needed was quite foreign to him.

Melinda, on the other hand, had shared a house with three of her friends from uni and had slowly been collecting everything she would need to move out on her own. Most of the furniture was either hers or what they'd been given through the gift registry for their wedding. Walking through a department store picking out items for the new house and then asking people to buy them as wedding presents had made his toes curl, but he had to admit that the house was taking shape and looked very nice.

'Making headway?' he asked when he finally found her in the bathroom, stacking toiletries into the mirrored cupboard above the basin.

As he'd left the station tonight, Spencer had offered to come around and help to move the furniture into place, but Dave had thanked him and said it would be best if he went home first and saw what was going on before he said yes. Now he was glad of that. It looked like Melinda had everything under control . . . Maybe. He couldn't be sure.

'Yeah, I think so.' Melinda turned around to face him, her face covered in dust and her cheeks red. 'I've got the bed in the right spot and made up, so at least we won't have to stay in the hotel again.'

The furniture had arrived yesterday just as the sun had been going down, so Spencer had suggested the department fork out for a night in the local pub. Dave had jumped at the idea; they didn't need to be unpacking well into the night after a day like they'd had. Leaving Bunbury that morning had caused floods of tears from both Melinda and her mum. Her father, Dave had noticed, had also teared up a little. Melinda hadn't stopped crying until they were a couple of hours down the road. Of course, she had started again when they'd arrived in Barrabine.

'What've you been doing?' Dave reached over to wipe a cobweb from her head. 'The house isn't so dirty that you should be getting cobwebs in your hair!' He grinned at her and tried to reach his arm around her waist, but she was too far away.

'Did you know there was a shed out the back? I didn't notice when we arrived. I went to have a look to see if we could store the suitcases and stuff in it, and it's filthy. Hence I look like this.' She spread out her arms and pirouetted on her toes.

Dave grinned. 'Well, I guess that's better than having rolled in the dirt.' He passed her a can of deodorant and a tube of moisturiser from the box at her feet so she could stack them where she wanted.

'How was your day?'

Dave reached back into the box and handed her more toiletries. 'Fine. Police station is okay. Met a couple of the other blokes, who seem nice enough. We went through some files Spencer is working on and had a bit of a drive around. But the most *interesting* piece of information I learned today is that the police station is haunted.'

'Haunted?' Melinda flicked her long hair over her shoulders and looked up at him, her tone disbelieving. 'Seriously?'

'Yep, apparently so. There was a gold squad detective back in the early 1920s who was murdered and—' he dropped his voice to a low rumble '—they say his headless body roams the station at night. There are noises and happenings that people can't explain.'

'Happenings? Really, like what?'

'Pieces of papers being moved, rubbish bins emptied. And it seems you can't leave a dirty mug on your desk overnight. The ghost is a bit of a clean freak. They always end up on the kitchen sink. The guys have tested it heaps of times, apparently. Every time there's a dirty coffee cup on a desk or somewhere other than the sink, it gets moved to where it can be washed.'

'Right.' Melinda drew out the word. 'I think everyone has a dose of the sun.' She reached into the box and picked up another bottle.

'Oh, I don't know,' Dave said. 'I thought I might test the theory myself.' He gave her a grin. 'Always wanted to know if I'm able to get in touch with my spiritual side!'

Melinda rolled her eyes at him and Dave knew the conversation was over. Spiritual was something Melinda didn't do. She was practical and didn't believe in anything to do with religion or an afterlife. Even when her oldest

22

nursing friend, Tash, told her the story of a man who had arrived on her ward in the hospital and stood in front of a patient who was stable and expected to make a full recovery. The man didn't say anything to the patient, who was asleep at the time, only stood and watched him for at least ten minutes, then left. Not ten minutes later the patient went into cardiac arrest and died, despite everyone's best efforts. Dave knew that to this day Tash still believed she'd seen the Grim Reaper. Melinda didn't.

He changed the subject. 'Did Kathy come over?' he asked. 'What was she like?'

'Yeah, she did. Turned up about ten this morning. She was nice enough. Much taller than Spencer—I think they'd look strange standing next to each other. And she was quite slim. I'd say the two of them are opposites in every sense of the word.'

Dave gave a chuckle. 'I'm looking forward to meeting her then.'

'Hmm. She asked lots of questions. Wanted to know how we got together and why you'd wanted to be transferred here. Said it was strange. Not many people ask to come to Barrabine apparently.' She raised an eyebrow at him, as if to say 'You're mad' and then stretched her back out before letting out a groan. 'My back is killing me.'

'Come on,' he said, reaching out a hand to help her over the box. 'Let's go and find a pub to have a drink. You look like you need one. And let's have tea there. Neither of us needs to be thinking about cooking tonight. If the bed is made up, that's all we need.'

Finally she smiled. 'That would be nice. I'm tired.'

The shrill noise of the telephone made Dave jump. 'Where's the bloody phone?' he asked, walking towards the noise.

'Kitchen,' she said. 'On the wall, next to the door going into the lounge.'

'Hello?' Dave answered, picking up the receiver.

'Dave, g'day. It's Mark Beattie. Settling in okay?'

Grimacing, Dave tucked the phone in between his shoulder and ear and reached down to pull his shoes and socks off. 'G'day, Mark,' he said to his new father-in-law. 'How's it going?'

'Fine, fine here. Although we're missing Melinda already.'

Dave noticed he wasn't included in that statement.

'Yeah, I bet you are,' he answered. 'I'm sure she's missing you too, although she's been pretty busy today.' He left out the 'so hopefully she hasn't thought about you at all' part. Dave hadn't liked his father-in-law from the moment he'd met him. Mark came across as a pompous arse—having made his money from good investments, he was always dropping hints about how intelligent he was, how he didn't need to work any more, he just did it for the enjoyment, and how his daughters had taken after him. After many hints about how Dave wasn't good enough for Melinda, the final straw had been when he'd suggested to Dave that his policeman's income wasn't going to be enough to keep his daughter in the way she should be looked after and perhaps the kindest thing would be for Dave to break off the engagement.

'Unpacked yet?' Mark asked, returning Dave to his tiny, weatherboard house in Barrabine.

'Well, Melinda seems to have done a great job already, but there's still a bit to go. Rome wasn't built in a day.'

'You're not helping her?' Mark's voice rose in surprise and Dave could hear the judgement.

'I've started at work today.'

'Ah. Yes, I understand. Some people have to work for a living.'

Choosing to ignore the implication that he wasn't helping his wife enough and only failures had to work, Dave asked politely, 'How is Ellen?'

'She's well. We had the grandchildren here this morning, so she's a little tired, but she's fine.'

'Good to hear.' An uncomfortable silence stretched out along the phone line before Dave said, 'Well, I'll just get Melinda for you.' Without waiting for an answer, he put down the receiver and went back into the bathroom. 'Your dad's on the phone.'

Melinda's face lit up and without a word she got up and jumped over the box and ran to phone.

Dave tried not to listen to their conversation, but he could hear her describing their arrival into town yesterday and the distaste in her voice. Her comments about the house were less than enthusiastic, and when he heard her say, 'Oh, no, Dad, don't even think about that. Dave would never accept it,' he wondered what Mark was offering. To buy them a new house? To make a 'donation' to their bank account. Indignation as well as a little rush of fear ran through him. What if she didn't settle here? Would their marriage be doomed form the start because he'd dragged her to the middle of Western Australia so he could become a top-notch detective and make it onto the stock squad? Would he have to put his aspirations aside again? Surely not—he'd already had his boyhood dream of becoming a farmer dashed by his father.

The little voice inside himself, which he was beginning to learn to listen to, told him no. They'd talked long and hard about the move to Barrabine, and Melinda understood why it was important to him, although naturally she'd had a lot of misgivings about giving up her own job. Especially after all her study. He hadn't wanted to come here by himself, but he would have if she hadn't agreed; eventually, after lots of thought and discussion, she'd told him she was up to the challenge. He'd been so relieved.

'I'm a bit over all the political bullshit that goes on at Princess Margaret Hospital,' she'd said. 'You know, having to deal with second-class equipment because the money isn't there to replace it and nurses being given jobs that doctors should do.' She'd wrapped her arms around his neck and stared up at him. 'Tash says country nursing is a lot more fun—loads of different things to try. She spent a year in Margaret River, remember? Having a couple of years in a country hospital will look good on my resume when we go back to the city. I don't like the idea of going out there without a job, but I guess I'll just have to hope something comes up.' Reaching up, she'd given him a kiss before whispering, 'So let's do it.'

Her brave words seemed to have deserted her now and no matter how much explaining he did, Melinda still seemed to think that Dave had asked to be transferred here. In fact, it had been the powers that be who had told him he was coming. So, whether she'd agreed to come or not, Dave would still have been transferred to Barrabine.

'You're going to be a great detective, Dave,' Terry O'Laughlin, his mentor, had told him. 'That's why I'm going to recommend you have a stint in Barrabine. You'll learn a lot there and it'll give you a lot of experience that you'll need as a detective. I'm partnering you with Spencer Brown. He's a good bloke, been there a few years and he'll help you get to know the area.'

'Barrabine, sir?' Dave had paused. 'That's a long way away. I'm getting married in a couple of weeks.'

'I know. We'll make sure the house is comfortable for you and your new wife, and this posting, well, it'll be your step up into the stock squad. I know you want to head there and we can use a bloke with your background as the lead detective. You know how to connect and talk with farmers and that's important.'

'The stock squad would be my ideal,' Dave answered, a bubble of excitement starting in his stomach. It was what he'd been aiming for since his dad had kicked him off the farm.

'Again, I know that. Barrabine for a year or two and then I'll get you shifted over. All right?' He'd nodded and then left the room. It had been a statement, not a question, and Dave hadn't been able to stop grinning for the rest of the day. If he were honest, he wasn't sure how much thought he'd given to Melinda's feelings about it all. He wanted to get into the stock squad and this was the way he was going to do it.

He focused on Melinda's phone conversation again. 'The garden is non-existent,' she was saying and there was silence while her father made a comment.

'Just lawn and a few garden beds without anything in them. I'd think it's too hot to grow anything right now. The seedlings would wither under the heat no matter how much water you gave them.' She lowered her voice. 'And, Dad, you should've seen it yesterday when we drove into town. Rubbish everywhere. The whole place is just so dirty, whether as a result of dust or garbage.'

There was silence again.

'No, it's okay . . . Honestly, Dad, it's fine . . . No, don't come and visit yet . . . I know, I know. Me too.'

Not wanting to hear any more, Dave let himself quietly out of the laundry door and went to have a look in the back shed Melinda had told him about earlier.

In the setting sunlight the whole sky seemed to be glowing pink. He'd heard the sunsets out here were spectacular. Maybe he'd take Melinda up to the lookout one night, with a bottle of wine and a beer. They could watch the sun sink below the edge of the earth together.

He sniffed the air, which was still and calm, and the temperature seemed to be dropping—just slightly.

The door of the shed creaked loudly as it opened and he peered into the dim light, seeing nothing but the dust and cobwebs Melinda had talked about. Well, he'd be able to store his camping gear in here no problems. And the suitcases. *Just need to buy a padlock*, he thought.

'G'day, mister.' Dave heard Ernie's voice from over the fence and ducked out, shutting the door.

'Hi, Ernie,' he answered with a grin. 'How're you?' He waved a couple of stray flies away from his eyes as Ernie gave him the thumbs up.

The back door slammed and Melinda came out, pulling her long copper-coloured hair out of her face. Wearing clean denim shorts and a sleeveless shirt, she looked cool and beautiful, but Dave could see she'd been crying. He wished Mark hadn't called.

'Hot day,' Ernie answered, seeming to ignore the question. 'Hotter tomorrow. No wind, see?'

Melinda beckoned to Dave without leaving the back steps.

'I see, so because there's no wind, it will be even hotter tomorrow than today?' Dave asked.

'Yeah, mister,' Ernie nodded, his hair bobbing up and down in time with the motion. 'Flies too. Lotsa flies. Need fly net. You buy a fly net.' He let out a loud cackle.

'Yeah, the flies are a pain. Never seen so many. Anyway, good to know about the forecast, mate, 'cause it was bloody hot today.' He took a couple of steps towards the house. 'Better get going. Still got a lot to do. Catch you later, okay?'

'Sure, sure,' he nodded and seemed to slide below the fence.

'All done?' Dave asked Melinda. He wasn't sure whether to mention her red eyes or not.

'Yep.' There were those one-word answers and thin lips again.

He decided not to do anything but take her hand and press it to his lips. She yanked it away from him and turned to stalk into the house and out the other side.

'Let's go then,' Dave muttered to himself, resisting the urge to sigh.

❧

Inside the pub there was a roar of laughter and voices. Dave felt Melinda press close to him and he realised there were mostly men in the bar. Last night the front bar had been empty save four old blokes who had had their eyes fixed on the TAB TV screen. They hadn't taken any notice of the couple when they'd walked in for dinner. Tonight was different.

'What would you like?' asked the bartender who looked in her sixties. She put her elbows on the bar and fixed Melinda with a stare. 'New around here, huh?'

Nodding, Melinda ordered a white wine and Dave a beer.

Without another word, she went to get their drinks.

'Want to sit where we sat last night?' Dave enquired, after glancing around, looking for tables.

'I'll go through.' Melinda seemed keen to get away from the front bar. Or perhaps it was from him. She hadn't said a word in the car.

'If you like. I'll grab the drinks.'

Watching as Melinda weaved her way quickly towards the dining room and the men followed her with their stares, Dave yet again wondered whether he'd done the right thing.

'Haven't seen you around before.' An unshaven,

dirty-faced man came up and leaned on the bar next to him. 'New, are you? Welcome to Barrabine.'

'Yeah, just joined the gold squad. Detective Dave Burrows.' He held out his hand.

There was a pause before the other man slowly put out his hand. 'Jeremy Maddison.' He lowered his voice. 'Ah, another one for the infamous gold squad. You detectives are well known around here. Do a good job, but I wouldn't go letting too many people know what you do, mate. You lot aren't our favourite people.' He took a long pull of his beer and looked at Dave over the rim.

'Miner, are you? Work for a company or yourself?' Dave asked, trying to work out what he should say so he didn't put his new acquaintance offside. Spencer hadn't warned him about this type of reaction.

'Something like that,' Jeremy said with a wink. 'I own a few leases up north and have me own smelter. That bloody Spencer Brown came and searched me shed a while back, but he didn't find anything. All the gold I had there was me own. Bloody git, he must think I'm stupid.'

Dave wasn't sure which type of stupid he meant—that he was silly enough to steal gold, or that he'd keep what he did steal in his shed.

Jeremy gave a nod towards his friends. 'Best get back, but I'm sure we'll see each other from time to time. You boys never seem to be able to stay away from me.' He walked back and said something in a low voice to the other men and there was loud laughing and two of the men looked his way before raising their drinks.

Dave wanted to turn away, feeling uncomfortable, but instead he raised his own hand in a way of cheers and gave a nod. Those fellas wouldn't get the best of the new bloke in town, Dave decided.

''Ere you go.' The barmaid was back with the drinks.

'Thanks,' Dave answered and took out a fifty-dollar note, gave it to her and waited for his change. 'I can take these through?' he asked, indicating to the dining room.

'Knock yerself out, love. I'll be in to take your order in a mo.' She smiled and walked off to another customer who was watching them curiously.

'I think we've made an impression,' Dave said as he set Melinda's wine down in front of her.

'I wish I'd worn a different shirt,' she said, pulling at the non-existent sleeves.

'You look beautiful.'

'I feel like everyone is undressing me.'

'They're not,' Dave said with a smile, wanting her to relax. 'They're actually looking at me. Wondering why a detective from the gold squad is in the pub. Apparently it's not the place for me. I just met some of the boys Spencer likes to keep an eye on.'

Reaching across the table, Melinda smiled. 'You always seem to know the right things to say.'

'That's my job,' he answered, raising her hand to his mouth and kissing her knuckles.

This time she didn't take her hand away. She kept it against his lips.

Chapter 3

After a week of bad coffee Dave had finally discovered the best place to go for his daily fix was at the Mug café. When he'd been told the name it had taken him a moment to work out whether his work colleagues were having a joke with him. Apparently not.

Now it was two weeks into his posting at Barrabine and the young girl behind the counter was already asking if he wanted his 'usual' and calling him by name. That made him feel good. Accepted. As if he belonged. He knew Melinda wasn't feeling like that yet, but she hadn't been out much. He hoped that'd change soon.

Last night, as they'd done most nights since arriving, they'd sat on the steps of their house, drinks in hand, and chatted about the day. Dave had asked what Melinda had done all day and her reply had been, 'Stayed in the house. Too hot to go outside.'

'Haven't caught up with Kathy again?' The one-word answer of 'No' had made him fall silent. He really wanted to ask her why she wasn't interested in making a new friend—in Perth she would have jumped at the opportunity. He couldn't understand why she wouldn't want to do the same here.

'What do you do all day?' he wondered out loud.

She looked at him. 'I phone my friends,' she said. 'Tash and my sisters. Mum. I do a lot of talking.'

But that's not helping you fit in here, he wanted to say.

Instead, he'd told her Spencer had taken him around to all the pubs within a fifty k radius and he'd been intro-duced to the owners. She shrugged and said, 'It's all right for some. You get paid to be introduced to people.'

For the millionth time, Dave wondered if he'd done the right thing by accepting the posting which would advance his career. Not that he'd had much of a choice. It seemed a long time ago that she had walked down the aisle with anticipation and a smile on her face. In only two weeks, it seemed like she'd lost weight and the fresh glow had gone from her cheeks.

'Here you go, Dave.' Layla broke into his thoughts.

'Thanks, Layla,' he said as she handed over the flat white in a large mug.

'Anything special on the go today?' she asked, ringing up his purchase.

'Not that I know of. I'm beginning to think all the stories I've heard about Barrabine and gold stealing are just tall tales!' He grinned, holding his hand out for the change.

'Uh-uh. No way,' she said. 'About three years ago there was a big police raid on the house next to where I lived.' Her face lit up as she remembered. 'It was really cool to watch—most exciting thing ever. I wasn't supposed to see . . .' she dropped her voice, confiding in him, 'but I couldn't help it. All the police car lights were flashing, making these funny shadows on my ceiling, so I had to go, didn't I?'

Dave smiled and nodded his agreement.

'So I snuck outside and peeped over the fence. The police were knocking the door in, and there was yelling and shouting. Then out comes the neighbour in only his shorts, with his hands handcuffed behind his back.'

'Sounds pretty exciting,' Dave said, taking a sip of his coffee and making a mental note to ask Spencer about it. 'Do you know what happened?'

Layla shrugged. 'Mum said he got charged with something, but I dunno what. I heard from one of my friends that he murdered someone who was on his mining lease, but another person told me that he only threatened to shoot them, so it wasn't that bad.'

'No, I guess not,' Dave muttered, trying to keep the laughter out of his voice. Civilians seemed to think there was a world of difference between threatening to shoot someone and actually doing it. Dave knew there wasn't. There was only about two millimetres—what it took to squeeze the trigger. 'Well, I'd better get on. Thanks for the coffee.'

'See ya tomorrow.' Layla flashed him a large smile, showing a set of perfect teeth.

'You will,' he promised and walked over to his normal booth at the front of the shop. He had seventeen minutes before he needed to be at the office, so he opened the newspaper that was sitting on the table. His day started at seven in the morning and yet he left his house every morning at six, to walk to the Mug, get a coffee, sit and read the paper, before leaving to walk to the office. Him walking meant Melinda had use of the car. Dave had been promised a work vehicle, but an endless amount of paper-work had to be processed first and Spencer had said it could take a while.

It wasn't bothering him too much right now. The walk was pleasant, the heat not as intense and he enjoyed the fresh air and peaceful start to the day. Having been raised on a farm, he was an early riser, so it wasn't hard for him, whereas Melinda found it a challenge to get out of bed before seven.

Today he'd woken her and spent a few minutes talking, encouraging her to go out with Kathy or one of the other policemen's wives.

'Spencer said Kathy asked you to go to lunch and you said you were busy.'

Sleepily she'd nodded. 'I still have things to do to organise the house.'

'It can't get any more organised, honey. Why don't you want to go?'

36

'I just don't. Please don't push me, Dave. All I want is you at the moment, okay?' She'd reached out and wound her arms around his neck, pulling him closer. He'd ended up being a little late in leaving the house, but he had the promise of lunch with her at one of the delis.

He resolved to talk to her then about the need to make friends. It seemed to him that if she did, she'd be happier. Although he did wonder whether she was content to wallow in her misery. Make him suffer a little for bringing her out here. She'd snapped at him last night at dinner, saying it was his fault they were in this one-horse town, then she'd immediately apologised. But if she made these accusations she'd been thinking them, Dave had realised later that night. She'd only been apologising for saying them out loud.

He glanced at the newspaper headline. He didn't care much about politics or the entertainment pages. He'd rather be reading *Farm Weekly* and catching up on stock and wool prices or agribusiness news, but it had been a while since he'd read that newspaper.

Glancing at his watch, he realised that being late out of the house this morning had made him late for the office, and if he didn't leave now, he wouldn't be there before Spencer.

Beating Spencer to work was important—it showed the older detective he was keen and he'd need Spencer's good opinion if he was going to make it to lead detective in the stock squad.

Dave folded the paper and drained his cup quickly, then hurried out onto the street towards the station.

The Barrabine Police Station was always bustling with activity. The constables and senior sergeants were in and out of the station, called out regularly to theft or domestic violence jobs. Then there were the offenders being arrested and brought into the cells, often yelling abuse in the process, ignoring the police's exhortations to calm down.

Pushing open the station door, Dave was hit with a blast of cool air. He nodded good morning to the constable behind the desk and put in the PIN code to get through into the detectives' office.

'Morning, Dave,' Terry Jasper said as he sat down and threw his feet on his desk. Leaning back, the wiry man ran his hands over his short dark hair and winked at Dave. 'Beat the boss man in again.'

'G'day, Tez,' Dave answered. 'Always the plan, mate.'

'You're making all of us look bad,' said Claire Steele, Terry's partner. Her voice was muffled as she shoved a piece of banana in her mouth. Dave glanced over at her and realised she'd had her hair cut. It was now very short and blonde.

'Nice hair,' he complimented her. She nodded her thanks.

Senior Sergeant Nathan Underwood called from across the room. 'Look! The new fella's trying to make good impressions on every front. It'll wear off!'

Dave laughed, enjoying the camaraderie. 'Can I just say that you're all here too. And a little bit before me!'

'That's a good point,' Claire said with a chuckle. 'What have you got on today, Dave?'

'I'm following up that burglary from a couple of nights ago,' he answered, switching on his computer. 'Got results from fingerprints. Known offender, so thought we'd go out and bring him in for a chat.'

'Who's the POI?' Tez asked.

'Person of Interest? Nathaniel Clarke. Eighteen-year-old from Calemalda Street. Been charged with theft before.'

'Yeah, yeah. He was up in front of the magistrate about twelve months ago for the same thing. Reckon it's probably his third time. He should go away, depending on what he stole.'

'Did the whole house: TV, computer, got the safe open and took about a grand in cash and the victim's rings from her grandmother.'

'Stealing to buy drugs. One of the biggest problems in this town, drugs. Because there's a high disposable income within the mining sector, the drugs get brought in, then the others—the unemployed or youth—get a taste for it and the crime starts because they need the money to buy.' He sighed. 'Never-ending cycle, unfortunately.'

'Same in the city,' Dave said, turning back to his computer. He hit the button to print out a few reports before making some phone calls to the pawnshops to see if any of the stolen goods had turned up. By midmorning he needed another coffee and had just taken orders from the rest of the crew when his phone rang.

'Reckon you've got a body on your hands,' said the voice on the end of the line.

'Sorry, sir, could you repeat that?' Dave's heart rate kicked up a notch and he reached for a pen. 'You're reporting a murder?'

'Not sure if it's a murder, mate,' the man drawled. 'But there's a heap of flies and an atrocious smell coming from a shaft on my lease.'

'And your name?'

'Tim. Tim Tucker.

'And whereabouts is your lease?'

'Twenty k north of Barra. Spencer Brown knows me. Send him.'

Dave looked up as the door swung open and Spencer strode in.

'Can I get your number, sir?' he asked, but realised he was talking to dead air.

'You've got a look of excitement on your face, Burrows,' Spencer said, mopping his brow. 'What's going on? Bugger, it's hot out there already. Morning all.'

'A body,' Dave answered, ignoring the comment on the weather. It seemed to him everyone knew it was hot and talking about it wouldn't make it cool down. 'Tim Tucker, you know him?'

'Sure do. Salt of the earth.'

'Says there are flies and a smell coming from one of the shafts on his lease.'

Spencer's eyebrows shot up. 'A body? Now how does young Tim know it's a human body and not an animal?'

'I guess he assumed,' Dave responded.

'Good thing he reported it; better to be safe than sorry. Although probably just some poor roo fell down the shaft and wasn't able to get out.'

Dave felt revolted. 'Really? Never thought about an animal tumbling into a shaft. S'pose I should've.'

'Unfortunately it happens more than you might realise. But,' he cocked his head to one side and held his finger up, 'I worked a case once where we thought a sheep had gone down a mine shaft. Turned out there was a body underneath it. The sheep was an afterthought to hide the body. Wool doesn't break down, you see. Always gotta keep an open mind.' He grinned. 'Come on then, let's go and check it out.'

❧

Tim had been right about one thing. The smell was sickening.

The three men stood around the shaft, swatting the flies away and breathing through their noses.

'Wish I'd brought the Vicks,' Spencer said. 'Got to be human, though, don't you reckon, Dave? They always smell worse than animals.'

'Never smelled a decomposing body before,' Dave admitted. He wanted to put his hand over his nose, but at the same time didn't want to appear weak and the new kid on the block. 'All the bodies I've dealt with have been found before too much decay had set in.'

'I reckon it's human,' Tim offered. 'Remember that lady I found, the one in the car wreck? She'd been there for a couple of days in the sun. Reeks just like she did. I've smelled plenty of dead roos, wild dogs, camels even, and they don't smell like this.' He reached down to pat a large red heeler sitting at his feet.

Dave glared at the dog from behind his sunglasses. His welcome had been a snarling ferocious bark which had sent ripples of fear through Dave, who was still sporting a deep puncture wound scar on his forearm. One of his father's kelpies had been caught in a fence and he'd tried to untangle it. The kelpie had been in pain when he'd latched on—Dave knew it never would have bitten him otherwise—but since then he'd kept dogs at a safe distance.

He shuffled to the side of the shaft, eyeing the red heeler as he went. Getting an unexpected whiff of the decaying body, he swallowed hard and turned away, trying to find clean air. The putrefaction hovered above the dark hole, just like the swarm of flies, and spread out from there.

Spencer slapped his hand onto his thigh. 'Yeah, yeah, I remember her. One car, fell asleep and drove off the road. Drove into a tree. Poor lass.' Spencer turned to Dave. 'This is going to be a bit tricky. We'll need to get the pathologist here from Perth. Got to get whoever it is outta this shaft, and forensics will have to come out.' He stared down into the hole again. 'Poor bastard,' he muttered.

Dave looked into the darkness then over at Spencer. He couldn't imagine anyone going down to recover a decomposing body in such a small space.

'How—' he started to ask, but Spencer interrupted him.

'I'll get on the blower to the mine, fire and rescue team.' He blew out air and rocked on his heels. 'We'll need their expertise in this. Before we go in.'

Dave wanted to shudder, only guessing what imagery would greet the poor person who entered the mine shaft first.

'How will they . . . ?'

'They'll use their equipment to make sure the walls are safe first. Once we know that, they'll send a team member down—remember, they're trained to work in small, confined spaces, in the dark or at least with minimal light. I've been meaning to introduce you to the team leader, Bluey. Looks like we'll be doing that on the job.'

His mind's eye conjured up an image of a man in a set of orange overalls being winched down into the dark, the foul stench of death encasing him. He assumed the rescuer would wear a breathing apparatus so the odour didn't overpower him.

Once the body had been enclosed in a body bag and hoisted to the surface, the decision would be made whether to send forensics down or not. Safety was paramount and, even though highly trained, if it wasn't safe, forensics and the pathologist wouldn't get to see the body in situ, which was fairly unusual. Bluey had expertise which the police didn't have.

The shaft was situated between an overhanging rock and soft red dirt, covered in what looked like blue metal, which the council would use to make a bitumen road. Dave squatted down and picked some of it up. As he looked more closely he realised it was nothing like blue metal, but small, dark and shiny. Quite heavy for the size of it. He looked up, wondering what could be seen from inside the mine: blue sky and trees, their red trunks smooth and tinged with green. Dave reckoned only the tops of the mulga trees would be visible from down in the shaft—they weren't as tall as the other species.

'What's this?' he held out the small stone to Tim.

'Ironstone,' he answered. 'Ironstone and quartz are good indicators that it's gold country.'

Dave nodded and considered the shaft, where someone who had believed there was gold under this ground had chiselled out a hole not much wider than a man's shoulders. He could see the thick wooden beams holding up the shaft, but, as much as he tried, he couldn't work out what would possess a person to climb down into a hole in the ground that small. Even the pull of riches beyond his wildest dreams wouldn't have induced *him* to go down.

Dave went over to their squad car and opened the back door, looking for the torch he knew was in the well-equipped car. When he found it, he walked closer to the shaft until his feet were almost hanging over the edge and flashed the beam down.

'Wouldn't do that,' Tim advised.

Dave looked up, puzzled. 'Do what?'

'Go too close to the edge.' He paused. 'Never know if the ground will give out from underneath you.'

Dave glanced at Spencer to make sure he was being told the truth. Trouble with the police department was that when a new fella turned up, everyone—crims and cops alike—loved to take the piss out of him. Until he worked out the ropes.

'He's right,' Spencer said as he squatted down a little way away from the mine and let his hands rest on his knees. 'Know how deep this one is, Timmy?'

'Nah, probably only five or six metres down.' The old man stared out into the bush. 'Haven't ever been down.'

Dave backed away carefully and glanced over at Tim, realising he was older than he'd first thought. Maybe seventy, older even. He had long grey hair pulled back into a ponytail and was wearing a pair of faded blue shorts and a grey T-shirt. His socks and boots were thickly covered in the red goldfields dust, and his skin seemed to have taken on the same colour as the land. Tim was looking down into the mine with a solemn face. Dave wondered what this man's story was; why he was still out here searching for gold. What had made him come here? Why had he stayed?

Spencer had told stories of men who had bought a lease, come to work it and never left. 'It's like something switches on in them and they can't turn it off. They have to search for more and more gold. When they find some, they're not satisfied. I guess it's a little like the gambler mentality. The next bet is always going give them the big win.'

Was Tim like that? He made a note to ask Spencer what he knew about the man.

'Do you go down them all?' Dave asked.

'Not all, lad. But most. There's lots to get through out here; and some, when you start to investigate them a bit further, you realise aren't safe. I leave those ones alone.'

'How many are on your lease?'

'Oh, I guess about thirty, give or take.' Tim brushed the flies away as he spoke.

'You didn't put the shafts down? Someone else did?'

'I've put all but two down. The old timers did those before I was even thought of.'

'Have you found gold in the ones you've been down?'

'Guess we'd better get forensics out here,' Spencer interrupted. 'And the rescue team. Take a few ropes to get whoever it is out from down there. Thank God I'm not the one who's going to have to go down that shaft.'

Dave agreed absolutely.

Chapter 4

Melinda walked into the Barrabine Hospital and immediately felt at home.

The smell of antiseptic was soothing to her and she took a couple of deep breaths to help calm the butterflies in her stomach. There was so much riding on this interview—her sanity and her self-worth—and she didn't want to think about what would happen if there wasn't a job for her.

She noticed her hands shaking as she held her résumé and she suddenly remembered arriving at the church for her wedding only one month ago. Her hands had been trembling from nerves then too, so much so that her flowers had shaken. Her father's words hadn't helped: 'Are you sure you want to go through with this? Life as a policeman's wife will be hard. Long hours, and he won't ever make much money. You'll always be waiting for a knock on the door to tell you something bad has happened.'

Her father's words had jolted her. She'd known there was tension between him and Dave, but how could he even entertain the idea she wouldn't marry him because of those minor things? Of course she would! The long hours and little money hadn't bothered her. Dave was her soulmate. She'd known that since they first met. They'd talked about everything—they didn't always agree, but their debates had been fun and interesting. He made her laugh and feel loved. Calmed her and convinced her she could do anything. He was the love of her life. Her strong, handsome man with his steady calmness.

She only wished Barrabine hadn't been on the cards for his first out-of-city posting.

'I told you,' a woman's screeching voice broke through her thoughts. She was standing at the admissions window. 'I told you! Stop asking questions. I'm here for me med'cine. No more questions, just me med'cine. I need it.' Her voice broke and it changed from loud to begging.

Melinda couldn't hear the soft answer, but whatever it was hadn't made any difference. The woman repeated what she'd just said. Then Melinda realised she was under the influence of drugs. Or was she just drunk? No, drugs, she was sure.

Melinda looked again. The woman wasn't the stereo-typical drug user: she was well dressed, with her nails painted and her hair neat, and yet here she was yelling like a banshee. Maybe she had a mental illness, Melinda thought as she observed the woman, testing her nursing skills.

A nurse from Emergency opened a door and ushered the woman through.

'See?' she yelled. 'Told you I was here for me med'cine. Don't need any help from you.'

The lady behind the window kept her head down and ignored the loud complaint.

Behind her, Melinda heard the sliding door open and screaming coming from outside. A young mum, holding a child who didn't look more than two, ran in and straight up to the admissions window.

'Please,' she pleaded, 'please, I need to see a doctor. Kate's hurt her arm. I think it's broken.'

Once again the woman took the details, ignoring the crying, and indicated for the two to sit in the waiting area.

'Someone will be with you shortly,' Melinda heard her say through the glass.

Shortly might not be soon enough, she thought as Kate continued to bellow. Poor love. Melinda tried to assess her arm, without looking as if she were staring at the crying girl. Her face was red with exertion and eyes puffy from crying. Her arm didn't look as if it was sticking out at a funny angle or swollen in any areas. If it was broken, Melinda thought, it would be a hairline fracture.

Glancing at her watch, she approached the window. 'Hello,' she said, smiling at the stern-looking lady. 'I have an appointment to see the director of nursing.'

'Take a seat,' she answered in a monotone before picking up the phone. 'Your ten o'clock is here.' Without waiting for an answer, she replaced the receiver and indicated for Melinda to sit. 'You'll be called shortly.'

Shortly? Was that the only word she knew for 'not long' or 'a minute'? Melinda nodded and went to the plastic seats which lined the wall.

Kate was still bawling and her mother was having a hard time soothing her.

'It's all right, love. It'll be okay,' Kate's mother said above the crying. 'The doctor will give you something to make your arm stop hurting.'

Melinda moved closer to them. 'Hi,' she said, trying to catch Kate's eye. 'I'm Melinda. Is your name Kate?' She noticed the mother frowned and tried to angle her body in between her daughter and hers in protection. She flashed a quick smile. 'I'm Melinda,' she said, this time to the mother. 'A paediatric nurse.'

The change in the mother was instant. She relaxed and gave her a wan smile. 'Can you get us in to see a doctor quickly?' she asked, rubbing her daughter's leg to try to calm her.

Melinda shook her head. 'I don't work here, but I thought I might be able to help with Kate. Is your arm sore, sweetie?' She directed the question at Kate, who didn't hear it through her tears.

'Kate,' Melinda tried to get eye contact with her and put her hand on her bare knee. 'Kate, I'm a nurse. Does your arm hurt?'

It was like turning off a tap. The crying stopped and Melinda's ears rang with silence. A couple of jagged breaths later, Kate nodded and pointed at her forearm, in between the wrist and elbow.

'Deary me. How did you do it?' Melinda gently traced the girl's arm to see if she could feel anything. She could see the beginning of swelling and bruising creeping up her arm.

'I felled off my cubby.' The admission brought a fresh round of tears.

'Oh no! That must have hurt. Is it very high, your cubby?'

Kate's mum nodded. 'About this high.' She held her hand up to shoulder height.

The door into emergency swung open and the nurse called out Kate's name. Quickly her mother stood up and gathered Kate into her arms. Without thanking Melinda, she almost ran towards the doors and the wailing started afresh.

'Good luck,' Melinda called, leaning back in her chair and letting out a deep breath. *Poor little mite*, she thought. *Well, nothing an X-ray and a few painkillers won't fix.*

'Melinda?'

She jumped up and saw a man standing in a doorway— she hadn't heard it open. 'Yes.'

'I'm Wes Corris. Please, come through.' He indicated down a brightly lit passage. 'Third on the left.'

Melinda gathered her folder and handbag and followed his instructions. As she started towards him, she heard the doors slide open and glanced over her shoulder to see her neighbour.

'G'day there, missus,' Ernie nodded to her.

Melinda realised he was holding a young child's hand. She nodded to him and matched Wes's steps towards his office.

'I understand you're new to Barrabine,' Wes said as he settled behind his desk.

With a quick glance, Melinda saw the back wall of the office was lined with medical books, while the right wall had whiteboards covered with staff leave and jobs to be done. His desk was ordered and the entire office held only one personal item: a photo of what she assumed was his family—a woman and two small children.

'Yes,' she answered, placing her handbag on the floor and sitting down. 'My husband,' it still felt odd saying the word, 'is a detective within the gold squad and we moved here a few weeks ago.' Melinda tapped one finger nervously on her knee.

'A big job,' Wes said. 'Bit of a wild west town this one.'

'So I keep hearing.' She didn't mention this was the whole reason she didn't like to go out or want to make friends. That and the fact she had come to realise if she made friends, once again she'd have to leave them. Melinda had come to the conclusion it was easier to keep her distance and not get too close to anyone.

There was a pause and Wes realigned his writing pad and pen into straight lines.

'How can I help you, Melinda? I understand you're looking for a job.'

She nodded. 'I'm a paediatric nurse.' Opening the folder, she brought out her résumé and laid it on the desk in front of him. 'I've also got my certificates here.'

Wes picked up her resume and started to read. 'Ah, you've worked under Tania Supple. I know Tania quite well,' he commented, his eyes still on the paper.

Melinda took the time to study the office a little more closely. The medical books were on obstetrics and palliative care. She wondered how Wes had ended up behind a desk, managing people and budgets. Most nurses didn't like the management side of the job.

Finally Wes put down the résumé and rubbed his eyes tiredly, even though it was only ten in the morning.

'I'm sure you understand, Melinda, that there has to be a vacancy for you to be able to apply for a job in the public sector.'

Melinda felt her heart sliding down into her feet, and the hope she'd held on to for so long disappeared with that one sentence.

'At this point I don't have a vacancy, as much as I need another three nurses and probably two emergency doctors. Budgets, God, don't even talk to me about the lack of money in health.' He let out another long sigh. 'I can't offer you a job, Melinda, as much as I need you and would like to. The hospital just doesn't have the money.'

Glancing down, she picked at the hem of her shirt, swallowing hard, while thinking of something to say.

'As soon as something becomes available, I'll let you know. You'd be a great asset for us.'

She nodded and looked up. 'Thanks for your time.'

'I watched you out there, with the little girl. I can see you're an excellent nurse. You've got an affinity with kids.'

'I love what I do,' she said simply. 'I loved my work in Perth and leaving my job at Princess Margaret Hospital was one of the hardest things I've done. I spent a lot of time studying to be able to get there.'

'Why did you leave?'

'My husband got the job here.'

'You gave up your career for him?'

Melinda paused. 'Not giving it up,' she answered. 'More like putting it on hold.'

'I hope he appreciates the sacrifice you've made,' said Wes. 'It's not always easy to get back into those good jobs like you had at PMH once you've been gone for a while.'

Panic flared in Melinda. She hadn't known that. What if . . . Anger burned at her throat.

'And you worked in the burns unit mainly?'

She refocused on him. 'Yes, but I started in Emergency. It's all in there.' She indicated to the résumé.

'Which did you prefer?'

Melinda gave a slight shrug. 'It's hard to choose. The adrenalin and rush of Emergency can be addictive, as I'm sure you're aware. Burns had its own type of urgency. The kids in burns, I'd get to talk to them a lot more, you know? Once they'd had their surgery or treatment, they were in the hospital for a while, often reliant on the nurses. They'd have long baths to wash away the dead skin, so we could assess the severity of the burn. Kids often got frightened, so I'd spend time sitting with them, talking to them.' She paused. 'Seeing them come back for more treatment was always great too. I guess we had a longer relationship with our patients than the ones who came into Emergency. Sometimes we'd see the same kids six or seven times a year.'

'Yeah, I understand what you're saying.' Wes stood up and Melinda followed his lead.

'I know this isn't what you're looking for, Melinda, but there is a position as a community health nurse going over at the community health campus. The job has a focus on babies and toddlers.' He leaned down and scribbled a phone number and some directions on a notepad then handed it over. 'At least it would keep your hand in. Keep you busy and working with kids.'

Melinda took the piece of paper and thanked him.

'Good luck,' he told her. 'I'm sure you'll find something which suits you.'

Out on the hot street Melinda walked quickly to her car, desperate to be inside where the air-conditioner would dry the sweat on her forehead and the tears that were threatening to spill over. She'd put so much hope into getting a job at the hospital and, although she understood everything Wes had said, still for some *stupid* reason she'd thought she'd be able to buck the system and walk right in.

Maybe not thought. Hoped.

In the safety of the car, Melinda let the tears fall. During the past month she'd been so lonely and bored. She was homesick and beginning to feel she'd given up her life to come to a place she hated. She'd only moved here for Dave. To help further his career, and now, according to Wes, she might lose everything as a result. Where was the fairness in that? *Maybe if I never fit in,* she thought, *I'll be able to go back home and Dave'll understand. Maybe if I'm quick enough they won't have replaced me at PMH and Dave and I could commute to see each other.*

Only three months ago she'd been racing in and out of wards, treating wounds, bandaging and offering pain relief. Soothing frightened children and explaining procedures to parents. She'd been involved in handover meetings and coordinating operations. And now here she was, sitting in her car on the wide street of Barrabine, the sun beating in through the windscreen, and nothing for her to do except go home and look at four walls. She knew very few people and none of them really interested her anyway. From what she'd seen, everyone was keen for a drink and that was about all. Around town she'd seen women pushing kids in strollers or stuck behind the counters of shops. And Kathy? Well, Kathy seemed to stay at home all day, doing wifely things. What could they possibly have in common? What could they talk about?

A little voice reminded her she really hadn't looked very far—the local supermarket, the pub and the parks. The mine museum, where she'd sat for hours in the Chinese garden, in front of the waterfall. The only water feature there was—again something she missed from Perth, which was on the sea. That was all. There was sure to be career women around here somewhere. There surely had to be someone she could have an intellectual conversation with.

There was a tap on the roof of the car and she jumped. Looking up, she saw Kathy smiling at her through the bug-splattered window. Melinda plastered a smile on her face, pretended to cough and quickly wiped her eyes, before winding down the window.

'Hello there, Melinda,' Kathy said in a pleased voice. 'I've been thinking about you. How's everything going?'

'Fine, just fine,' Melinda answered through gritted teeth. She really wanted to scream out she wasn't fine at all. 'And with you?'

'Oh, you know, just the normal things. Getting Spencer organised for work, washing, cleaning. We've started ballroom-dancing lessons, so I've been practising a little while Spencer is at work. It's such fun. You and Dave should come along. Get out and meet people.'

'Spencer is ballroom dancing?' she asked. The very thought was too improbable to imagine.

'Oh yes. Despite his looks, he's very light on his feet.' She paused. 'Would you like to have an early lunch with me? I'd really love to hear how everything is going for you.'

Melinda felt the hotness of tears behind her eyes again and shook her head very quickly. She couldn't afford for anyone to be too kind to her today. She'd start crying again and probably wouldn't be able to stop. 'No thanks, Kathy. Not today. I've got another appointment to get to. But thanks for the offer. Maybe next week.'

Kathy gave a small smile. 'Sure, Melinda whenever you'd like to. I know you might find this hard to believe but I think we have some things in common. It's not too long ago I moved here, you know.' She put her hand in the open window and squeezed Melinda's arm, then readjusted her handbag safely on her shoulder and left.

What was that supposed to mean? Melinda wondered. That she understood what she was feeling? Ha, unlikely! No one could. No one had given up the same sort of job she had and followed their husband to the ends of the earth. Melinda watched her walk down the street, trying to fight the isolation that swept over her.

Chapter 5

Dave was scrutinising the surface around the mine shaft when he noticed the two sets of footprints. They weren't his or Spencer's—the grips on both were wide and jagged, although one set was smaller than the other.

He stared at them for a minute, trying to work out why they looked familiar, then he realised they had the same tread as his brother's Rossi boots. Different to the Blundstone boots he and Spencer wore. He made a mental note to look at the soles of Tim's boots, then grabbed his camera.

Snapping a couple of close-ups of the outline in the dirt, he hoped he could get a cast made and they'd be able to confirm the brand of shoe and size of the foot. He glanced at Tim's feet, trying to see what type of boots he wore, but they weren't anything like Rossi boots. His were ankle-high lace-ups with the Blue Steel logo sewn to the tongue of the boot, and his feet looked like they were larger than the biggest print he'd found.

'Got prints here, Spencer,' he called, following the trail of footprints. In this type of dirt, the feet seemed to sink in a little more than usual, leaving clear outlines of the sole.

'Go anywhere?' Spencer called back.

'I'll follow them.' Dave hoisted the camera over his shoulder and brushed the tiny black bush flies away from his face, remembering Ernie's advice about buying himself a fly net. He would find a camping store when he got back to town and do just that. Spencer and Tim were both wearing one, so they wouldn't take the piss.

As he walked, he drew a line with a stick, separating his prints from the others. They couldn't get confused that way. He followed them through bushes and trees until he hit a little dirt track. Looking up and down it, he couldn't see a car or even vehicle tracks. The outline of the prints seemed to start from the edge of the bush and end at the mine shaft. He stood still and let his eyes look at all the aspects of the thick scrub, then took a couple of steps into it. He could see where the footprints started from—or finished. He couldn't be sure if they started at the mine or the bush. Or vice versa.

Curious, Dave thought as he snapped more photos and went to report his findings back to Spencer.

He wanted to know a lot more about Tim Tucker. Most murder investigations began with the person who had seen the victim last . . . but this wasn't a murder investigation.

Yet.

❧

The hut Tim Tucker lived in was nothing more than a permanent tin shed, with a mud and water mix plastered over the inside of the tin and coated with a lime whitewash. To Dave it looked like something out of the 1920s. There were three tiny rooms—a bedroom, a kitchen and a laundry, all sparsely furnished—but it seemed to have everything a person could need: a hand-operated washing machine, an oven (albeit a bricked-up fireplace with a frying pan hanging over it), and a modern-day travel fridge running off battery power, which to Dave's thinking looked completely out of place. He was sure Tim's living area could have been an exhibit in the mine museum!

The only other thing that looked out of place was a polished piano wedged hard up against the wall, taking up at least half the living area. It seemed like the most cared for item in the house. The mahogany was polished and there wasn't a skerrick of dust on the outside.

'Couldn't ask for a better view,' Tim said as he put the kettle onto his gas burner and lit it. 'Tea?'

Both the detectives nodded their thanks and Dave turned to look out the door. Tim was right. The red earth was scattered with saltbush and broombush, blackbutt and gimlet trees. While the trees stood tall, the bushes grew in clumps beneath, creating what looked like paths, which made Dave want to head out and follow them. The iron-stone sprinkled across the soil still looked like it could be an abandoned asphalt parking lot, but Dave knew better now and saw beauty in it.

'It's very picturesque,' he said. 'How long have you lived here?'

'Bought my lease back in 1938 and haven't moved from here since.' He put three pannikins out on the handmade wooden bench and threw a handful of tea leaves into the boiling water. Dave watched the bubbles boiling up the sides of the billy, mesmerised. He hadn't seen tea made this way since his granddad had taken him camping up in the north of Western Australia.

'Nineteen thirty-eight?' Dave finally asked, surprised. 'You must have been young.'

'I was eighteen then.' Tim turned and looked out the door, his faded blue eyes clearly seeing a scene from the past. 'I'm seventy-seven now. Been here fifty-nine years.'

'Fifty-nine years? And you've never left?' Dave was incredulous. Fifty-nine years living out here, without any luxuries, without company. He found it hard to fathom.

'No. I love it here. The country, the landscape. You know. I'm happy in my own company. Couldn't imagine living in town with neighbours after all this time. Even a trip into Barrabine for supplies is an effort for me.' He looked around and sighed contentedly. 'No, this is where I'm happiest.'

'And mining?'

'Mining doesn't matter to me the way it used to.'

There was another heavy sigh, this time from outside and Dave turned to see the red heeler asleep in the sun. He looked very relaxed and nothing like the fierce dog he had encountered when he'd first arrived.

Spencer got out his notepad. 'Righto, you know the drill, Timmy,' he said. 'We need to ask you a few questions.'

Tim poured the tea and put the mugs on the table. 'Sugar? Milk? I've only got long-life.'

'Just sugar for me. Thanks,' Dave answered.

'Same,' Spencer said.

Tim turned and took a bag of sugar out of the fridge and put it on the table. He saw Dave looking. 'Stops the ants from getting into it,' he said by way of an explanation. Leaning against the bench, he took a sip of his tea. 'What do you want to know?'

'How did you discover the body? I'm going to say body because we don't know what is down there. Might be ten people for all we know.'

'Geez! I hope you're wrong,' Tim said.

'Me too.' Spencer was quiet while he waited for Tim to answer.

'I've had a few nightly visitors lately. You know how it is.' He talked straight to Spencer. 'Fellas walking onto the lease with detectors in the dark. Looking around. I don't mind if they want to have a look on my lease—you know, the amateurs. They've only got small detectors which go maybe a half a metre down—they're not going to find the mother lode. If they find a piece, there'll be something bigger there, more than likely. All I ask is they pinpoint the site they found it and then I can take my machines in and have a look. But they keep sneaking onto the place when I'm not looking. When it's dark or they think I'm not around. Sometimes I see little pinpricks of light. If you

63

watch for long enough you can see them moving slowly across the land.'

'Pinpricks?' Dave asked.

'They wear headtorches so they can see where they're walking,' Tim explained. Then he gave a wicked laugh. 'Sometimes I send Chief out to give 'em a bit of a scare.'

Spencer shook his head, disgusted. 'It's not only you. We're getting more and more complaints about this. They've got the fever and they get greedy. Don't take notice of the boundaries. We've even had bigger mining companies complaining of people walking out onto their tenements. Too many people straying over the borders.'

'Chief here,' he nodded to the dog, 'he usually gets rid of them, but if it's further over, he won't hear them. Last night he got a bit excited, barking and carrying on. Kept running off into the bush and coming back as if to get me. Reckon it was about ten, so I got in me ute and followed him. Didn't see anyone, or any lights. Thieves are too clever for that, so whoever was there last night wasn't an amateur.'

Tim put down his cup and wiped his hands across his eyes, getting rid of the sweat which had pooled there. Dave did the same—it was bloody hot under this tin roof. Probably forty-five if not more. He wondered how Tim could live out here without air-conditioning and other mod cons. Then his grandfather's voice stopped him. 'All he's ever known, lad.' His wise words often returned to Dave when he was dealing with people.

'Chief put up a hell of a racket at the shaft, so I stopped near it and got out to have a look. Black as the ace of spades it was, but I could smell it. No mistaking. Came back here this morning and checked it all out. I heard the flies first. Like a swarm of bees, they were. Course, by the time I drove into the local to use the payphone to ring you fellas, the morning had got on a bit. And this didn't happen last night, 'cause you and I both know bodies don't pong this quick.'

'And did you have any idea who Chief was barking at?'

'Never saw or heard anyone,' Tim answered, his face grim. 'I tell you, Spencer, they want to be careful 'cause I'll take to them with my gun.'

'That won't help anything except get you slapped with a charge, Timmy. Put that thought out of your head. You just gotta ring us. We don't mind coming out and handing out some warnings or slapping the cuffs on the ones who give us lip.'

'I know, I know,' he reluctantly agreed.

'I'm guessing the body's been there maybe three or four days in this heat,' Spencer said.

Tim nodded thoughtfully. 'Might be a little more, maybe. Don't be forgetting it's cooler down there than up here. Not that I'm an expert in these things, but I've seen a lot, you know?'

'Sure do.' Spencer jotted down a note.

'So, you've had people coming onto your place on and off over the last two weeks, yeah?' Dave asked.

'Since time began, lad, but more so over the past month, I'd say.'

'Going back to the body and time of death: you don't remember seeing or hearing anyone nearby in the last week then? No tyre tracks, anything out of place?' Dave wanted to know.

'Nope. The last midnight visitors I *heard* were about two weeks ago. There was an engine noise—just a steady engine noise as if it were on the road—but it was chugging like it was going slowly. The next day I came across tyre tracks and footprints about four or five miles from here. Didn't see any lights. And Chief had a few woofs but didn't get too upset, so they couldn't have come within his protective range. Then there was last night, but that was Chief getting upset—I didn't see or hear anything.'

'Did you recognise the tyre tracks you saw a couple of weeks ago?' Dave asked. 'Could have they been from a vehicle you know?'

'Nah. Just normal four-wheel drive tracks. Could have been anyone.'

'Are there any mines around where you found the prints and tracks?'

'Nope, there's not. I followed them until they left my place and onto another mining lease—one of the big company ones. They didn't go near any of my shafts. They were just working the surface.'

'What about gold, had you found any pieces where the tracks were? Had you told someone you'd found something?'

'Young man, the first rule you learn about gold is you never tell anyone when you've found some and never where you found it. If you do there'll be twenty other blokes in the same spot by morning, or some bugger'll do you over searching for what you've already found.'

'That's a no then.' Dave gave a grin.

'That's a no,' Tim answered without smiling back.

'There been any other reports from other leaseholders, Killjoy or China? They had the same types of visitors?' Spencer asked.

'Haven't seen either of them in a couple of months.'

'Due for a catch-up?'

'Next Saturday.'

Spencer gave a laugh. 'Well, look out Barrabine. You'll all be painting the town red, I got no doubt.'

Tim gave a gentle smile. 'I think we're past all that, don't you? A few quiet beers off the wood and a feed is more our style. And I reckon we'll be at Oakamanda. Not as far to go.'

'Don't kid yourself. I know you fellas know how to have a good time.' Spencer looked down at his notebook. 'I need you to think back and see if you can come up with exact days when you heard the vehicle.'

'Which time?'

'The last one, two weeks ago, would be helpful. Sounds like that's the closest we have.'

'Cor, that's asking a bit.' He rubbed his hand across his face again. 'All the days run together out here, you know that.'

'Just try.'

'What's today? Wednesday?'

Dave and Spencer nodded together.

'Right, so yesterday I went to the western side, and the day before over to Mari's Find.' He continued to talk to himself and tick days off on his fingers, until he said,

'Right-oh, best I can do is I reckon it was Friday night, so twelve days ago.'

'Full moon?'

'Do you want me bowel movements too?'

Dave let out a chuckle and Spencer snorted. 'Just your weather report.'

'Reckon it was. Moon's only about half now. You should have been able to work that out yourself.'

'I want to know what you remember.'

'That's about it, really. It was hot. Maybe twenty-five and I was sleeping outside on the camp bed. Been doing that a bit lately.'

'Last night, you didn't hear any engines, just Chief barking?'

'That's right. And he doesn't bark at wildlife.'

Spencer nodded his understanding. 'You haven't upset anyone you know of? Someone who might have come looking for you?'

'Not that I know of, but I'd be the last one to find out. If someone wanted to have a go at me, I'm sure they wouldn't let me know about it first.'

'But you'd know if you'd had words or a disagreement with someone,' Dave said.

Tim sat back in his chair, quiet. His fingers were steepled as he tapped them against his lips, thinking. 'I can't think of anyone and I know no one has upset me.'

'No one who thinks you stole gold from them, that type of thing?' Dave pushed.

Tim leaned forward and looked Dave in the eye. 'I don't steal gold,' he said.

Spencer snapped his notebook shut. 'That's it for the time being,' he said. 'I'll leave a message for you at the pub if I need you again, all right?'

'No problems. I won't be going anywhere.'

Dave and Spencer shook hands with the old man and climbed into their four-wheel drive.

'You know Tim Tucker pretty well?' Dave asked as they set off, although it was more a statement than a question.

'Met him the second day I was here, so six years ago last month.'

'Good bloke?'

'One of life's gentlemen,' Spencer answered as he flicked on the left-hand blinker and turned down a disused road. 'I don't think I've ever heard him swear, and he's one of the most honest miners out here. You know how I know that?'

Dave glanced over at him. 'How?'

'He doesn't get frightened when the gold squad turns up. Some of the fellas will start shaking and working out a lie before I even turn off the car. Tim, he's different. Ask him a question, he'll tell you the truthful answer. I've never caught him in a lie and he even gives me a bit of inside info when I need it. There is absolutely nothing crook about Tim Tucker.'

'You don't think we need to keep him in mind if it turns out to be a murder? You know as well as I do that the murderer is usually the last person who has been seen with the victim.'

'Yeah, yeah, and of course we've got to have an open mind, but we don't know who the body is yet.' He shrugged. 'Too many questions for the autopsy to answer before we can start. Anyway, like I said, Tim Tucker is as honest as the day is long.'

'Not many people like that around anymore.'

'Not out here, Dave. Farming areas, now most of those blokes are salt of the earth. And the women too. But anywhere there is money to be made there are people who will tell lies and choose greed and power over truth and justice.'

'Never pegged you for a cynic.'

'Not cynical. Realistic. I'll tell you another thing about Tim Tucker.'

'Hmm?' Dave was watching the road wind deeper into the bush and wondered where they were going.

'He's a millionaire twice over.'

It took Dave a moment to compute what Spencer had told him. He looked over at his partner.

'A millionaire?' he asked.

'Twice over.'

Chapter 6

'Where are we?' Dave asked as Spencer pulled up in front of an old rundown pub. He was still trying to get his head around why a twice-over millionaire would live in the middle of nowhere, in a tin shed, without air-conditioning and with only a dog for company.

'This, my friend, is the Oakamanda Pub. And Dee is one of the best informants around. Local knowledge is king. Nothing gets past this bartender.'

Looking around, Dave tried to work out if the pub was operating or not. It must be if Spencer said it was, but it really didn't look like it. There didn't seem to be any other liveable buildings nearby, only the stone one which had a peeling sign hung from the gutters stating it was the *Oakamanda Pub. Cold beer and friendly service.* There were wrecked cars piled on top of each other to one side, and beyond that he could see the glint of a tin roof. He looked again. Three small houses were situated on the edge of the bush. Beyond that there was only more bush stretching out as far as he could see. The dirt road they had arrived on seemed to continue through the tiny town and off into the scrub. Dave wondered where it went. It obviously led somewhere, so maybe the clientele came from that way too.

'And the Oakamanda Pub is . . . ?' he finally asked.

'One of the best little pubs in the area and Dee owns it. Got a bit of history about it. Bikie history. You'd probably know the story. Was owned by the Demon bikie gang a few years ago. Back in the seventies, I suppose. They pissed off another lot . . .'

'Yeah,' Dave broke in. 'Nomad Rebels turned up and there was a shoot-out between the two gangs. Four people dead and three injured. The police couldn't break through the code of silence to find out who started the shooting, or what initiated it.'

'Dead right.' Spencer nodded.

'I reckon I was about seven or eight when that happened and we didn't have TV on the farm then, but I can remember Mum talking about it. You know, "What is the world coming to" type of thing. Then there were the war stories of the older detectives I worked with.' Dave opened his door and got out, shielding his eyes from the sun. It hadn't got any cooler.

Spencer pointed to the front verandah. 'Demons took the heaviest losses. First shot fired was into Fast Frankie Appleton's chest there, underneath the window. Fast Frankie was known for his gun-toting ability, but they didn't stand him in good stead that day. He died instantly, according to all reports. He was the ringleader and manager of the pub. Damien Appleton, Frankie's brother, went down next in the front bar, then Kev Grant. Dazzling Darryl Punter, or DD as the blokes here called him, from Nomad Rebels was just coming in the back door when one of the others shot him through the neck. Bang!' He made the action of a gun. 'Bang, bang. Then one more for good measure. Bang.' Each time he said the word, Spencer aimed his fingers at the spot the men had died.

'Found drugs in the pocket of Fast Frankie and more in his bedroom. Not enough to be saleable, which is why we still don't know what it was all about. Cold case now, of course. Only personal use.' He paused. 'More than personal use,' he amended, 'but you gotta remember he would've stocked up when he came out here. Like farmers' wives do when they go to town to do the weekly shopping. Anyway, not enough to make it saleable.

'There was a gun we couldn't trace on DD, but that was all. If the argument was about drugs or a sale gone wrong or women, the coppers up here at the time couldn't find a speck of evidence. Couldn't charge Frankie for possession because he was dead!'

'You sound like you worked the case.'

Spencer shook his head. 'No, mate, but one of the fellas I worked with up in Karratha did. He told me all about it. One of the first things I did when I turned up here was to come out and see it for myself.'

'People still come here? You'd have thought that the murders would have put people off.'

'To the contrary,' Spencer said, hoisting up his shorts and starting to walk over to the pub. 'It makes the place more attractive to them. Dee's done the whole pub up on this incident. Kept the bullet holes in the wall, found all the newspaper articles and pinned them up around the bar. It's almost like a living museum. Tourists seem to love it.'

'But is it worth it? I mean . . .' Dave looked around. It was so quiet, he could hear the flies buzzing. 'There's no one here, Spencer. She can't get too many people through in a day. How does she make a living?'

'I asked her last time I was here. Thirty to forty tourists a day stop off in the hotter months and anywhere from eighty to one hundred during the height of the tourist season. When the grey nomads get going there's heaps of trade. All that area out there,' he motioned with his hand to the large gravel pad which seemed to have no purpose, 'can be full of caravans and four-wheel drives. The Oakamanda Pub is a tourist attraction as well as the local watering hole for the miners who live around here.' He pushed open the door and went in. Dave was pleased to feel the blast of cool air on his forehead.

'G'day, Dee,' Spencer said to the woman behind the bar.

Dave watched as she looked up and gave a broad smile. 'Well, well, well, if it isn't Spencer Brown. You lost or something?' Her ample breasts and stomach shook as she started a rough whiskey and cigarettes laugh. 'What you doing here, honey?' She came around from the bar and held out her arms.

Spencer grinned and gave her a smacking kiss on the cheek. 'Do I need a reason for popping by?' he asked.

'You've always got a reason. Unless you're thirsty and that's still a reason.' Her gaze flicked over to Dave. 'And who's this handsome man? Geez, the police force is training them young these days.' She held out her hand. 'I'm Dee, owner of Oakamanda Pub.'

'Dave Burrows. Detective. Spencer's partner.' They shook hands and Dave smiled at her.

'He's not that young,' Spencer put in. 'Looks younger than he is. Aren't you? How old again?'

Dave laughed uncomfortably. 'Thirty.'

'Thirty,' Spencer confirmed, turning back to Dee. 'There you go, and he's just got married a month ago.'

'Oh, you're a late starter,' Dee said as she flicked him the once-over.

'You reckon,' Dave said. He wasn't about to tell a perfect stranger how he'd worked for his dad until he was twenty-three and then one day, out of the blue, he'd been told there wasn't room at home for him. How he'd had to find a way to stay involved in agriculture and he'd chosen to aim for the stock squad. That's where he'd be next year or maybe the year after, depending on how this year went.

'So, what do you think of my little pub? I guess Spencer has filled you in on the history,' Dee asked Dave. 'I had the bloodstains removed from the floor,' she looked down at the uneven wooden floorboards and scratched at a spot with her worn-out sandshoe. 'But you can still see the outline. See? It was there. And one of the bullet holes? Over there just behind the bar near the mirror.' She pointed.

Dave looked around. Photos lined the walls, as did pictures of large nuggets: *Found, 8oz nugget, 5km from Oakamanda* or *2oz nugget, found 9km from Oakamanda.* On one wall there was an old rusty rabbit trap pinned to the wall. Under it was written: *Tap here for complaints.*

'It's great,' Dave said and he meant it. Even though the pub had the wild-west feel he was beginning to get used to, it was clean and cool and Dee had obviously gone to a lot of trouble to display the place's history.

Dee turned her attention back to Spencer. 'Drink or business?' She flipped a tea towel over her shoulder and went back behind the bar.

'Business,' Spencer said, hoisting himself up onto a bar stool and helping himself to a handful of peanuts which were sitting on the bar.

'And here I was thinking it was my good looks that had brought you all the way from Barrabine.'

Spencer grinned for a moment and then turned serious. 'Heard anything about people going onto leases they shouldn't be?'

Dee let out a loud laugh. 'Only every day, sunshine. You'll need to be a bit more specific.'

'Unusual happenings . . . Anyone come in here complaining of seeing tracks the morning after type thing?'

Dee stared at Spencer, her wide smile gone, replaced by a frown. Then she leaned forward and picked up a large plastic display folder, thumping it in front of Dave. 'There's all the history of this joint. Newspaper articles, court documents, you name it, it's in there. Knock yourself out. Have a read. Interesting stuff in there. By the time you finish that, your partner here might have a sensible question to ask me.' She folded her arms over her breasts and stared at Dave with a grin.

'Um, thanks,' he said, glancing over at Spencer, who was beginning to open his arms in protest.

'Ah, come on, Dee. Don't be like that,' Spencer said, his voice cajoling. 'I can only tell you so much and you know it! Just thought I'd see if you've heard any more discontent than usual. Any mutterings from the locals or bragging from the tourists. That sort of thing. People camping in wrong spots or locals overreacting.'

'Nothing more than usual, and that's a fact, Spencer. Timmy Tucker must have a problem, though,' she said. 'He was in here this morning ringing you guys on the pay-phone. Don't take a detective to work out it's his joint you're asking about.'

Spencer held out his hands in a 'you got me' way.

'Seriously? I've heard there're a few blokes pushing the boundaries. Walking onto leases at night, but no one ever seems to be able to catch them,' Dee said. 'Old Brandy up on the hill said he met one carload coming in his driveway 'bout two or three days ago. Got the gun out, I reckon, 'cause they came in here to get a drink and calm their nerves! Never said much 'cause their English wasn't too good, but they were as white as ghosts and their hands were shaking.

Think they might have got the full force of his hospitality. I'm sure they were only backpackers looking for a place to park their van for the night and there wasn't anything too sinister about them.'

'Geez, I wish he wouldn't do that!' Spencer said, frowning.

'Only been doing it for the past twenty years. Old habits are hard to break, you know.' Dee looked steadily at him. 'I'll tell you something interesting though. I've heard four-wheel drives coming past the pub in the early hours of the morning for the last couple of weeks and that's pretty unusual. Even with the mine shift changes, when they're running twenty-four hours a day, I don't hear cars after three in the morning. There were two cars last night. One at three-thirty and the other at four.'

'You're very precise with your times,' Dave said.

'Sweetheart, when you're my age, you don't sleep so good. Anyway, Mary's been waking me up a lot more recently. She's pretty bloody noisy with that mop and bucket of hers.'

'Mary?'

'Our resident ghost.'

Dave managed not react. 'I see.'

Spencer opened his mouth to say something, but Dave beat him to it. 'And how does, uh, Mary wake you up?'

'You don't believe me, do you?' she said with a grin. 'I know people think I'm mad, but I don't care. I haven't been out in the sun and had me brain fried. I've heard her.

Even seen her once. One night in the hallway. I was getting up to my sick grandkid, but she'd already beaten me to it.'

Dave felt goosebumps spread across his skin and looked around as if Mary might be standing behind him.

'Mary lives here and has done for the whole time I've owned the place,' Dee continued. 'I've done research on her and everything. She's a chambermaid from the late 1800s and she used to rattle her mop and bucket when it was time for everyone to leave.' She leaned closer to Dave. 'That's what I hear. The rattling of the mop and bucket,' she whispered.

Spencer cleared his throat. 'You'll have to work harder if you want to frighten Dave. He used to be a farmer and now he's a cop, so he doesn't frighten that easy.'

Dave nodded in agreement, pretending her story hadn't affected him.

'I'm just telling it how it is,' Dee said. She gently thumped Spencer on the arm. 'You know about Mary, dontcha?'

'I do and I've heard her,' Spencer said quite seriously.

'Hey, I didn't say I didn't believe!' Dave put in.

Dee burst out laughing. 'No need to sound so defensive, love! Gotta tell you my stories while you're here. Now, back to poor Timmy Tucker.'

'Yeah, let's focus on the work,' Spencer said. 'You heard one vehicle at three-thirty and one at four?'

'Yep, sure did.'

'Both coming from the same direction?'

'Nope. One came in from west of town and the other came in from the main road to Barrabine.'

Dave wrote down the information in his notebook. 'Was it strange enough for you get up and have a look?' he asked.

'Only because I had to get up and go to the loo. It was a red wagon of some sort. Not a mining vehicle.'

Dave looked at her quizzically and Spencer explained quickly, 'There's a difference between leases, tenements and mines. When people talk about the mines it's the big company-owned mines, like the ones I showed you on the first day. They have shift changes every twelve hours and mostly the blokes drive around in white single- or dual-cabs with orange flags on them. Sometimes they have an orange flashing light on the roof. Not all, admittedly, but ninety percent of them. When Dee says it wasn't a mine vehicle, she's saying it didn't look like a vehicle which would be carting mine employees around.'

Dave nodded. 'Okay, so red? Nothing to do with mining. Privately owned then?'

'I couldn't say that, but certainly not a mine one. And it's not local 'cause I would've recognised it otherwise.' She took the tea towel from her shoulder and started to wipe the bar.

'How can you be sure it was red? It would have been dark.'

'There was enough moon to see. I couldn't say it was fire-engine red, but red, burgundy,' she shrugged. 'You know what I mean.'

'China or Killjoy been in recently?' Spencer asked, switching subjects.

'Nope. Not for about a week. Killjoy said he was heading north to work his lease up outta Karralie.' She mentioned

a town about two hundred kilometres away. 'He'll probably only be gone a couple of weeks though. And I don't
reckon he'll be leaving until after the social club catch-up
on Saturday night.'

'Social club?'

'All the locals come in once a month and have a catch-up.
It's this Saturday night, so he won't be going until after.'

That tied in with what Tim had told them about meeting
his friends this weekend. Dave ran through what he knew
and at this point it wasn't much.

'Do you think it could have been the same car?' he asked.

'What, going to somewhere and back again?' Her smoky
voice held a ring of disbelief. 'Can't get anywhere out here
in half an hour, love.'

'What if they were going somewhere and had forgotten
something, so turned around to go back and get it?' he asked.

'If you live out here and are driving around at that time
of the day, I'd think you're going to be a lot more organised
than that. Who'd want to start off at three-thirty and have
to turn around?' she said in a scornful tone.

'Point there,' Spencer said.

Dave jotted down: *Camped one side of town, killed on
the other, back again?* He'd talk more to Spencer about it
when they were in the car.

'Oh, bugger me,' Dee said and put down her tea towel,
wide-eyed. 'I'll tell you what I just remembered. Couple
of nights ago there was a bloke in here who had a huge
nugget, and I mean huge.' She held her fingers about an
inch apart and Spencer whistled. 'He was bragging about

it and no one does that. Not much anyway. I did hear him say he'd heard a dog barking in the distance that had put the wind up him, so he hightailed out of wherever he was.' She turned excitedly to Spencer. 'Timmy's not the only bloke who's got a dog, but he's probably the most ferocious one I know of out here. He brought Chief in with him last time he came and he put up a bit of a woofing when my new barmaid walked in. Scared the pants off her, poor love. So they might have been talking about Tim's place!'

Chapter 7

'Okay, one body only,' said Shannon Wood. The forensic pathologist had come straight from the plane to the scene, then on to the hospital. It had taken nearly twenty-four hours from the first phone call to the mine, fire and rescue team to bring the body to the surface. Shannon had arrived just as the all clear had been given for her to descend into the mine and look for evidence. Two days later and Dave was keen for news on what she knew. 'Male. That's nearly all I know right now.'

The photos both Shannon and Dave were staring at were graphic against the glare of the whiteboard in the detectives' office at Barrabine Police Station.

Dave recalled how a man from the mine, fire and rescue team suited up and was winched down the hole. It had been his job to get the remains into a body bag, secure it and get it to the surface. Once the body was retrieved, Shannon had been given the all clear to be lowered down to examine the site, complete with high-powered torches and camera. The inspection had been time-consuming and tedious work under trying conditions.

To Dave, who wasn't an expert like Shannon was, it didn't look like they would be able to get any information from the body. The decomposition was advanced, despite the coolness of the underground grave. The facial features were unrecognisable from bloat and skin slip, and the body was coloured a bruised red and green. Of course, even though it looked unidentifiable, with modern methods he knew Shannon would be able to get a lot of info from the body.

'I'll take the body back to Perth and finish the rest of the examination there. I just don't have the facilities here to run the types of tests I need and do a full exam. He's possibly between the ages of thirty and sixty,' Shannon said, breaking into Dave's thoughts.

'Male, then. Anything worth mentioning with the body? I guess you've gone through his pockets? Or did you pick up anything down the mine shaft?' Dave asked. The office was stifling, with the afternoon sun on the west-facing windows, and the air-conditioner wasn't keeping up. He could feel the sweat running down his spine and he wanted to wipe it away, but he focused on the details Shannon was giving him.

'Over here.' She indicated for him to follow her. 'There are a few things—watch, pen, set of keys, they look like house keys or something similar.' She poked at them through the bag.

'We should be able to work out when we've got the right person, then,' Dave joked. 'We'll be able to get into his house.'

'But look at this.' Shannon took out another bag from underneath the top one. It held three small pieces of gold.

Dave gave a low whistle. 'Would you look at that,' he said softly, leaning closer to inspect the nuggets.

'Pity we don't know where he got them from,' she said.

'Yeah. Spencer said to me once that gold doesn't come with an address or GPS coordinates. Would make life a lot easier if it did!' He continued to look at them for a few moments longer before turning back to the keys. 'I'll talk to Spencer but I think we can analyse gold and find out what general area it came from. Whether or not it can be narrowed down to sections of the goldfields, I don't know, but if we can, I'll get it done. Where did you find them?'

'Left-hand pocket. Strange really. They were loose in there. I would have thought someone in possession of gold would have had it in a plastic bag, or wrapped up somehow. Loose in a pocket, anything could happen to them—fall out, get lost right in the corner, you know what pockets can be like.'

'That is weird. Spencer has said a lot of the prospectors carry film canisters—you know, the sort that hold camera film?'

'Yeah, I know the ones you mean.' Shannon bent over and put her face close to the plastic bag. 'It's a lot darker than I thought gold would be, dull is a better word.'

'The jewellers haven't got hold of it and given it a good polish yet.' He leaned forward too. 'And it's still got dirt ingrained in it. See here?' He pointed with the end of a pen.

Her hair brushed against his arm and he moved a little to the side.

'Yeah, yeah. Interesting thing, with all the holes and gouges. Some of it looks like there've been bubbles inside and burst!' She straightened. 'Anyway, how are you liking it out in the sticks?' she asked.

'I'm loving it,' Dave said honestly. 'Don't miss the city one bit.'

'The morgue is so much quieter without you around,' she elbowed him gently. 'Always knew when you were coming because your boots clicked loudly on the floor and your laugh was really loud. You've got a lovely laugh.'

Dave straightened up and grinned. 'Don't mind being known by my laugh. Laughing is much better than frowning.' As he said it a flash of Melinda's face from the night before hit him. She'd been standing at the window in the lounge, scowling as some kids walked up and down the street. They didn't have shoes and were yelling loudly, one was bouncing a football. Two of them had come to the front gate and tried to open it until Ernie had called out over the fence and scared them off. When he'd turned back her face had been contorted into an ugly grimace.

Shannon stood up too and patted his arm. 'Anyway, we miss you.'

'You know I have to ask,' Dave said, changing the subject.

'Ask what?'

'Is there a cause of death?'

'Nothing obvious,' she said, moving away. 'No gunshot wound, stab marks, ligature marks. I'll need to run toxicology and do a proper autopsy. Should have the prelim results to you in two days. Depending, of course, what's backed up when I get there. I had a phone call yesterday saying we had twelve on the waitlist.'

'Twelve?'

'Suicides, unexplained deaths. No murder. Your John Doe should get priority. We're booked on the flight back tonight.'

'We' meant Shannon and the body. One of the frustrating things about policing so far from the city was the lack of resources and the delays this caused. Lengthy time delays meant more decomposition, and the killer, if there was one, would be getting further and further from their grasp, as evidence disappeared, swallowed up by the bloat and active decay of the body.

'You've never told me why you became a forensic pathologist,' he asked. 'I mean, how long have we known each other? Two years?'

Shannon thought before nodding. 'Something like that.'

'And this scene, it's not your average one—pretty scary going down into the shaft with the smell and flies. Not knowing what you were going to find. Being so dark. Why'd you sign up for that sort of thing?' He remembered some of the younger officers ogling the pretty pathologist when she'd first arrived. Betting each other who was going to get her out on a date first; admiring her curves and long hair.

He might have been interested himself if he hadn't been seeing Melinda by then.

Shannon pulled her hair back and curled it into a bun at the back of her head before securing it with a hair band she had on her wrist. 'My grandmother,' she said. 'She was found in the state forest three months after she'd gone missing. She had dementia and had wandered off. The police and SES spent days looking for her but it wasn't until a couple of hikers came through that she was found. And then it took a little while for her to be identified.' She shrugged. 'I don't know, I just wanted to make sure people were looked after when they were brought into the morgue and identified as quickly as possible. It's awful not knowing what's happened to your loved one, and I can say that from experience. When Nana wasn't found, it was like a big question mark hanging over our heads, and the fewer people who have to go through that the better.'

They left the office and walked out into the hallway. The sun didn't penetrate into the middle of the building and it was much cooler. Shannon walked to an air-conditioning vent and stood underneath it, her head tilted backwards to catch the cool air.

'That's much better! What about you?' she asked. 'I always knew you were a country boy, so I guess I'm not surprised to see you out here.'

'How'd you know that? I didn't tell too many people.' He'd still been smarting from the injustice of his father's dismissal when he'd arrived in Perth and had kept his past to himself.

'The way you dressed. Your *boots*! And your casual demeanour. I had cousins who were from a farm and you all act the same.'

Leaning against the wall with his arms crossed, Dave answered, 'I always thought I was going to be a farmer. That's what I *wanted* to be. Dad has five thousand acres at Northam. He does a bit of cropping but the main business is merinos. Wool and wethers.' He paused and scratched his head. 'Got two older brothers, one who's married, and they got the berth, not me. Not enough land for four families to make a living.'

'Tough,' she said.

'Yeah. I worked around for a bit—you know, working on other people's farms. Even toyed with the idea of trying to buy a bit of land myself, but I couldn't make it work. So I had to think of another way to be involved in agriculture and live in the country.'

Shannon looked up at him. 'How does being in the police force keep you involved in farming?'

'The stock squad,' he answered simply.

Realisation dawned on her face. 'Oh, I get it.' She nodded. 'Yeah, I really do.'

He started to walk off down the hallway and Shannon followed.

'How'd you go down the shaft?' Dave asked.

'Just got to focus on what needs to be done. Interesting though, one thing I can tell you—and the guys have photos of this—there aren't any scratch marks at the bottom of the mine, but there are on the way down. I can see where he's reached out and tried to stop himself from falling—you know what I mean?'

Dave nodded.

'The pools of blood I found down there were small. His heart wasn't beating or didn't beat for long when he hit the ground. There were splatters of blood and scratch marks on the upper part of the mine walls. Even with the decomposition, I can tell his fingertips are very badly grazed, but I'm really hoping I'll be able to get partial prints at least. Anyway, what I'm saying is he hadn't tried to get out of the mine once he'd fallen in, so he wasn't unconscious or dead when he first fell but he was by the time he got to the bottom.'

'Do you have a time frame?'

'Hard to tell with the differences in temps but I'd guess maybe five days. Possibly six.' She shrugged and gave him a half-smile. 'Dave, you understand that I'll know more when I get back to Perth.'

'I know, I know, just thought I'd push it as far as I could.'

'You detectives are all the same!' She glanced at her watch. 'You've got to wait for the science. Anyway, I've got two hours before my flight leaves. Do you want to have a drink before I go?'

Dave realised the day had flown and it was now past six o'clock. 'I'd love to, but I'd better go and catch up with Spencer, then get home. Melinda will be wondering where I am.'

Shannon's face flamed red. 'Shit! I'd forgotten you'd got married. Sorry! Well, I'd better get organised. I'll send through the results as soon as I have them.'

Dave opened his mouth to ask why she was apologising but Shannon turned quickly and disappeared into the ladies' toilet.

He frowned. She'd always been shy around him, but completely professional. Never once indicated she'd been interested in him. Dave admitted to himself that if he hadn't been with Melinda he would have asked Shannon out on a date. It had been her eyes which had caught his attention first—vivid pale blue but always sparkling, no matter how awful the case was. It had taken Dave nearly eight months to realise she had long black hair under the medical cap she always wore, and was slim and pretty beneath the gown and mask. She also understood his work. To someone who worked strange hours and seemed to be on call twenty-four hours a day, that was attractive.

'Anything?' Spencer asked, interrupting Dave's thoughts.

Dave shoved his hands in his pockets, trying to put the curious interaction with Shannon to the back of his mind, and followed Spencer back into the detectives' office. 'Pen, keys and a watch.' He then told him about the scratch marks and approximate time of death and age. 'Still not much to go on, really.'

'Hmm.' Spencer walked over to a map on the wall with three pins stuck into it. He held a ruler to measure the distance between one pin and another and jotted a note on the whiteboard beside him. 'Murder?'

'Can't be sure yet. Shannon said there were no obvious signs but, as you know, she has to do the full lot of tests.'

'The question here, Dave, is what was a man doing out on a property which wasn't his, near a mine shaft which wasn't his, and how did he end up down the bottom, dead?'

'All good questions,' Dave answered. 'Shannon did come up with something interesting, though.'

'Hmm?' Spencer said distractedly.

'Spencer?' Dave said sharply, wanting his full attention. 'Three gold nuggets.'

Spencer didn't move for a moment, then slowly turned around. 'Nuggets?'

'Yeah. Three. Shannon said they came out of his pocket. Not in a canister or plastic bag or any container at all, just loose.'

'Unusual.' He frowned, then turned back to the board. *GOLD* he wrote in capital letters then ringed it three times. 'Might be nothing. He could be a prospector who found something that day or days before. Might not be murder, he could have just fallen down the shaft.' He tapped at the whiteboard.

'But he didn't have any gear,' Dave said suddenly. 'There wasn't a detector found, was there?'

Spencer shook his head. 'Nothing in the shaft or within a five-hundred-metre radius. Still, just because there wasn't any prospecting gear with him doesn't mean he wasn't a prospector. It might be at his camp . . . if we could find it.'

'Bit like looking for a needle in a haystack. We've got a backyard of a million acres and the rest to search!'

'Ah, don't be despondent, Dave. We'll turn up something.'

'We've still got the footprints,' Dave said.

'Yep, we do. Did you ask forensics to make casts?'

'I did that when we came back in from the scene. But we don't know which way the vic came from. The tyre tracks Tim told us about couldn't have anything to do with *this* body because they were in a different section of the lease. We have footprints, which start at the road, but no car tracks. He had to have walked in. But how did he get to that part of the road in the first place? Do you think these tracks are even involved? Could they be some random tracks? Has he parked a vehicle a long way away and walked?'

Spencer stuck his tongue out of the corner of his mouth as he thought. 'Yeah, and yeah. Long distance walking might be the answer. Or, it might not. Could certainly have been a prospector moving through—especially with all the reports we're getting about people straying onto areas that aren't theirs. However, it may be too coincidental. My question is, if the vic was by himself, how did he get there? There weren't any vehicle tracks and footprints don't appear out of nowhere unless you're a ghost or alien. And if he wasn't by himself, who was with him?'

'I think I've just solved it,' Dave said in a serious tone.

Spencer frowned. 'What?'

Dave nodded to emphasise his point. 'Mary.'

'Who?'

'Mary, Oakamanda's resident ghost. Obviously, these are her tracks—she followed him, pushed him down the mine and disappeared. You said yourself, it had to be a ghost or an alien. I'd rather go with ghost scenario, because aliens aren't my thing at all.'

Spencer laughed loudly. 'Get away with you, cheeky bugger!'

The humour faded from the room as they both continued to look at the map.

'Identification,' Dave finally said.

Spencer pointed the whiteboard marker at him. 'Correct. We have to identify him before we can do anything else. Maybe the autopsy will turn up a barcode we can scan and it'll be easy.'

'Ha! Every detective's hope. Or at least arrive in the morgue with a wallet and driver's licence. I'll check the missing persons reports. What are you doing here?'

'Okay, this pin is Tim's mine and here,' he slid his finger over the map, 'this is the Oakamanda Pub. There's twenty kilometres between the two. I was trying to work out if there was enough time to get to Tim's place and back through Oakamanda Pub within that thirty-minute time frame.'

'Going back to the red vehicle that Dee heard? What do you think?'

'It's possible, but the driver wouldn't be able to do much there. Unless he already had a body in the back of the car and he pushed it down.'

'Different nights, though,' Dave pointed out. 'And Shannon seems to think that he wasn't unconscious or dead when he went down, but certainly was by the time he hit the bottom, so a body in the back of a car probably isn't what we're looking for.'

'Agreed, but Dee also said she'd heard vehicles frequently over the past couple of months, didn't she? On that, a body in the car doesn't have to be dead. Held against their will maybe, or unconscious, but not necessarily dead.'

Dave nodded his agreement. 'Mmm, so you think this car might have something to do with this death?'

Spencer shook his head. 'I can't say that until we know if the poor bugger was murdered or accidentally walked down a mine shaft.'

'So we've ruled out that he died elsewhere and his body was dumped. We already know that Shannon indicated there was only a small amount of blood from the fall. He wouldn't have bled if he was already deceased because there's no heart action to make him bleed.'

Spencer nodded slowly as he put his marker down. 'See?' he said with a grin. 'That's why you're one of the hotshots in Perth. You're quick and onto it.'

Dave felt his face redden. 'Don't know about that.'

'Credit where credit is due. You'll probably be wasted here, Burrows.'

'I don't think so. I'll just check those MPs, okay?'

Dave sat at his desk and pulled up the Missing Persons Register on the police database and typed in what he knew, which, as he kept telling himself, wasn't very much.

Scrolling through he looked at the ages because that was the best thing he had to go on. Occasionally he glanced at the photos but, not knowing what the man had looked like before he'd died, he couldn't make a connection.

Twenty-seven, no good.

Nineteen.

Thirty-four . . . Dave stopped to read the information:

Jack Doust, reported missing on 10 September 1996 from Perth. Last seen wearing a red windcheater, denim jeans and sandshoes. Disappeared after a disagreement with wife. Missing ten days before reported.

Dave printed it off, knowing it could be a possibility, then went on to the next one.

Fifty-two-year-old Ian Shipe. Reported missing on 5 June 1995. Wearing tracksuit pants, possibly grey, black jumper and runners. Requires medication. History of mental health problems.

He was a possibility too.

'Dave?'

He looked up at the sound of his name and realised an hour had passed and he only had two possibilities.

'G'day, Nathan,' he said to one of the other detectives. 'You off?'

'Yeah, you in for a quick drink?'

Dave glanced at the screen and saw he had thirty files still left to go through. It would be better to have the whole lot sorted and all the possibilities ready for Monday morning. Hopefully by then they'd have Shannon's report and they'd be able to discount half of the possibilities and work on the others . . . if it wasn't murder. 'Nah, mate. I want to get through this lot tonight. Next time?'

'Sure. Catch you on Monday.'

Giving him the thumbs up, Dave checked the time and picked up the phone to ring Melinda. When she didn't answer, he left a message on the machine: 'Hi, honey, I'm going to be a couple of hours late tonight. Still working on that body we picked up Wednesday and I want to do some final checks. Hope your day was great. See you tonight. Maybe about seven or just after.'

As he hung up the phone he wondered where she could be. Usually she was sitting by the telephone, waiting for her parents or sisters to call. Maybe she was hanging out a load of washing or talking to Ernie over the fence.

He chuckled to himself, knowing that wasn't a possibility; so far, the Indigenous community seemed to make her uncomfortable. He wasn't sure why—perhaps because she hadn't grown up knowing any Aboriginal people, whereas he'd had Aboriginal friends at school. Turning his attention back to the computer screen, he continued reading the files.

Chapter 8

Melinda heard her husband's message and scowled. She'd been sitting on the couch for the last three hours, crying and hitting the cushions. Dave being late was the last straw. She needed him at home. To yell and scream at. For him to be able to calm her down and make her see sense.

Trouble was, she didn't want to see sense. She wanted to hit out. Let him know she blamed him for this. For her unhappiness. Her lack of career.

Was she overreacting? She didn't care. It was how she felt.

She stomped across the lounge and picked up the wedding photo sitting on the dresser, wanting to throw it across the room. There was no way, when they'd driven out of Bunbury, she'd ever envisaged being unemployed, lonely, homesick and angry at Dave. Certainly, she'd been nervous about the move and, if she was truthful, appre-hensive. Her meeting with Wes had upset her more than she'd anticipated—especially when he'd told her it was hard to get back into good jobs once she'd resigned.

Instead of having a fulfilling and challenging job to go to every day, she was holed up here, looking at four white walls while the world went on without her.

'Bastard,' she hissed and threw the photo towards the kitchen with all her might.

The photo hit the bench and shattered, sending glass splintering across the kitchen.

'Bastard,' she whispered again and burst into loud, noisy sobs.

❧

'Hey, Mr Dave?' a voice whispered through the darkness as Dave hurried up the path to his front door. 'Mr Dave?'

'Evening, Ernie,' he answered as he continued to walk. Dave didn't want to get stopped in conversation right now. He was tired and had the beginning of a headache, along with an aching back from sitting all day.

'Got sad missus, yeah? Sad missus,' the low voice said.

That made Dave stop. He turned and went over to the fence. 'What do you mean?'

'Crying. Lots of crying. Then I heard glass break. Uh-huh. Glass break. I knock on door, you know? To see if I can help. No answer. Ah nuh. No answer.'

Closing his eyes, Dave rubbed the back of his neck and let out a heavy sigh. 'She's not settling in well.'

'Take time. I bring her present, next time I out in bush. Yeah? Present.'

'You're a good neighbour, Ernie. Thanks, mate. Have a good night.'

Dave walked in the door and was greeted by broken glass and an empty house. He slowly looked around and realised the glass in the kitchen had come from a framed photo of the wedding.

'Melinda?' he called, stepping over the glass and walking down the hall. Fear trickled through him but everything was in place and it didn't look like anything had been stolen. So where was Melinda? Had she left him? Had he destroyed their relationship by bringing her here?

'Melinda?' he called again. Again, no answer. Just a house so silent he could hear the tick of the clock in the kitchen.

He checked the bathroom and pushed open the toilet door but both were empty. In the spare room there was a suitcase half packed, but still no sign of his wife.

Unsure what to do, he looked through the case. He was relieved to realise her grandmother's ring and watch set weren't packed. If they had been, he would have known their marriage was over before it was even a few months old. The ruby-studded ring and watch were Melinda's most prized and loved possessions and she never went anywhere without them.

'Hi,' her voice was suddenly behind him.

Spinning around, his arms outstretched, Dave started to smile, but his smile faded the moment he saw her face.

'Hey?' he said uncertainly. She was wearing her grandmother's jewellery and her face was puffy.

'I didn't get a job,' she said.

'Oh.' He suddenly understood.

'I'm really angry.' She stared at him, heat in her eyes.

'I'm sure you are—'

'No. At you,' she interrupted. 'Do you realise I may never get another job like my old one now I've resigned?'

'I'm sure that's—'

'Wes Corris told me today. He's director of nursing, so he'd have a pretty good idea.'

He reached out for her, tried to pull her into his chest, but she twisted away.

'I've given up everything for you,' she said, her tone changing from angry to icy cold. 'Everything.' She turned on her heel and left the room.

Dave stood still, staring at her retreating back. He had no idea how to deal with this; he'd never seen Melinda this unhappy.

'Honey?' he said, following her.

She was standing in the middle of the lounge room, tears rolling down her cheeks. This time she let him put his arms around her and hold her. He kissed her forehead and rubbed her back, trying to make the anger go away. For his sake as much as hers.

'Thank you,' he said. 'Thank you for moving here with me. For supporting me the way you always do. I'd be lost without you.' He kissed her forehead again. 'I'm sorry if you're angry with me. I never wanted it to be like this. I just assumed you'd get a job and everything would be fine.'

'How can it be? I might never get a job like my old one. All the training I've done will have been for nothing.'

He shook his head. 'No, it won't. Something will come along. I know it will.' Even to his ears that sounded like empty promises, but he had to say something. To help her.

Dave could see everything from her point of view. She had given up everything precious to her to come to Barrabine, to be with him. His grandfather's voice whispered: 'Melinda didn't give up everything. She's still got her qualifications. She just needs to find her fit.'

'It'll be okay,' he said gently. 'We'll be okay. You just need to find your fit.'

❧

Feeling like her eyes were gritty and swollen, Melinda picked up the phone and punched in the number Kathy had given her on one of her earlier visits. Dave had left early for his usual Saturday routine of a run and coffee. He hadn't wanted to leave her, but she'd insisted he go.

'Go and do something today, by yourself. Just give me some time,' she said to him. 'I need time by myself.' She knew he'd been upset when he'd walked out the front door, but she couldn't help that. She had thinking and working out to do. And that included a phone call.

She'd argued with herself for the whole morning about whether to make the call or not, but finally she'd given in to her need to speak to someone other than her family. The last phone call she'd had with her dad had ended in him suggesting she come back to Bunbury to live with them. Her father wouldn't like to know this but as soon as he'd said the words, her world had come into focus. He was still pushing her to come home, as if she were a child who didn't know what was best for her. As if she'd made a silly decision and needed help to get out of a 'situation'.

She didn't. She'd decided to marry her soulmate. And if it meant living here in Barrabine with him, Melinda just had to deal with that. She didn't want her marriage to fail. She loved Dave too much.

She thought back to the phone call she'd made to her sister yesterday. Sarah had told her in no uncertain terms it was time for her to pull herself together. 'You can't just keep ringing me up daily and saying how much you hate Barrabine. It's dirty, or hot, or you can't get a job. Life is what you make it, Melinda,' she'd said.

Her family couldn't really understand what she was feeling, but she did know someone who might.

'Hello?'

Melinda paused before saying, 'Um, hi, Kathy?'

'Yes?'

'It's Melinda Burrows here.'

Melinda could almost feel Kathy's pleasure down the line. 'Oh, Melinda, it's great to hear from you. How are you?'

How was she? Did she tell the truth?

'Um . . .' A lump swelled in her throat, closing it over.

'How about I pop over?'

'Thank you.' She put down the phone and burst into tears again.

By the time Kathy arrived, Melinda had regained some composure but she was sure it was clear to the older woman that she'd been crying.

'I'm guessing you'll find it hard to believe, Melinda,' said Kathy as they sat down to a cup of tea, 'but I felt miserable when we first moved here too. Angry at Spencer for dragging me to some godforsaken place where there were more flies than people. Angry I had to leave all the friends I'd made in Margaret River. Ha! Couldn't get two more different places—the cool, rainy climate of Margs to here.

'It took me a very long time to settle and make friends. I love it here now, but it certainly does take some getting used to. Policemen's wives have to try hard with every new town. We need to settle, to make friends, to fit in. We are constantly being moved from town to town, and if we don't make the effort to establish ourselves, we run the risk of always being on the outer. That's a lonely place to be.'

Melinda nodded and sipped her tea. 'Have you made good friends?'

'Have I? Of course! I started off by volunteering for Meals on Wheels. Met some lovely like-minded people that way. Within time I found a job I love—only part-time, but enough to get me out and meeting people—and from then on I was away.' She paused, reaching for her cup of tea, then changed direction, putting her hand on Melinda's knee. 'I know you're unhappy, Melinda, but this is your lot for the next year or two. You can't keep hating it and not trying. You've got to get out there and meet some people. How about volunteering for Meals on Wheels with me, or something similar? Get involved. Do you like sport? We're always looking for new tennis players down at the club.'

Melinda grimaced. 'No, I'm not a tennis player, I'm afraid.'

'But you love working with children?'

'I spent lots of years training to get the qualifications I have now.'

'Then apply for that job, Mel.'

'Melinda,' she said automatically.

Kathy cocked her head and looked at her. 'Then apply for that job, Mel,' she repeated. 'You're in the country now.'

There was a silence between the two of them and Kathy reached for her cup and took a sip.

'How are things between you and Dave, if you don't mind me asking?' Kathy finally asked.

Melinda thought about that. Dave was being as supportive as he could be. She was the one being the prize bitch. 'He's being the supportive, caring, gorgeous man I married, ignoring the fact that I'm be awful to him all the time.'

'Have you ever thought he might be missing Perth?'

'Ha! Not a chance. You should have seen his face light up when we first got to town. No, he wants to be here.'

'Better than still pining for the farm,' Kathy said gently.

That made Melinda pause. Dave didn't talk about missing out on the farm to many people, so if he'd told Spencer and Spencer had told Kathy, Dave must think they were good people. 'Yeah, that's true.'

'Here's an idea for today—Saturday. How about getting up off that chair and coming out with me. I'll take you on my Meals on Wheels round and you can meet a few people, then you can come home and cook a nice dinner for Dave. Talk to him. Tell him how you're feeling without being angry. Be present in your new life, your marriage. Nothing will slip away if you do that.'

Chapter 9

'Got a 3-3-8 at one of the brothels,' Spencer said, walking into the office. 'All the others are out, so it's you and me.'

Dave had been staring at his new email program, waiting for responses to a couple of enquiries he'd sent out, but his inbox had remained empty. Not that he'd really been concentrating on it. He'd been thinking about the previous evening and Melinda. His fear of her leaving had only increased when she'd asked him to spend the day away from the house because she needed time to think. He'd started off with his run, but couldn't settle so had decided to go into the office for the day. He'd been surprised to find Spencer there working on an old file.

His colleague had looked at him over the tops of his glasses but not commented on his appearance at the station.

Dave had a constant feeling of anxiety in the bottom of his stomach and half expected that when he went home tonight Melinda wouldn't be there.

'A 3-3-8?' he asked. It was code for a sudden death. He pushed his chair back and grabbed his gun holster before shrugging into it and following Spencer out of the room.

'Reckon we might have a stiff.' Spencer laughed. 'That's what you go to a brothel for, hey. Jeez, I crack myself up!'

'A body?'

'You'd be surprised at the number of people who die while having sex, Dave. Anyway, Madam Narla has called saying they have a body in one of their rooms. The girl is hysterical. Apparently they came back from the showers and he lay down. Next thing, he was dead.'

They climbed into the car and Spencer put his foot down, making a squealing noise as they left the parking lot.

Glancing over at Dave, Spencer finally asked, 'What's up with you? You look like shit.'

Dave stared out of the window, wishing Spencer hadn't noticed. 'I didn't sleep too well last night.'

'Woman trouble, huh?'

'Why do you say that?'

'Can read it all over you. New copper in town. The place isn't quite what the wife thought it would be. Left her family and friends . . .' He shrugged one shoulder. 'See it all the time, mate, and you've got that look.'

Dave clenched his teeth. 'You ever have the same problems?'

'Not when I shifted here but I did in our first posting. Kathy really struggled. New mum, away from her family. We were based in a tiny town—not even five hundred people—all the way back in South Australia. It was tough going for a while.'

'What got you guys through?'

Spencer swung the car around the corner of Plenty Street and came to a halt in front of a bright red door. 'Kathy had to get out and make friends. I made sure she met other policemen's wives and knew she wasn't the only one struggling.' Spencer's face became grim. 'Come on, let's check this out.'

Madam Narla met them at the front door full of apologies.

'So sorry, Spencer,' she said, putting her hand on his arm. 'He's gone.'

'You told me that when you rang, Narla. Don't worry, we'll get it sorted. I'll call the ambos once I've looked at the scene. Just need to talk—'

'No, I mean, he's not here,' she interrupted.

Dave noticed the madam's face was very pale and she looked like she might have had a shock.

'Not here?'

'He wasn't dead?' Dave put in.

'We thought he was. He wasn't responsive or breathing. I even held a mirror under his nose to make sure! I don't know what happened but he suddenly just sat up!'

Spencer looked beyond her and into the dim light of the passageway. 'Where is he now?'

'I don't know. He got up and dressed and practically ran out the door.'

'Better put a call out in case he's lying unconscious on the street somewhere. What's he look like?'

'Early twenties, I guess. Blond hair, well built. Had the hands of an underground miner.'

'Right, so ingrained dirt, cuts, callouses and so on,' Spencer said to Dave. He directed his next comment to Narla. 'I have heard of this type of thing happening before. Some little vein in the back of your neck closes when you get overexcited. Makes you look dead but you're not, then someone moves you and the vein opens and everything carries on as it was before.'

'I've never seen it,' she answered. 'It really gave me a fright!'

'And where's your girl?' he asked.

'In the bedroom. As soon as you've finished talking with her I'll send her home. She had a bigger fright than I did, poor love.'

Dave went out into the bright midday sunlight and requested a 7-0-1, relaying the details of the young man.

He gave a smile. *Must be the unluckiest fella in Barrabine*, he thought. As he walked back into the brothel he heard Spencer ask how business was.

'Busy,' Narla answered. 'I have five girls working today and another five starting at six tonight. They're all booked until two am tomorrow.'

'Lucky you've got good girls, Narla,' Spencer said. 'We'd have riots out here if you didn't.'

'I know. We service the need. Now, Kiri is this way.' She turned and indicated for Dave and Spencer to follow her.

In the bedroom, which was lit by a warm light on the bedside table, Kiri sat in a bathrobe. Her arms were around herself and it looked as if she had been crying.

Spencer went to her and squatted down, looking her in the eye. 'I'm Detective Brown. You must be Kiri?'

She nodded.

'Can you tell me what happened?' he asked gently.

'I don't know. He came back from the shower and stretched out on the bed. I turned away for a couple of moments to put the towels away and asked him if he wanted anything in particular. When he didn't answer, I looked around and he . . .' She broke off, taking a few deep breaths. 'He looked different. I slapped him on the face a couple of times and nothing happened, so I called Narla.'

Narla took up the commentary. 'After I phoned you lot, I did the checks I told you about, then we turned him on his side . . . His eyes opened and he took one look around and jumped up. Ran like a frightened rabbit, he did, after he'd got dressed.'

'Did you catch his name?'

'He didn't give me one,' Kiri answered. Without warning, she started to laugh. 'It's a bit funny, isn't it? Like, he was dead, then he wasn't!' She laughed harder and Dave and Spencer smiled with her, knowing it was probably shock.

They asked a few more questions and decided there wasn't much more they could do: the man was alive and there was nothing to investigate.

'Look after your girl in there,' Spencer said to Narla as they were leaving. 'Nip of brandy might help.'

'I will. Thanks for coming out so quickly. Before you leave, I wanted to mention that we've had a stranger in here recently. He's been visiting twice a week or so. Very flashy. Tossing big notes around. The girls say he's a bit rough. I'm keeping an eye on it, but I thought I'd let you know in case I need to call you in. I won't stand for roughness with my girls.'

Spencer nodded. 'We'll come immediately if you need any help.'

'Thank you, Spencer.' Narla inclined her head towards him as a thank you, then turned and went back inside.

The men climbed into the car and looked at each other.

'I want to laugh,' admitted Dave.

'So do I,' Spencer said with a chuckle. 'I wonder what his first thought was when he woke up.'

'Obviously the need to get out of there on the double,' Dave laughed, then sobered as Melinda's face flashed in front of him.

Spencer looked over as silence filled the car.

'Don't worry, mate. She'll get sorted.'

'I hope so,' Dave muttered.

Melinda re-read the application letter, making sure there weren't any spelling or grammatical errors.

Everything Kathy had said to her today had hit home. Who was she to complain? She wasn't the only woman who had had her life upended. Kathy told her she'd shifted six times in the twenty-five years she'd been married to Spencer.

And Dave. Her gorgeous, driven Dave. He'd been kicked off the farm without warning. His dream of being a farmer had been shattered by his father, but he'd set a new goal and was heading for it. Barrabine was a step along the way.

Maybe there wasn't a job in paediatrics at the hospital, but there was one in community health. Kathy had driven past the community health centre on the way to pick up the meals for delivery. Melinda had been surprised to see a line of cars parked out the front on a Saturday. Two grubby, wild-haired children were in a playground inside the fence, while a woman sat in the shade of the verandah and watched them. She was sure if she'd wound the window down she would have heard their shrieks of laughter. The building looked new and freshly painted, even with the lining of red dirt on the walls that she'd come to expect on every building.

Sitting in the car with Kathy, she'd felt a bubble of excitement. She could almost smell the disinfectant and hear the hum of busyness inside the walls. She craved the work environment. Before Kathy had dropped her home, she'd decided to apply.

Now, here in front of her computer, she felt the buzz of adrenalin begin to kick in. Dealing with children every day was what she loved and there were plenty of kids at the community health centre. Along with parents who would need a kind and caring ear.

Melinda printed the rest of her résumé and she couldn't wait until Dave came home so she could tell him her plans.

Switching on the TV, she saw the six o'clock news was on. Melinda frowned; Dave was late. Well, could she really know when she would expect him today? She was the one who had told him to go because she needed some time. Maybe she'd been such a bitch he wouldn't come home. That stopped her in her tracks. She remembered her mother telling her once you could only push people so far before they didn't come back.

Where would he be? she wondered. Walking the streets? In the pub? Should she go and see if she could find him? She paced the kitchen and lounge room, fear rolling around in her stomach.

There was a gentle tap on the door and she stopped, wondering who it could be.

'G'day, missus,' Ernie said, holding out a parcel wrapped in newspaper. 'Kangaroo steaks. Good tucker, yeah? Good tucker.'

'Oh,' Melinda stood at the door, not knowing what to say. 'Um, kangaroo?'

'Yeah, missus.' Ernie shook the parcel. 'You take. Good tucker. Food.'

Good manners made her reach out and take his offering. 'Um, thank you.'

Ernie nodded at her and turned to leave. 'You be right, missus. Time is all. Just time.' He left her standing on the step, staring out into the dimming light. How had he known? She smiled a little as she realised she may have made her second friend. What a nice feeling.

Closing the door gently, she decided to make tonight special. She'd experiment and use the kangaroo steaks. She knew Dave had eaten them before and liked them;

she never had so tonight could be the start of many new firsts for her.

Feeling like an old-fashioned housewife, Melinda found the linen tablecloth her grandmother had left her and spread it over the kitchen table. She brought out the good cutlery they'd been given for their wedding and set two places; she'd make the table look pretty and inviting.

Humming to herself, she danced over to the cupboard and pulled out the crockery set her parents had given them. It was white with gold edging. For a moment she was thrown back to their wedding day. She remembered walking down the aisle towards Dave. His hair had been slicked back and he'd looked so handsome in his tuxedo. When she'd stopped beside him at the altar he'd looked at her like she was the best thing that had ever happened to him.

Her wedding dress had held shades of Princess Diana's—ruffled sleeves and neck. And the train . . . well, it had been far too long, but after being transfixed by the royal wedding as a child, she'd wanted something similar. Her brides-maids, sister Sarah and best friend Tash, had screwed up their noses as they'd held up the train while Melinda went to the loo. They both had probably taken on more than they'd bargained for being the bridesmaids for Melinda, who had a two-metre train hanging off the end of her wedding dress!

A jingle came on the TV and she gave a little wiggle of her hips and said out loud, 'Come home soon, honey. I can't wait to see you.'

She found candles and placed them in the middle of the table, then went looking for one of the potpourri bowls that had been on the tables at their wedding. She knew she'd kept three of them—they'd been full of rose petals and lavender flowers and smelled divine. The clear bowl would look nice on the table tonight.

The news had finished and the familiar strains of *Hey Hey It's Saturday* filled the room. Melinda stopped setting the table and looked at the clock to make sure she wasn't wrong. It was six-thirty now. Was he even coming home?

All her positiveness started to seep away. Part of her wanted to crawl into a ball and cry. She wanted to tell him about all the good decisions she'd made today and what her plans were for the next week.

Just then she heard the squeak of the gate and a few moments later the door opened. She met him at the door and they looked at each other uncertainly.

'Hi,' they both said at the same time.

'I'm sor—' Melinda tried, but Dave put his arms around her and pulled her into his chest, muffling her words. Returning the hug, she closed her eyes and breathed deeply, peace finally descending over her. They stood like that without speaking for a long time, then Dave gently pushed her back and looked down at her.

'How was your day?' he asked quietly.

'Good. Really good. I did a lot of thinking.'

'And what did you work out?'

'I've been disgustingly selfish and I'm sorry.'

Dave went to say something but she shushed him by putting a finger over his lips.

'I realise it's got to be me who makes the effort to meet people and fit in and I'm going to be doing that.'

Pulling away, she went to the fridge and grabbed out the kangaroo steaks. 'Ernie dropped by tonight and gave us these.'

'What are they?'

'Kangaroo steaks.' She put them on the counter then reached back in for a beer and a bottle of wine.

'And you're going to cook them?'

Dave looked around the kitchen, then leaned forward and whispered playfully, 'Where's my wife?'

Melinda smiled at him. 'The new wife is right here. The other cranky, dismal wife has gone. Well, you never know, she might turn up again, but hopefully she's gone for good.'

'Tell me about today,' Dave said, taking the beer with a 'Thanks'. He looked at her. 'I'm just so glad you're still here. I was frightened that when I came home you wouldn't be.'

'And I got scared you wouldn't come home tonight. Come and sit outside.' She took his hand and led him to the backyard. 'What did you do today?'

'Went into work,' he answered before taking a long swig on the beer. 'But I'm more interested in hearing about yours.'

'I'm going to apply for the job at the community health centre,' she said, grinning.

Dave let out a breath. 'God, that's good news. What made you change your mind?'

'Kathy,' she answered simply. 'I spent most of the day with her.'

Dave regarded her steadily. 'Kathy changed your mind, what, just like that?' He snapped his fingers. 'In one conversation?'

'Yeah—well, no. It was lots of different conversations, but I realised I was being stupid too. I'm sorry. It's not that I don't want to be here with you. Not at all.' She reached out and grabbed his hand. 'It's just taken a little adjusting to. So,' she straightened up, 'if I don't get the job, I have a plan B. I'll join Meals on Wheels with Kathy, or volunteer to listen to reading at schools. And I'm going to start a sport again. I've always liked swimming and that's a good sport for the middle of the desert, isn't it?'

Smiling, Dave leaned over and kissed her. 'The best, I would've thought.'

Chapter 10

Dave looked across at Melinda—she was still asleep. His stomach flipped as he looked at his wife, her copper-coloured hair spread out across the pillow. She was beautiful. Sometimes he felt he was punching above his weight when he looked at her, or when he saw other men staring. Which they did. Often. She was a tall, slim woman who carried herself with poise and self-confidence and Dave found that very sexy. Especially when her hair was out of its usual ponytail and she let it hang loose over her shoulders.

Quietly he slid out of bed and pulled the sheet up to her chin before kissing her cheek gently and pushing a stray hair from her face.

In the kitchen he put on the new electric drip coffee maker bought with some of the money they'd received for their wedding. Leaning against the bench in his boxer shorts, he thought back to what Melinda had said last night.

He was sure if she got a job she would be happier. A job would mean meeting new people, potentially making new friends. And there couldn't be much happiness in staring at four walls every day, he supposed. But there was something different about her—almost like she'd found a new energy. The glow was in her face again, and her grandmother's jewellery was back in the safe.

Opening the fridge, he saw there was bacon. After rustling around a little, he found the eggs. A few minutes later the bacon was sizzling and the coffee maker had produced its second cup. Taking it to the bedroom, Dave put the cup on the bedside table before sitting on the edge of the bed and kissing Melinda awake.

'Good morning, sleepyhead,' he said softly.

Melinda groaned and opened her eyes. 'Morning. What's the time?'

'Just after eight. I've got bacon cooking and I'm about to throw on the eggs. I thought I'd take you for a drive. How does that sound?'

'Where to?' Melinda sat up and pushed her hair out of her eyes.

'A little place I've been to on an investigation. Oakamanda. Got a cool pub. I reckon you'll like it. And it's a really pretty drive out there.'

'Sounds like fun.' Melinda reached for her coffee. 'God, that's good,' she said after her first sip.

'Yeah, God bless all the people who gave us money as a present,' Dave laughed. 'Couldn't have bought it without them.' He got up. 'Breakfast won't be long.'

Melinda reached up and ran her hand down his chest and looked up at him from under her lashes. 'Got time for you to come back to bed?'

Dave groaned and bent down to kiss her. 'The bacon will burn,' he whispered.

'Let it,' she sighed against his lips.

❧

Dave cranked up the stereo as they left the town behind, John Williamson blaring.

Melinda reached over and took his hand. 'This country is stunning,' she said. 'Really vivid. The redness of the earth is beautiful.'

'I know. Even in the Flinders it's not like this—well, that country is more purple than red, but the colours aren't as intense.'

'What are the trees called?'

'The shiny-trunked ones are gimlet trees. And the ones that only have the bark on the bottom, they're blackbutts.'

Melinda giggled. 'Never thought about a tree having a butt,' she said.

'Can't say I had either.'

'What grabbed your attention about this little pub?' Melinda asked, turning in her seat to face him. She kept hold of his hand and brought it up to kiss his knuckles. Dave felt a thrill run through him again.

'There's loads of history there and it's got a lovely little beer garden out to the side. But the main reason was Dee, that's the publican, mentioned she runs what she calls

"Contiki tours" around the town. I wanted to take you on one.'

Melinda smiled at him, then dropped her eyes. 'Thanks for putting up with me when I was being such a cow.'

'Don't be silly. I didn't "put up" with you. And you weren't a cow. Just a bit stressed and sad.'

He started to slow down just before the town sign and turned the stereo down.

'Look, there's a cemetery.' Melinda pointed to the sign on the left-hand side of the road. 'Can we have a look there when we come back? I love old cemeteries! I bet there are some stories in there.'

'I'd reckon.'

Pulling up at the pub, Melinda let out a gasp of awe. 'Look at the stonework. I wonder if it was built by hand?'

'It's over one hundred years old, so I'd guess it was. They would have got the rock from around here. This crime scene I went to last week—the mine was under an overhanging rock, chiselled out between the ridges of granite. Amazing.'

Melinda fiddled with her camera and took a couple of photos before taking his hand and walking across the road to the pub.

There were five cars parked out the front and loud music pumped from inside. Dave pushed open the door and ushered Melinda inside.

As he stepped into the cool, he blinked a couple of times to adjust to the dimness and realised Tim Tucker was sitting at the bar. Beside him sat a man of Asian descent, his brown hands wrinkled, bruised and cut. On the other side sat an Aboriginal man with greying hair and a beard.

'G'day, Tim,' Dave nodded. He wondered if this was China and Killjoy. He remembered Tim saying they were going to catch up this Saturday. Maybe they'd decided on Sunday too.

Tim looked over his shoulder and nodded. 'G'day there, cobber.' His gaze rested on Melinda for a second. 'Brought the missus out to see our little local?'

'Sure have. We're still sightseers. Haven't been here long.' As he talked, he realised Melinda hadn't stiffened at the word 'missus'. 'Tim, this is Melinda.'

'Pleased to meet you, I'm sure,' Tim said, tipping an imaginary hat.

'Hello.'

Dee came out from the kitchen, the tea towel over her shoulder. Dave hoped it wasn't the same one from when he'd been here last time.

'Well, bugger me dead, look what the cat dragged in. Didn't you get enough of my history lesson the other day?' Dee put her hands on her large hips. 'And you've brought a different sidekick. Who might you be?'

Dave glanced at Melinda, who had a half-smile on her face. 'I'm Melinda. The wife of what the cat dragged in.'

Dee gave a chuckle. 'Hi there, Melinda. Welcome to the Oakamanda Pub, where the beer is cold and the service warm.'

'Geez, Dee, can't you do better than that?' Dave asked, dragging out a bar stool and sitting down.

'Why would I want to do better? It's all true! What can I get you both?'

'Have you got a white wine?' Melinda wanted to know.

'Sure, love. We're not as uncouth as we look. Dave?'

'Just a lemon, lime and bitters. Driving.' He glanced at Melinda and saw she'd flushed at Dee's words, even though they were friendly. 'I was telling Melinda about your Contiki tours. We were hoping you might have time take us on one.'

'Can do. I'll get my daughter to come and mind the bar.' She plonked the drinks on the bar and picked through the change Dave had put down. 'What do you want to see?'

'Whatever you want to show us,' Melinda answered, picking up her glass. 'The country is so pretty and I haven't seen a mine shaft yet.'

'Dime a dozen round these parts. Gotta be careful walking around out here. Can easily fall down into one if you don't know what to look out for. Like the poor fella you guys brought up the other day.' She nodded at Dave.

Immediately Dave wanted to ask how she knew the dead man had fallen in but as he opened his mouth the Asian man next to Tim spoke up.

'Now, Dee, you're jumping to conclusions again.' His accent was pure Australian, which took Dave by surprise.

'What do you mean?' he asked the man.

'Just that. You got no idea whether he was out walking in the night and fell in or was pushed down there on purpose.'

'China, this fella here is Dave Burrows, Spencer's new sidekick,' Tim quickly put in.

China turned and regarded Dave silently before saying, 'You'll have your work cut out for you then,' without offering his hand.

'Meaning?'

'Lots of blokes around here are sick of people trespassing. You lot don't seem to do much about it. We're getting a bit fed up with calling the coppers and no one turning up to help.'

Dave felt Melinda shift uncomfortably next to him. He fished around in his pocket and brought out his wallet and handed over three business cards. 'You have any problems, you ring me. I'll come out straightaway.'

The other man reached out and took one. 'It's hard to do anything, China. You know that. By the time the coppers get out to us, the trespassers have usually pissed off. Especially if they know we've rung and made a complaint.'

Dave held out his hand. 'Dave Burrows.'

'They call me Killjoy.'

'Are you?' he asked with a grin.

'I don't reckon. My dad called me that when I was a young fella. Been called it for so long I've forgotten me real name.'

Melinda laughed. 'Why did he call you that?' she asked.

Killjoy gave her a wide grin that showed two missing teeth. 'Apparently I wouldn't sleep at night and I stopped my parents from conceiving any other siblings.'

Dave and Melinda were the only ones who laughed; it seemed the others had heard the story before.

'I take it there's only one of you then?'

'They broke the mould when I was born,' Killjoy answered, raising his glass in a salute.

'And thank God for that,' Tim said, clapping his mate on the shoulder.

The back door opened and Dave felt a blast of hot air follow the young woman who walked in. Tall and slim, she was smiling and immediately he could see she was related to Dee. It was the smile: wide and welcoming. Holding her hand was a little boy, blond hair sticking out in all directions and his cheeks red. It looked like he'd just woken from sleep.

Dee held out her arms to the little boy and he shook off his mother's hand and ran to her.

'How's my little man?' she asked. 'Have you been asleep?'

'Tim!' the girl said. 'I haven't seen you in an age.' Rounding the bar, she gave him a hug before giving one each to China and Killjoy. 'Had any luck?'

'The luckiest I've been is since you walked in,' Tim answered with a grin. 'How are you, my girl?'

'Aw, you old silver fox.' She patted his shoulder with fondness. 'Always know how to make a girl feel special.' She sighed. 'I'm fine, although I wish Jasper would sleep a lot more.'

'Giving you a hard time, is he?'

Dave listened to them chat as he wandered around the room and looked at the pictures and slices of history on the walls.

The small town of Oakamanda and its pub is at the centre of attention as detectives and forensics swarm over it looking for clues as to why a shooting occurred there last night, one newspaper article wrote.

Police are at a loss as to why the shooting, which claimed three lives, took place at the Oakamanda Pub three weeks ago. They are calling for more witnesses to come forward, appealed another.

Dave felt Melinda come and stand at his side. 'Have you seen the other room?' she asked quietly.

'Haven't been in there yet.'

'Come and have a look.' She took his hand and led him through a doorway. The first thing that struck him was the coldness of the room.

'Maybe it's the presence of the ghost,' Melinda said in a stage whisper, then rolled her eyes.

Giving half a chuckle, he glanced around and pointed at the air-conditioner on the wall. 'Not unless her spirit is coming out there,' he said.

'And the walls. They're really thick—much thicker than the ones in the front bar, so they'll help keep the heat out,' Melinda suggested.

Dave ran his hands over the pool table as he walked around. There were old couches and stuffed chairs pushed up against the wall. They looked like they'd been there since the pub had first opened. The fireplace had a large spray of dried flowers and gum leaves in the hearth, and even though the room looked very old and worn, it had a welcoming feel to it. A display cabinet showed off relics from the area: old mining picks, broken cups, a photo of a woman sitting on a log by a campfire.

'Wonder who that was,' he said, pointing at it.

'That's our resident ghost, Mary,' Dee said, coming into the room. 'She died right in this room, you know. Dropped dead while she was mopping the floor. Obviously loved the place so much she didn't want to leave.'

'You don't really hear her at night, do you?' Melinda asked, disbelief in her voice.

'Sure do! Lots of clattering about.'

'I don't believe in ghosts. There must be some kind of logical explanation for the noise.'

Dee gave her a hard look. 'There is a logical explanation,' she said. 'It's Mary. Now you ready to go? Caitlyn is looking after the bar so we can head off.'

Chapter 11

Dave and Melinda followed Dee outside, walking over the carefully mowed lawns and through the gardens, which had the old staples that would survive the summer heat: geraniums, bougainvillea and gums. The outdoor tables were covered by shade cloth, and fairy lights hung from the trees. Dave could imagine it would be a beautiful setting to have beer on a warm evening.

'Hopefully the old bitch'll start,' Dee said as a battered old ute came into view.

At a glance Dave could see it wasn't roadworthy; the front end looked like it'd had a collision with a roo, and there didn't seem to be any glass in the front windscreen. He watched as Dee put her hand in through the window and yanked on the door handle. She didn't seem worried he'd put a sticker on it.

'You'll have to do the same,' she indicated. 'Handle's given up. Unless you want to sit in the back. I wouldn't today though. The sun's got too much bite in it for your skin.' She aimed the comment at Melinda. 'But if you really want to, I've got sunscreen somewhere.' She looked under the seat in a half-hearted effort to find the tube, then knocked the gear into neutral.

'We're fine in the front. You let people ride in the back? That must be a bit dangerous,' Dave ventured.

'What do you think the couch is for?' Dee asked as she turned the key. They listened as the engine turned over without firing. It didn't sound very healthy.

Dave wondered if it would even get them to where they were going, never mind back again. He counted ten empty Four X Gold cans on the couch, which was tied onto the tray with a piece of rope. Dave felt a glimmer of excitement. He remembered the fishing trips he and the footy team had taken when he was a teenager, the sand dunes they'd driven over, the drinking they'd done. The ute reminded him of those times and he was sure this Contiki tour was going to be fun.

Taking them by surprise, the ute suddenly roared to life and Dee gave a whoop. 'Good girl!' She got into the driver's seat and patted the steering wheel. 'Never let me down, do you?'

Melinda climbed in, kicking a few more beer cans out of the way. Dave followed, slamming the door behind him.

'Right, I'll take you to the first mine I ever came across,' Dee said. 'Mel, have you ever seen a mine before?'

Dave was about to correct her with the name, knowing how much Melinda hated her name being shortened, but Melinda spoke before he could.

'I haven't. They sound fascinating.'

He wanted to raise his eyebrows in surprise. Could one pep talk make all the difference? Would this new 'Mel' last? He hoped so.

'Oakamanda has a really interesting history, even without the shooting. The town used to be about ten kilometres from where it is now. There was a mine right on the edge of it. People lived there in canvas tents and cooked over campfires. This is back in the 1800s when gold was first found. But then a miner by the name of Wallace Parker found a larger reef where the town is now.'

'They moved the town?' Dave asked in surprise.

'Sure did. Packed up and shifted everything. There was water here, see? And water is almost more precious than gold out here. No point in walking an extra ten k to work and water, not when the town was moveable. That's when they built the pub.'

Dee changed gears and the gearstick struck Melinda's leg. She tried to shift closer to Dave. 'Sorry,' she apologised.

'Always a bit of a tight fit in here. That's another reason for the couch,' Dee said, crunching gears again.

'Great idea,' Melinda agreed, smiling. 'There is something about this country. I don't know what it is, but it's so picturesque. Even with the heat.'

'I know what you mean. Gets under your skin. I fell in love with it the minute I came here.' She veered off to the left, throwing Melinda against Dave's shoulder. 'Mine's down this way,' she pointed, following a track that didn't look like it'd been used in years.

'What brought you here in the first place?' Dave asked.

'My mum and stepdad owned the pub. My stepdad won it in a card game. I'd had a marriage break-up and didn't really know what to do with myself. Tried living in Perth and didn't like that, so I moved to a little country town called Wickepin and liked that even less. Caitlyn was off my hands—had her young—so one day I jumped in me car and drove up here to see the olds. Haven't left since. Don't want to be anywhere else. Enjoy talking to the people coming through. Met some interesting ones, I tell you. When it's tourist season, the hustle and bustle of this joint is more than enough for me. Here we are.' She pulled up with a jerk and threw open her door before Dave and Melinda could say anything.

Melinda looked at Dave. 'A card game? Hustle and bustle? There isn't any of that out here!'

Dave shrugged. 'That's probably what she means. She doesn't like hustle and bustle. And this is the wild west. Card games and gambling are normal.'

Dee was already a way in front of them by the time they tumbled out of the ute and got their footing. Dave felt his feet sink into the dirt a couple of inches and once again marvelled at the softness. *Good soil to roll a swag over*, he thought.

'This way,' Dee called. 'Watch your step. There's no rails or anything flash out here to stop you from falling in.'

'I reckon occupational health and safety would have a field day with you,' Dave called as he realised Dee was wearing thongs.

'I'd be the least of their worries,' she laughed. 'They're more concerned about the mines and the workers than a little Contiki tour that I don't charge for. Here you go.' She pointed down.

It took Dave a moment to see what she was pointing out. A tree root had grown over the entrance and it was clear this shaft hadn't been used in years.

'Wow,' muttered Melinda, getting out her camera. 'And people used to go down these?'

'Still do.' Dee walked along the top of the ridge and looked down. 'If you come up here, you'll be able to see it follows the line of rock.' She held her hand out in the direction the shaft ran. Dave took a couple of steps and jumped up.

'I see,' he said half to himself. 'The shaft is long rather than deep.'

'This one runs for about one hundred metres along this ridge. If you go up a little further, you'll be able to climb in a way. Dunno how deep it is. See, in the old days the miners would put false floors in their shafts, so even if you chucked a rock down, you could never be sure when you heard it drop whether it was the real bottom or not.'

'Why'd they put false floors in?' Melinda asked, shooing away the flies which kept clustering around her eyes.

'They'd know if someone had been there. If there was nobody to stay and guard the mine, people would come along and have a go at seeing what they could find, even if it was registered to another miner. If someone was at the bottom of the mine when they came back, they'd either be dead or badly injured, depending on how deep the shaft was. It made people think twice about raiding someone else's property.'

'Severe.' Melinda grimaced a little.

Dave walked ahead, loose stones scattering under his feet. He could hear them tumble down into the darkness and thought about the old blokes, the ones who'd lived out here in the heat and flies, without water and company, looking for that one piece of gold which would make them rich.

Coming to the crevice where Dee had told him he could climb in, he looked down and saw the clear lines of quartz running through the rock. He clambered down and ran his fingers across them, feeling the coolness of the stone. Had a miner stood here decades ago, with excitement in his belly? Filled with equal parts hope and fear? Had he wondered, as he climbed down into the darkness for the first time, whether he'd be going home that night, or had that thought never entered his mind? Did it even bother him? Was he prepared to die trying to find the prize?

Dave tried to conjure up the sounds of the gold rush. Men laughing and calling to each other. The tinny noise of pick on stone and the groans as they shovelled the soil into buckets and tied the rope to the handle and called up for their partner to pull it out and comb through it.

Hearing it all in his head, he had flashes of men, filthy with red dust across their faces and sweat lines across their brows. The smell of campfire smoke and chatter of children laughing as they hauled buckets of water back to their tents. The sobs of women who were burying their men or children, and the silence of men grieving.

Taking a few deep breaths, he became aware of the muted sounds of the bush as he climbed down that little bit further. There really wasn't anything but silence. A heavy silence; no birds or crickets. Occasionally the wind rubbed the leaves of the trees and bushes together.

A stone dislodged from the wall of the mine and skittered down the side, causing Dave's heart to stop for a moment in case there was more above him that could come down on his head.

He peered up and could only see trees and blue sky, and although it was an odd feeling not to be able to see across the land, it was strangely peaceful and calming.

'There you are.' Melinda's head appeared over the top. 'Ugh, that looks a bit scary. Nothing but a big black pit.'

'Pass the camera down if you don't want to join me,' Dave called up. 'It doesn't look like this one has got any timbers reinforcing the sides.'

'It will have further down,' Dee answered; she was at Melinda's side, scrutinising where he was. 'But it's best not to go any further. Got no idea what's down there, hey.'

Dave picked up a stone and tossed it into the inky blackness, listening. He didn't hear it land. 'Must be bloody deep!' He started to climb out, slipping and sliding on the steep walls. He put a foot wrong and slid all the way back down, fear stabbing through him. Dave tried to reach out and grab something to stop his fall, imagining he was going to end up like the stone, but there was nothing but loose stones and solid wall. Without meaning to he let out a small cry of alarm.

'Shit, shit, shit!' he muttered. His fingers finally found a tree root and he hung on tight.

'You okay there?' Dee called down, laughter in her voice.

Dave wasn't sure why—he didn't think it was a laughing matter! 'Fine,' he answered, but his heart was beating so fast he felt it was going to come out of his chest.

'Sweetheart?' Melinda's voice held dread.

'I'm okay, don't worry.' He started up the side again, this time watching his footfalls. Finding a solid piece of stone to use as a hand grip, Dave hoisted himself up, finally reaching the surface.

Wiping the sweat from his forehead, he grinned at them both. 'Wasn't sure what was about to happen then,' he admitted.

'It's scary when you slide back down, I know,' Dee said. 'I've done it heaps of times, but you couldn't fall in because the ledge you were standing on while you were down there would have stopped you. Doesn't stop you from freaking out though.'

'Dead right.'

'Come on, I'll take you up to the wedding hill.'

Piling back into the ute, Dave turned to Dee. 'You said the pub was won in a card game? That's pretty intriguing.'

She nodded, crunching through the gears as she drove towards a large hill on the horizon.

'Yeah, the guy who owned it had a gambling problem.' She looked over at him, a humorous look on her face. 'I know you'll find that hard to believe since he bet his own pub!'

Melinda gave a shout of laughter and reached out to hold on to Dave's arm as they went through a bumpy river crossing.

'Anyway, he didn't have anything else to put up and he wanted to be in the game. He'd lost his car, savings, some of the stock from the pub—mostly rum. Had nothing left. My stepdad just played his cards right and won it.'

'Just won it?' Dave said, shaking his head.

'Can you imagine it? Four fellas sitting around a campfire in the middle of the bush, drinking, watching the flames, and someone pulls out a deck of cards. They were playing poker. Unusual for out here. Two-up is more the go. Probably a good thing there were a few others there because otherwise he would have been in danger of being shot or murdered somehow so the owner didn't have to pay up!'

Dave glanced across at Dee but he wasn't seeing her, he was seeing a campfire. Men silhouetted by the flames, the glint of knives and guns, the distrust between men palpable. The cards were held by each man and a look of disbelief passed between the players as Dee's father laid down the winning hand. He could hear the crackle of the fire, the hiss of anger as the previous owner stared at the cards.

The black cloud of flies above Tim Tucker's mine shaft flashed into his mind's eye and suddenly he realised how many complicated motives for murder there could be in this area he now called home.

Chapter 12

Tim Tucker sat out on his verandah, listening to the sounds of the bush. The sun had started to dip below the trees and the darkness was beginning to spread across the land. On the opposite horizon, the hint of the coming moon smouldered a deep orange.

He'd left his mates at the pub, deciding he really wasn't in the mood for drinking and talking to people. That was one of the reasons he lived where he did—he didn't like the energy it took to deal with people, and he was used to being in his own company. Miners had to be like that. Loners.

He hadn't always been that way, but time changes people and he was a different man from the one he'd been in his younger years.

Taking another sip of his beer, he savoured the coolness as it slid down like a balm. Chief was lying on the dirt near his chair, waiting for him to move—he shadowed his owner everywhere. His was the sort of company Tim liked. Not the people who asked questions and used up generosity. Not the ones who promised things and didn't deliver. Chief loved unconditionally. He protected, warned and adored. And he'd never let Tim down.

The tinkle of a piano seemed to filter through on the evening breeze and he turned his head to listen. Immediately it disappeared. Even after so many years, when his mind played tricks like this he still thought Marianne was here, playing the melodies she'd treasured and knew by heart. Filling the evening air with the music that made the birds' song sound like sirens.

The familiar ache of grief sat in his stomach every day, but it was worse on nights like these.

He'd met her when he was only nineteen and he remembered the day so clearly. The Barrabine north wind had tossed his hat from his head and it had skipped across the dirt road, becoming covered in red dust—even more than it was already. As he'd chased after it, he'd heard the music. He hadn't known what the instrument was, or who was playing it, but the notes were sweet and sad at the same time. It'd made him imagine raindrops, even on that hot and dusty day when he'd felt grimy and gritty.

Tim could see himself stopping and picking up the hat, slowly walking towards the music. Why the window was open on a day like that was beyond him, but he stood there for nearly twenty minutes . . . stood in the sun even, and listened.

Then he saw her. She was standing in front of the window, reaching up high to pull it shut. Raven black hair falling over her shoulders, deep olive skin and a flash of silver-blue eyes. Eyes that looked straight at him as she was closing out the heat, closing out the dust and snatching the music away.

A mopoke called loudly from the tree above him and Tim was brought back to the present. Realising there were tears on his cheeks, he stood up quickly, annoyed with himself. He tried to keep Marianne out of his thoughts these days, for thinking of her served no purpose. She'd been gone for so much more time than they'd had together.

Another reason to stay out here. No one bothered him with questions. Although it had been a long time since anyone had asked about her. Marianne would be forgotten by most of the old-timers now. Remembered only by him, her husband. The one who had loved her the most.

Trying to dispel the memories, he walked out into the night—it had cooled down from the heat of the day, but it wasn't so chilly that he needed a jumper. The moon cast a white glow across the land; the shadows of the trees were slim and long.

Not needing a torch, he kept walking, one foot in front of the other, sidestepping bushes and trees and keeping an eye on the moon so he knew which direction he was going. Chief walked silently at his side—the dog was as fit and lean as he was. He'd heard Caitlyn say at the pub earlier that you could boil both of them down and you wouldn't get enough fat to make a cake of soap. He'd grinned at that, knowing he was wiry, but he had never thought about making a cake of soap out of his fat!

Chief went in front a few steps and looked back to make sure he was following and knew where he was going.

'Where are you off to, old mate?' Tim said, his voice sounding loud against the bush silence. There was a flutter of wings suddenly overhead; he must have disturbed an owl.

The dog didn't stop walking, just kept in front, following the invisible track. Tim walked behind him, enjoying the freshness of the night air against his skin. As he got older, he was finding each summer a little harder to bear, but he'd already decided to stay where he was until he died. What else was there for him to do? He didn't like Barrabine; there were too many people on the pathways to walk in a straight line. The noise of the cars had given him a headache the last time he'd stayed for more than a day. No, that place was not for him.

Dee had suggested he buy a small block on the outskirts of Oakamanda and build a house. 'You could have air-con and be comfortable,' she'd said. 'Build a smelter shed. You'd still be able to do all the things you want. You could still go out and mine—use your loader and dry blower. Find gold in an easier way rather than being underground.'

Air-conditioning was tempting, to be sure, but living so close to people, even to people who were his friends? No, that didn't interest him either.

Nope, it was the bush for him, no other place.

Tim knew every stone and shrub on his lease, which was why the nightly walks he took didn't frighten him. Fifty-nine years he'd been here and during that time he'd learned the land had her moods. Watched her bloom in spring and die in summer.

Chief stopped, the hackles rising on his neck, and he growled a low, long snarl. Tim stopped too, his hand going to his belt for his pistol. His eyes darted from one side to the other but he couldn't see anything. He sniffed quietly, trying to see if he could smell campfire smoke or body odour or something to indicate there was a person in the blackness.

That was how he'd caught the bloke who'd been in his hut back in 1962. Body odour.

Tim'd had a win. His third big win. Forty ounces of gold. He'd told no one but, still, somehow word had filtered out— he guessed the bank manager or gold buyer had opened their mouth a little too wide. Confidentiality had had a different meaning in the goldfields back then. There were very few secrets and nothing could be done about it. Since he'd been to town to put most of the gold in a safe box and cashed in the smaller nugget for groceries and a few essentials, he'd had a few blokes come to ask if they could help him mine. He always said no, happy on his own and happy he didn't have to share what he found with anyone.

This particular night, about two weeks after his visit to town, he'd arrived home from a long day down the mine. Again, he'd had some luck—this time he had thirty ounces in his pocket—the reef he'd stumbled across was proving very profitable.

It was spring and the wildflowers were out, covering the country with white and pink, the green leaves of the trees standing out against the deep red of the earth.

Tim had thought something was a little odd when he'd first walked in through the front door—the mat was a little crooked. He had stood at the door for a while, casting around, making sure he couldn't see anyone. Nothing else seemed to be out of place—the floor still had the sweep marks of the leaf broom he used, and there wasn't any noise. Even so, a little sense of worry had itched at the back of his neck and he'd kept his hand on his gun, watching, waiting.

That was how it had to be out here—always watchful and mistrusting.

He had taken a small step inside the hut and stood still again. Then another. And another.

Then he had smelled him. A stink so bad it had made him want to throw up. It wasn't him; a fox can't smell its own scent. There was someone inside. Inside his house.

Quietly he had backed out of the hut and went around the back where there was a slit in the tin. Tim had peered through and had seen James Bell crouched behind the wall in the bedroom. He had slowly cocked his gun and fired it into the dirt at James's feet.

Tim smiled as he remembered the terrible scream the man had made and the dust that had ballooned up into his face. Rotten bastard, trying to get in and steal his gold. He wouldn't try that again!

James Bell had taken off before he had got back around to the other side of the house, running out into the bush, not stopping to look behind him. Tim hadn't bothered to chase him.

He stood still in the darkness, listening for a stick cracking or any tiny noise that wasn't the bush. All the while reliving the memory of James Bell. Chief had stopped growling, he realised. There couldn't be any danger or he'd still be on guard. He started to walk again, lost in memories.

Those were the good old days. Anyone could fire a gun and no one got upset. Except the fella you were firing at! People could protect their property however they wanted to. He gave a little satisfied grunt. James had never come back to bother him. In fact, not too many people had after word had got out.

Tim brushed his fingers over a broombush and felt moisture on his hands. He looked up and assessed the moon again. *Going to be a dew tonight*, he thought.

Chief gave a bark and bounded out of sight. It was then Tim realised where he was.

He stood still, not wanting to go any further. But somehow his feet continued to walk of their own accord. They took him closer to Pammy, Kenneth and Kelly.

The ache started in his heart once more. The one he'd felt when he'd heard the ghostly tunes from the piano. His mouth opened slightly, wanting to apologise again; but what was the point? The twins had been gone for fifty-three years, while Kelly, fifty-two. He'd apologised every time he came. Didn't make any difference. They were still in the ground. His regret didn't bring them back.

The wire that held the rough handmade wooden crosses together glinted in the gentle light of the moon and distracted

Tim from the deteriorated fabric of the teddy bear and the faded plastic flowers he'd bought once on a whim.

Everything about these graves spoke of neglect and disinterest. But that couldn't be further from the truth. He chose to remember his children in his heart rather than sit and stare forlornly at their graves.

He wanted to remember Kenneth's wicked giggle and the way he'd followed Tim around, wanting to be just like his dad. His favourite saying had been: 'Dad, don't walk so fast, I can't keep up with you.' Tim had always slowed down and taken his hand. Walked him back to his mother or to somewhere safe.

Pammy had idolised her twin brother—he was five minutes older and she followed him everywhere. Which was why when Kenneth had toddled out into the bush at age four she'd followed. It was also why, when Kenneth had peered over the edge of a mine shaft, she had too, and it was why they'd in fallen together.

Born together and died together. The family of five had suddenly been reduced to three.

Marianne's ready smile had been replaced by deep lines and grief etched across her lovely face. Tim had worked harder to forget the pain. Kelly had tried so hard to bring her parents back, to get their attention.

Tim ran his hands over his head as he squatted in front of the graves.

'Sorry,' he whispered. 'God, I'm so sorry.'

How it had come to be that not eight months later a king brown had been found curled up in Kelly's makeshift cot, the child dead inside, no one would ever know. But Kelly hadn't been the first child to die from a snakebite and she wouldn't be the last—the houses weren't snake proof by any stretch of the imagination. The shack they'd lived in then hadn't even had doors on it.

Three to two.

Two empty shells.

Marianne had wept and stormed, furious with Tim for bringing them out here, into the heat and flies, in the search for gold. Was gold more precious than his family? she'd screamed at him.

Tim hadn't known how to answer. He'd always thought not, but hadn't his actions proved it was?

Had he ever thought the precious mineral could cost him his family? Never. Not once. And it hadn't been just his children. It had ended up being his wife too, but not in a way he had ever dreamed possible.

Chapter 13

Dave straightened his tie as he walked into the station on Monday morning. It was a little cooler than usual and he thought, since he was hoping for details on the body today, he should dress as he would've every day in Perth. Professionally. It reminded him he was a detective and had an important job to do. If he was going to be out interviewing people then he had to look the part. Shorts and an open-neck shirt would have been frowned on in Perth, but he'd fallen into the casualness of the country since he'd arrived and it was what Spencer wore day in and day out.

The casualness appealed to him much more.

As usual the station was humming with busyness. Uniforms were dragging in a drunk and disorderly, who seemed to be putting up a fight, and there was a woman in one of the interview rooms as he walked by. The low drone of people working and computers humming filled the air.

'Morning.' He nodded at Tez and Claire who were poring over a witness statement.

'Dave, how goes? Good weekend?' Claire asked around the pen in her mouth.

'Great. Yours?' He switched on his computer and put his coffee cup down on his desk.

'Fine,' she answered before Tez said, 'Hey, you don't have a lead on your stiff down the mine, do you?'

'Nah, not yet. Hoping to have all the info this morning. Shannon would have done the PM on Saturday at the earliest, and she mightn't even get to it until this morning. She did say that John Doe would have the priority.'

'It's all round town.'

'Course it is.' Dave sat down. 'Wouldn't expect any less. What's the deal here?' He nodded towards the woman in the interview room.

'Looking at a fraud,' Tez said.

'Fraud?' Dave turned around and looked at the well-dressed woman who was sitting with a straight back, her hands linked together in front of her on the table.

'Yeah.' Claire grinned and rubbed her hands together. 'But it sounds worse than it is! Between you and I, I'd say she was being entrepreneurial, but I'm pretty sure the people who have made the complaints about her wouldn't see it my way.'

'Sounds interesting. What've you got?'

'She runs prospecting tours. The complaints against her are they never find gold.'

'Them and the rest of the world, I would have thought!'

'Turns out one of the tourists she took out saw her hide a piece of gold in the ground. What she does is charges to take them out into the field and lets them loose with detectors. Part of the deal is the first nugget they find is hers. From then on in, they keep the rest. They only ever find slivers of gold—not worth ten bucks—but because they find something big the first time, they recommend the tour to others.'

It took Dave a moment to work it through. Then it dawned on him and he grinned. 'She's planting the gold and pocketing the money and they never find anything worth much?'

'Spot on. Clever, wouldn't you say?'

'That's gold!' he said in a tone which was half laughing and half amazement. Then he realised what he'd said and groaned. 'Sorry, pardon the pun!'

Claire cracked up laughing. 'I hope your jokes are better than that!'

Dave held his hands up in surrender. 'Melinda would say they're not, but I don't think they're that bad. Here, let me tell you this one: what do you call a man who lies under leaves?'

Everyone in the room looked at him blankly. Then Claire dropped her head into her hands and said, 'I think my ears are going to hurt.'

'Drum roll . . .'

'The suspense is killing me.' Tez's sarcasm was like water off a duck's back.

'Russell.' Dave held out his hands, waiting for applause.

Tez looked at him deadpan, while Claire peered at him from between her fingers. Neither of them had a smile on their face. They hadn't even groaned.

'Yeah, that's not good,' said Tez, turning away.

'I'm not giving you the job of organising the entertainment for the Christmas party,' said Claire. 'You might hire yourself and we'll all be crying into our beer within the first five minutes.'

Laughing, Dave said, 'Okay, okay, I admit it. Telling jokes is *not* my forte. My brother told me that years ago.'

'You surprise me,' Tez answered in the same deadpan tone.

'Okay, so back to Barrabine's newest hotshot entrepreneur. Got any ideas on how you're going to prove it?'

'Thought she could sweat it for a bit. We'll go and have a chat in a couple of hours, probably caution her. Maybe put out a warning to the tourist bureau so it shuts her little business down. Don't think we need to charge her with anything.'

'Never ceases to amaze me how crims evolve,' said Dave. 'They just keep coming up with new ways of ripping people off.'

The phone rang and Claire picked up it, while Dave grabbed his empty paper coffee cup and threw it across the room and into the bin.

'Better basketballer than you are comedian,' Tez quipped.

Dave harrumphed good-naturedly and turned to the computer and put in his password. He could hear Claire on the call.

'Uh-huh.' Pause. 'Right, and when was it supposed to be returned?' Pause. 'And your name?' Pause. 'Right, right. Can you give me the details: who hired it, plate number, et cetera?'

Dave could hear Claire's pen scratching across the page as he scrolled through his emails, hoping to see something from Shannon. Nothing with her name on it. Damn. He really wanted to get going on this. Maybe he should check the fax. Emails were so new, Shannon might have sent it by fax instead.

'Look, I think we'll send a detective out to see you. Might match up with an investigation we've got going on already.' Pause. 'Detectives Burrows and Brown.'

Dave looked up at the sound of his name.

'Yes, sir, they'll be out there shortly. Thanks for calling.'

Claire put the phone down and looked at Dave. 'Just got a report from the Avis mob at the airport saying there has been a rental car not returned.' Excitement lit her face. 'Maybe that's your John Doe. Said you'd go out and see him.'

A familiar thrill of discovery flowed through Dave. 'A hire car not returned? Sounds good.' He stopped. 'Unless we've got a body in a motel room somewhere.'

Claire shook her head. 'If there was, it probably would have been found by now. This car should have been returned four days ago. White Toyota four-wheel drive.' She reeled off the numberplate and the vehicle identification number. 'Most of the hotels here service the rooms daily. I reckon we'd have heard about it if there was another body some-where. Anyway, I think one's enough, don't you?' she asked.

'More than,' Tez said, looking up from the book he was writing in.

'Did you get a name of the person who had hired it or a DL or DOB?'

'A Mr Glen Bartlett. Thought you'd get those other details when you went out.'

Dave frowned and swung his chair around and with two-finger typing entered the name into the Missing Persons Register but didn't get a hit. From there he did a search to check whether the man had a record or anything that might give him some information as to whether he could be his John Doe, but without a date of birth or driver's licence number, he couldn't be sure which of the five Glen Bartletts who appeared on his screen would have had reason to be in Barrabine and not return a hire car. None of them had theft on their record. Driving under the influence for two, and drunk and disorderly for the other three.

'Okay, I'll head out there and talk to the manager,' he said, then remembered the autopsy report. He checked his pigeonhole in case someone had picked the report up off the fax machine, but it was empty. Over at the fax he leafed through the pages on the tray. Nothing for him or Spencer.

Instead there was the regular police newsletter, which no one read, and an enquiry from the Karratha Police Station addressed to Tez.

'For you,' he said, putting it down on his colleague's desk.

'Cheers.' Claire put her hand out for it. 'That'll be the details on that stolen truck they're looking for. Need to let patrols know.'

There wasn't any answer from Tez, who was reading something intently. Dave grinned as Claire picked up a piece of paper and scrunched it into a small ball before throwing it at her partner. 'Oi!'

'What?' Tez looked up at her with a wounded look on his face.

'You're not listening.'

'Shit, for a moment I thought you were my wife. That's why I didn't take any notice.'

'You dickhead,' Claire answered good-naturedly. 'Here.' She pushed the fax towards him. He flashed her a cheeky grin and took the pages. They had a great partnership.

'Morning, morning,' called Spencer in his loud voice as he pushed the door open and came into the detectives' office. 'How's everyone this morning?'

'Fine, boss.'

'Good, and you?'

'No worries.'

They all spoke at once. Spencer sighed, threw himself in the chair and looked over at Dave.

'What's going on? You look excited. Got the PM results?'

'Not yet, but there was a phone call reporting a hire car that hasn't been returned. Been missing for four days. Out at the airport.'

Spencer pursed his lips and nodded. 'Interesting.' He seemed to think for a moment then asked, 'What did you do for the weekend?'

Dave blinked at the change of subject.

'Ah, took Melinda to Oakamanda for one of Dee's Contiki tours.'

'And you survived? You'd better buy yourself a lottery ticket. Did you see the couch on the back?'

Dave grinned. 'Oh yeah, and all the beer cans! She'd go for a row if we wanted her to.'

'Got to pick your battles, mate.'

Dave nodded. 'We right to head out to the airport?'

Spencer adjusted the waistline of his shorts. 'I've got something to do here. You head out and do the interview.'

The phone on Dave's desk started to ring and he snatched it up.

'Burrows.'

'It's Shannon.'

'Morning. What've you got?'

She paused and he heard her intake of breath. 'You've got yourself a murder.'

Dave glanced up at Spencer and nodded, before grabbing his pen and paper. 'Hit me with it.'

'I'll send everything through by email.'

'Great, but give me the basics now. I'll read your report when it comes in.'

'Okay, your John Doe has had a blunt force to the head, which cracked his skull. My measurements and research make me believe it was a flat-mouthed shovel. The type you can buy from any hardware store.'

'And the type which would be a dime a dozen in a mining town.'

Shannon gave a small laugh. 'Yeah, I don't suppose I've given you an unusual murder weapon.' She paused and Dave could hear the rustle of paperwork. 'The decomposition hid the damage to the side of his head, which was why I couldn't determine whether it was murder or not.'

'It's no problem. Some clever pathologist told me you had to wait for the science anyway.'

'Very clever pathologist that one,' she quipped. 'So, the blow was on the left-hand side. It measures one hundred and fifty-two millimetres across on a downward angle, so I'm wondering if the vic was starting to bend or bending down as he was hit.'

Dave exhaled loudly.

'I've managed to pull some partial prints, but again the decomposition has hurt. I've run what I've got through the database and not got any hits. We ran him through the X-ray machine and he had a broken leg when he was young. Maybe twelve or fourteen.'

'Other than a run in with a shovel, he'd still be alive, yeah?'

'Exactly.'

'Any scars or tatts?'

'Nope, he's a cleanskin.'

'Right, I'll wait for the rest of your report then. Thanks for the heads-up. It's good to know what we're dealing with.'

'I'll email it through to you now.'

'No worries.' Dave paused and turned his back on Spencer. 'And, Shannon, it was good to see you last week.'

The line hissed quietly and Dave felt her embarrassment all over again. 'Yeah, you too,' she said finally. 'Sorry . . .'

'Nothing to be sorry about. Nothing wrong with two work colleagues going out for a drink. I'll give you a ring when I get back to Perth next. See if we can round up some of the old crew and have a catch-up.'

'Sounds good. Talk to you then.'

Dave hung up the phone and relayed the information to Spencer. 'Need to ID him,' he finished with.

'So she didn't come up with that barcode I was hoping for?'

'Apparently not.'

'Shit,' Spencer complained, then seemed to gather himself. 'Better get out to the airport and see if you can get a match that way.'

Chapter 14

Melinda smiled broadly and held out her hand to her new boss, Patricia Adams.

'Thank you,' she said. 'Thank you very much. When would you like me to start?'

Patricia smiled. 'Right now. I'll get the forms you need to fill out and hopefully we can have you on the floor in a couple of hours.' She stopped and smiled. 'I've got to tell you, Mel, you're a godsend. I didn't think I was going to fill the position. Community nurses are hard to find out here.'

Melinda ignored the shortening of her name and touched Patricia's arm instead. 'You might be my godsend,' she said truthfully.

'Call me Patti,' Patricia said and indicated she follow her down the hall. 'Patricia sounds so formal, and you've probably worked out by now that no one in Barrabine is formal. We'll shorten or lengthen any name. Anything to make a nickname!'

'I've noticed everyone's pretty laid-back. My husband used to wear a tie to work; everyone did in Perth. It was expected. Today's the first time he's worn one since his first day and I'll bet he's the only one in the office wearing a tie.'

Patti gave a bark of laughter. 'Yep, you'd be right there. I know Spencer and I don't remember him ever wearing a tie. In fact, I bet he doesn't even own one.'

'You're probably right,' Melinda agreed, looking around and taking in her new workplace. The walls were lined with posters imploring mums and dads not to smoke or drink. The heavy black writing shouted about passive smoking in cars and showed photos of babies and young children stuck inside with the windows up and smoke filling the vehicles. Others encouraged healthy eating and exercise or stressed the importance of immunisation.

'I'm sure you understand I'll have to put you on a three-month trial,' Patti said, breaking into Melinda's thoughts.

'Um . . .' She didn't get to ask why because Patti continued talking.

'Yeah, the government has just brought it in: mandatory three-month trial. I'm sure you won't need it, though. It's not a hard job. I guess you'd say it's more of an early child-hood nurse rather than a community nurse. You'll need to weigh the babies and track their growth. Talk to the mums and make sure they're managing okay. Not suffering depression or baby blues.

'You'll be able to make referrals to other professionals if you think there's something developmentally wrong with the baby.' Patti walked fast and Melinda almost had to jog to keep up with her. 'Just last week I recommended a two-year-old see a speech pathologist. The child wasn't showing any signs of forming words, but I knew she could understand what I was saying to her. I'm more than aware children develop at different stages, but by eighteen months they should have a couple of words.

'The grandmother had come in with the mother and said she felt there was something not quite right with the toddler. Of course that upset the mother, and within moments the whole appointment had deteriorated into a sobbing mum, screaming child and a grandmother trying to talk over the top of it all.' She shook her head. 'God, it was awful.' She stopped at the entrance to a small office and indicated Melinda should go in.

'What did you do?' Melinda asked, finding a chair and sitting down.

'First thing was to get rid of the grandmother. She wasn't being at all helpful. I think the mothers and mothers-in-law often forget how frightening it can be to be a new mum, and when they keep telling them what to do or that they're doing something wrong, it makes the mums anxious.

'The grandmothers are all bravado and full of advice, which,' she turned and looked at Melinda with her eyebrows raised, 'I must say, is *not* always the best guidance. We've moved on from thirty years ago. And, as much as they're trying to help their daughters, they're not always the best person for the job.'

'Sounds like it can be tricky.' Melinda felt a tremor of uncertainty run through her. She was used to following protocols or instruction from doctors. From what Patti was saying, in this role she would be expected to trust her own instincts and make her own decisions.

Her thoughts must have shown on her face because Patti turned from the filing cabinet and said, 'Oh now, don't you be worrying about what I'm saying. If you get stuck or aren't sure of anything—any tiny little thing—you come and get me and I'll check the mum or bub out. In fact,' she handed over the employment forms that needed filling out, 'if you like, I'll sit in on the first few appointments. Would that make you more comfortable?'

'That would be great,' Melinda said, relief filling her.

❧

'Hello,' Melinda greeted her first client in the waiting room. 'You must be Rachael.' She flashed a large and what she hoped was a comforting smile at the new mum. 'And who do we have here?'

Melinda peered into the pram to see a tiny baby dressed in a pink sleeveless jumpsuit staring at a moving toy, her arms and legs flailing about gently. When Melinda popped her head into view, the baby took her eyes off the toy and cooed at her.

The young woman stood up quickly and smiled. 'Yeah, hi, I'm Rachael. This is Taylor.' She grabbed hold of the handles and started to push the pram towards the weighing room.

Clearly she'd been here a few times before. Melinda waited until the two were inside her new office, which was decorated with bright colours and mobiles hanging from the ceiling.

'It's nice to meet you, Rachael,' Melinda said, sitting down at her desk. She took Taylor's baby book from Rachael and flicked it open to the recording page. 'How have you been?' Looking up, she focused on the woman, who looked tired but was smiling.

'I've had a great month,' she said. 'Taylor is beginning to roll from side to side and she even slept through for the first time last night.'

'Well, aren't you a clever girl!' Melinda said to Taylor. She reached down and held out her finger for the baby to grip hold of and refocused on Rachael as Patti had instructed—these sessions were as much about checking in with the mothers as they were about assessing the babies.

Having offered to sit in on Melinda's first few appointments, Patti had been called away to help her elderly mother, who had had a fall. Melinda was on her own.

'Don't show fear,' had been Patti's parting advice. 'New mums are like horses—they can smell fear a mile off. Act confident and sure of yourself. If you have any problems or think something is wrong, ask them to make another appointment for next week.' She'd smiled. 'You'll be fine. You're a paediatric nurse, so you know all of this. It's just a matter of applying it in a different context, okay?'

'How is Taylor sleeping generally?' Melinda asked in her most professional tone.

'Okay. I mean, she still wakes up three or four times a night mostly. Last night was out of the ordinary and . . .'

She stopped as her eyes filled with tears. 'I had a bit of a freak-out this morning when I first woke up and realised she hadn't woken.'

Melinda understood. 'You thought the worst? That's perfectly normal.'

'Yeah, I did. Stupid of me. She was still asleep, breathing away just fine. Then I felt bloody ridiculous.' Rachael brushed her tears away and smiled again. 'Crazy, huh?'

'Not at all. It would've given you a fright. However, you *can* probably expect she'll do this from time to time now. In fact, with any luck, she'll do it every night from now on and last night wasn't a once-off! How old is she again? Seven weeks?' Melinda glanced down at the book to check.

'Eight,' the new mum answered.

'A lot of babies can have a night here and there of sleeping through at her age.' She paused. 'But all babies are different.' She focused on Rachael. 'What about you? How are you feeling?' She picked Taylor up out of the pram and held her over her shoulder.

Rachael sniffed. 'Mostly I'm okay. Just sometimes when I get a fright or she doesn't feed easily, I get a bit teary. It's not often, just . . .' She broke off and it seemed to Melinda she was unable to finish because she was working overtime not to cry.

'That's common too, you know. Having a new bub is a big change for everyone and these little cherubs don't come with a manual.'

Rachael seemed to gather herself. 'It was just the fright I had this morning.'

'Crying is healthy,' Melinda reassured her. 'As long as you don't do it all day, every day.'

'Marty is such a help too,' Rachael said. 'He baths her and changes nappies when he's home. I really don't have anything to complain about. Do you know, my friend,' she seemed to brighten, 'she had her baby two weeks ago and her hubby hasn't changed a nappy yet!'

'He might need some practice,' Melinda said dryly, happy to see Rachael was recovering herself so quickly. She made a mental note to ask about this again at the next appointment, but she didn't see anything out of the ordinary here.

'Right, maybe you could undress Taylor and we'll pop her on the scales.' Melinda gave her another big smile and handed the baby to her mum.

'How's your husband coping with the new routine?'

'I think he's getting used to it. It's a bit tough when he's on night shift and needs to sleep during the day. I try to make sure she doesn't cry very much then, so she doesn't wake him. If she's unsettled I put her in the pram and take her for a walk. Makes it easier to sleep when it's quiet.'

'Sleeping during the day is hard work,' Melinda said. 'Even when you're used to it.'

'Yeah, Marty said as much, but every time I go past the bedroom door I hear him snoring, so she can't be keeping him awake all the time!' she laughed.

'I know when I was working night shift at the hospital, I'd sleep like the dead for the first few hours after I got home, but then noises would wake me quite easily.'

Taylor started to cry as her jumpsuit was taken off. Melinda watched as Rachael expertly removed her nappy and popped her onto the scales.

'Have you got any concerns about Taylor at all?' Melinda asked while she waited for the scales to freeze on the weight. 'Ah look, there we are. Four point six kilos—a gain of about six hundred grams. Very nice.'

'Oh, that's great! I always feel it's a bit like a test coming in here—you know, how good I'm doing as a mum. As soon as I know she's put on weight, I relax!'

'I hope I'm not as scary as a test. That wouldn't be cool!' Melinda flashed a large grin and repeated her previous question.

'No, no concerns.'

'How's everything for you since the birth? No pain or discharge?' She started to work her way through the list of questions that Patti had left for her.

Within another ten minutes she had everything wrapped up and she was showing Rachael out of the door.

A feeling of triumph surged through her. She'd got through her first appointment as a child health nurse and she'd nailed it!

Chapter 15

1945

The man finished burying the woman's body and placed his shovel in the back of his old car. He wiped the sweat from his brow and took a long swig from his water bag, then started the engine.

Following the rough track towards Barrabine, he kept an eye out for any humpies in the bush, somewhere the woman could have lived. Every mile or so he stopped and sniffed for campfire smoke, but he didn't come across anything that gave him any indication of life.

The road got smoother closer to the town, and just as the sun was setting he parked in front of one of the three pubs and turned off the engine, sitting there in silence. He kept wondering who the woman was and why life had got on top of her to the point she thought death was the easier option. He couldn't get the image of her body swaying from the tree branch out of his mind and he was finding it hard to concentrate on what he was doing.

He rubbed his face hard, as if trying to scrub away the memory.

Gathering himself, he sniffed at his hands to make sure they didn't smell and walked into the pub. He looked around to see if there was anyone he knew at the bar, but he didn't expect there to be. Barrabine was a transient community; people came and went on the whim of gold fever. And they died easily here too.

He heard his name called out and turned around.

'Paddy, how yer goin', mate?' A man with curly red hair came over to him, his hand outstretched. 'Let me buy you a beer.'

'G'day, Rocco. Didn't expect to be seeing you here. Where was the last time I saw you? About fifty miles north, wasn't it?'

'Last night here, mate,' Rocco answered, looking sad. 'The missus is crook and I got to get her to Perth, so the doc says. Don't want to leave, I love this place, but she can't cope without me.'

'Sorry to hear that,' Paddy answered, his thoughts immediately flying back to the woman he'd buried today. If she'd had family who had cared for her as much as Rocco cared for his wife, maybe she wouldn't have died the way she did.

'Yeah, even sold me lease. Don't reckon I'll be back.' His face was grim and Paddy could see it was hurting him to leave.

'Hard decision to make. Don't envy you having to live in the city. Full of bloody cars and people walking too fast.'

Rocco looked at him solemnly. 'I hope it don't kill me up there.'

Paddy patted him on the back. 'You'll be right, mate. Be settled in no time. First find yourself a local watering hole and then everything'll fall into place.'

'Maybe you're right. Anyway, what's your news?'

'Not much. On my way to the Ballarat goldfields. Hoping for better luck over there. Now tell me, do you know of anyone living about twenty miles out to the north-west of here?' Paddy asked him as they moved towards the bar. He took a roll of notes out of his pocket and peeled one off.

Rocco took in the roll and whistled softly. 'You have a win somewhere?'

'I bloody wish! Doesn't matter how hard I look, I don't seem to be able to find any of the yellow stuff. Beer, please, love,' he said, turning his attention to the barmaid. 'And one for my mate here.' He turned back to Rocco. 'Nah, I sold some of my gear so I could get across to Victoria and have a crack over there. My grandfather left me a lease and I thought I'd have a go at that.'

'Victoria, hey? I met a bloke from there the other day. Said there's still lots in the ground, so you might be lucky.' Rocco clapped him on back. 'Why you asking about people living out north-west?'

'Had to bury a woman today.' As he said the words, she flashed in front of him again. The slow gentle sway, the crow on her shoulder. The ants. He took a long pull on his beer to wash away the vision. 'Want to find her family and let them know where she is.'

'Shit, really?' Rocco's face became sad. 'Snakebite or something?'

'Or something. She was hanging in a tree.'

'Holy Mother of Mary. She killed herself?'

'Looked like it.'

Rocco crossed himself, shock clear on his face. Paddy appreciated that—not because he wanted Rocco to be upset but because it showed he hadn't become immune to the fragility of life. When men failed to react to shocking stories, that's when the harshness of the goldfields had claimed their humanity.

Death was commonplace out here and everyone knew it. Look at the man who'd been killed last month—a mine had collapsed on him and by the time the blokes from nearby mines had managed to get him up, he'd suffocated. Then there was the child who'd cut himself on a piece of tin and died from blood poisoning, and the woman who'd died in childbirth. It was harsh and tough and really, Paddy thought, nothing should surprise anyone, but they should always *feel* the tragedy of it.

'You know of anyone out there?' he asked again.

'Nope. Didn't think there were any leases pegged out that way yet. I know there's been some fellas exploring, but . . .' He trailed off. 'If you go and ask at the mines office, they'll be able to tell you if anything's been pegged and who the owners are.'

'I might do that. Thanks, Rocco. I'd want to know where she was if she were my family. They mightn't even know she's gone.'

Rocco brightened as another man gave him a secret nod. 'You want to have a bit of fun tonight?' he asked, lowering his voice.

Paddy wiped the condensation from his glass of beer. 'What'd you have in mind?' he asked, thinking of the roll in his pocket.

'Just a little gambling. Away from prying eyes.'

Paddy raised his glass to him. 'Here I was thinking you meant the ladies!'

'Well, you could do that if you want, you being single 'n all, but two-up's more exciting as far as I'm concerned.'

'Pulling your leg, Rocco. Ladies of the night don't interest me. I'm in. Always happy for a bit of fun.' Maybe a night with the boys would help him forget.

About four miles from the centre of town, the group of seven squatted down under the drooping branches of a coral gum. The ring was drawn with a stick. Then a bottle of rum was passed around in the firelight. They drew straws for the first spinner. It was Paddy. It didn't bother him that he wasn't going to be able to bet at the start. They would all get their turn eventually.

'Who's got the kip and coins?' he asked, looking around the group—he realised out of all the men there, he knew only Rocco. Two he knew by sight, but the rest were strangers. Apprehension trickled through him—he hoped they were all as trustworthy as Rocco. Why hadn't he checked before they'd left town? Probably because he was too busy trying to forget the woman.

The crazy idea of giving her a name popped into his head. He couldn't keep thinking about her as 'the woman'. She was somebody's daughter. Maybe someone's sister, wife or mother. She would have a family somewhere. Everyone did.

Rocco passed over the piece of wood and Paddy took it, glad of the distraction. He inspected it; it was about seven inches long, worn smooth at one end and with impressions for the pennies to sit in at the other.

'Looks like you've used this a bit, Rocco,' he said with a grin, indicating the smooth handle.

'Who me? I'm a law-abiding citizen,' he answered, returning the grin.

Everyone knew that two-up was illegal—gambling was illegal—but it didn't stop them. For some, the need to have a wager burned in their bellies like the fever to find gold. Paddy remembered one man he'd shared a campsite with who'd been like that. He recognised his own addiction and tried to sabotage his gambling urges by putting his savings into a box that couldn't be opened unless it was cut open by a blacksmith. This worked well until he ran out of the allowance he'd given himself for betting. Then he'd run around like a man possessed, trying to convince someone to open it for him.

'Mate,' Paddy said, turning to one of the other men, 'you be my ringy and boxer.' He polished the two coins and placed them in the tray.

Another of the men looked up from the swig he was taking and frowned. 'They can't be the same person,' he said.

The boxer was supposed to oversee the game and wasn't allowed to participate. He had to be neutral, while the ringy looked after the coins in between throws to avoid interference.

'No rule that says that,' Rocco answered.

'It goes without saying.'

'Come on, we're all men of honour here,' Rocco said, spreading out his hands. 'It's a game to celebrate my farewell. I don't wanna get bogged down in rules. Let's just play.'

The men glanced around at one another and Paddy decided to take the lead. 'Place your bets, gentlemen, and may your night be lucky.'

The men threw their money into the hat and watched in silence. Paddy tossed the coins high, firelight glinting onto copper-coloured pennies. In silence, everyone followed their path, watching them twirl in slow motion. They started their downward spiral, still spinning, and landed on the soft earth with a gentle 'thwack'.

'Odds!' yelled Paddy and loud chatter and groans broke out between all the men. One man threw up his hands in excitement and grabbed the hat full of coins.

'Next bets,' Paddy called again after the ringy had collected the pennies and given them back to him.

It went on like this until the rum bottle was empty and the men were falling asleep at the edge of the ring.

'I'm out,' slurred Rocco.

'Me too,' said Paddy, sitting down and pulling another smaller bottle out of his pocket. He offered it around to the men, but only he and Rocco took sips. The others faded away to their swags.

Paddy leaned against the trunk of the tree and looked up into the night sky. A shooting star streaked across the diamond-studded blackness. He remembered his mother saying he should make a wish when he saw a shooting star.

What to wish for, he thought. His mind was muddy from all the rum. He could wish for fortune when he got to Victoria, for a long reef of gold that would make him rich. He could wish for the comfort of a woman, one who loved him and was prepared to live with him on the goldfields. Or he could wish to find the family of the woman he had buried today.

Paddy didn't need to think too hard. Before the shooting star disappeared, he wished to find the family of the dead woman.

Chapter 16

When Dave pulled up at the airport, he spotted an Ansett plane on the ground and people climbing the stairs to board. Inside the airport building people were milling around; some had coffees in their hand and others beers. Dave wondered if they'd just come off night shift and were having their 'nightly' beer, even though it was only nine in the morning.

'G'day, I'm Detective Dave Burrows,' he said to the man behind the Avis counter, offering his hand.

The elderly man immediately stood up and grasped his hand. 'George Robertson. Thanks for coming.'

'No problems. What's happened?' Dave asked, getting out his notebook.

George pushed over the paperwork and Dave looked down. He saw the handwritten name: Glen Bartlett, a driver's licence number, address and phone number. A heavy, scrawly signature was at the bottom of the page. It appeared Mr Bartlett hadn't wanted to take out extra insurance and he was happy with the terms and conditions. He'd hired a white four-wheel drive wagon and the numberplate was listed.

Damn! Dave had hoped it might be the red vehicle Dee had told them about.

'Do you know what flight he got off?' Dave asked, still looking at all the information in front of him.

'Afternoon flight from Perth two weeks ago. I remember him because he was a very nice man. Most people are in a rush and too busy to talk, but he wasn't. I do this job so I can talk to people. I'm on my own, now, see. Not much conversation at home. That's why I remember him so well.

'He said he'd be here for about two weeks, maybe a little longer if he found who he was looking for, and he'd be staying at the Federal Hotel. Hadn't booked a return flight.'

'Did he say what he was looking for?' Dave asked.

'It was a who. But that was all he said.'

'Uh-huh. And why didn't you report the vehicle missing when it wasn't returned on the day?'

'I'd organised with him to give me a call if he was going to be over the time frame and he asked if I could give him a two-day grace period, just in case he was out in the bush.' George frowned.

'Is that normal practice?'

'Not at all. He seemed like such a good bloke I told him no worries. Apparently I'm either too nice or too naive. I assumed he'd let me know, and when I hadn't heard from him on the second day, I thought I'd give him two more . . . Just in case, you know? I guess he could be in the

Northern Territory by now.' The old man sighed. 'Reckon head office will probably give me the flick if I've had one of my cars stolen.'

'What makes you think he might be in the Territory?'

George shrugged. 'If he wanted to steal the vehicle he's got nineteen days, hasn't he? Could be anywhere. I just picked the Northern Territory out of the air. He never mentioned anything about it.'

'I see.' Dave glanced up at the ceiling. 'Any security cameras aimed at your desk?'

He nodded. 'That one up there.'

'I'd like to get the footage, please.'

'I guess you'll have to talk to the airport people about that. Avis just rent space here. The rest is up to the airport.'

Dave had expected as much. 'And this vehicle, it was in good condition, no known problems? Reliable? Couldn't have broken down and he's stuck somewhere?'

'If he broke down it wasn't because the car wasn't in good nick. All my vehicles are in tiptop shape and serviced regularly. It'll be because he's got a flat or put a branch up through the radiator or something like that.'

'Does that happen often to the vehicles you rent out?'

'More than you'd think. Especially if the renters aren't four-wheel drivers and don't know this country.'

Dave paused, gathering his thoughts. 'Did Mr Bartlett have any distinguishing features?'

'What do you mean?'

'Tattoos, scars, that type of thing.'

George narrowed his eyes, trying to remember. 'I don't think so,' he said slowly. 'But I couldn't be sure.'

'Okay, thanks for this. I'll be in touch once I've got something. I'll go and find out who to talk to about the video footage.' He reached into his pocket for his wallet and took out a business card. 'If he turns up or you remember anything else, make sure you give me a call. I'll send you through the stolen vehicle report so your company can get on with an insurance claim.'

'Great, thanks.'

They shook hands and Dave walked away.

Three hours later he was back in the station, looking at the security footage. It had taken an age to find someone who was authorised to give it to him, but he'd persevered and left the airport with video tapes of the day in question, plus the ones for a day either side. One thing Dave had noticed since his move to Barrabine was that the people out here were never in a hurry—they seemed to run on their own time. The balding man who oversaw airport security seemed to be on 'go slow mode'. There was certainly no sense of urgency.

'What have you got?' Spencer asked, looking over his shoulder.

'Nothing yet.'

'Run his driver's licence?'

'Yeah, he hasn't got a record or anything of interest. Speeding ticket in his home town of Ballarat three years ago, but that's all. Not married.'

'Any next of kin?'

'None who I've found yet.'

Spencer went over to the whiteboard and wrote Glen's name up on it, along with the details of the missing vehicle. 'Put out a 4-2-4 on the radio. Get everyone to keep an eye out for the vehicle.'

Dave jotted a note to remind himself; 4-2-4 was a report of a stolen vehicle. 'Will do.' He swung the chair around to look at Spencer. 'Find anything of interest in the PM report?'

Spencer scratched his head. 'Not really. Pretty healthy fella by all accounts. Like you said, a cleanskin, so no identifying features. However,' he held up a finger and pointed at Dave, 'the broken leg will be helpful in identifying him if nothing else turns up.' He paused and squinted at the whiteboard. 'I think I'll get the gold analysed,' he said slowly. 'See where it's come from. Might at least give us an idea of where he's been.'

'Good. That'll be helpful.'

Dave turned back to the television screen and continued viewing the security footage. He watched as Glen Bartlett approached the Avis desk and smiled at George Robertson. There was no sound to the tape, so he couldn't hear what they were saying and the pictures had been taken from too far away to be able to lip-read.

Glen looked to be about the height and weight of his John Doe and George Robertson was right: he smiled a lot. He'd spent a good fifteen minutes chatting with George compared to the five or so minutes most people took at the desk, signing papers and getting their keys. Having seen the interaction, Dave wasn't surprised George remembered him as well as he did.

'I'm going to the Federal,' Dave told Spencer after he'd finished examining the footage. 'See if I can get any information there.'

'Good idea. You right by yourself?' asked Spencer. 'I've got court this afternoon.'

'Sure, no worries.'

Outside the air was cooler than it had been since he'd moved to Barrabine, so Dave decided to walk the two blocks to the Federal Hotel. He nodded to a few people whose faces he knew and thought how nice it was to be able to do that. In Perth, when he'd walked down the street there had only been blank faces, averted eyes and the roar of buses drowning out the possibility of any conversation.

He jogged up the steps of the pub and pushed on the door, noticing the peeling paint as he did so. The whole building looked old and tired, as did a lot of the shops in the main street. *An overhaul wouldn't go astray*, he thought. *It's not like there isn't any money around.*

The moist air-conditioning hit him in the face as he entered the bar, as did the smell of stale beer and vomit. Didn't seem to matter how clean these pubs were, they still stank.

'G'day, Charlie,' said Dave, nodding at the middle-aged man standing at the end of the bar, watching a horserace on the TV.

'Dave,' Charlie answered without taking his eyes off the screen.

In the reception area he was glad to find Ginger behind the desk. Thanking his lucky stars it was someone he knew, Dave hit her with a large smile. He was sure he'd be able to talk her into showing him Glen Bartlett's room without a warrant.

'G'day, Ginger. You're looking busy there.'

She looked up and returned his smile. 'Hello, Dave. Always busy. Keeps me off the streets! How're you?'

'Fine, fine. You?'

'Under the pump, as always.' She indicated the paper-work spread across her desk. 'Trying to get everything ready for the accountant. I'm a bit late. Like about six months!'

'Can't be on top of everything all the time,' he said. 'You booked out at the moment?'

She shook her head. 'Nah, only got nine rooms filled out of thirty. Not the busy time of the year. Too hot for tourists and school holidays are over.' She narrowed her eyes as she glanced at the folder he was carrying under his arm. 'But I'm guessing you haven't come to enquire about booking a room.'

'You'd be right there, although I'm still very grateful you found Melinda and me a nice room when we first arrived. Trying to put our bedroom together that night would have been a disaster!'

'Ah, go on with you,' Ginger said with a wave of her hand. 'What can I help you with?'

'Have you got a Glen Bartlett staying with you?'

'Not now. He checked out about a week ago. What do you want with him?'

'Can't tell you that right now but could I have a look at the room he stayed in?'

'Sure, although it's been cleaned. I don't think I've had anyone in it since he left. Hang on . . .' She flicked through the register book and found the right page. 'Hmm, nope. Haven't had anyone in there since.'

'Excellent. Do you know why he checked out? Was he on his way home?'

Ginger reached under the desk and pulled out a key before turning the desk sign to *Back in five minutes*. 'I don't rightly know. He didn't say he was on his way home. I did notice on the morning he checked out his hire car was loaded with camping equipment, which I thought was a bit strange. He'd said he was from Victoria and he'd never mentioned he was going to drive home. I would've thought he had to return the hire car to where he hired it from, and he did tell me he flew in to Barra. Oh, listen to me, I'm rambling. This way, room twenty-one,' she said and led the way outside to the units at the back of the hotel. 'But you know what this town is like, Dave—everyone holds their secrets close to their chests and no one asks questions.'

'Yeah, tight-lip syndrome, we coppers call it! Can you remember much about him?' Dave asked as they walked across the asphalt.

'I only saw him a few times. He was very friendly when he first checked in and I spoke to him a couple of times on the phone when he rang for room service, but that's about it.'

'Did he say what he was doing here?'

Ginger brushed her long red hair away from her face and scratched her elbow. 'He was looking for someone, from what I recall. He didn't say who, just that he was hoping to catch up with an old friend. Here.' She indicated a door and put the key in the lock.

Inside there was a sagging double bed and grey walls. Towels were arranged in a fan shape on the end of the bed, and there was a TV on the bench next to the mirror.

Dave looked around slowly. He took in the smell and atmosphere and checked to see if there was anything disturbed. Nothing. He put his hand between the mattress and bed base, feeling to see if anything had been left behind. Then he opened drawers and cupboards and checked the bathroom.

They were all empty and clean.

'My girls would have put anything they found in the lost property,' Ginger said. 'I don't remember anything from this room, but I can check when we go back.'

'That would be good. Cheers.' He was just about to leave when he saw a scrap of paper poking out from underneath the curtain. He pulled out the pair of rubber gloves he had in his pocket and put them on. Bending down, he drew it out and looked at it. There were numbers scrawled on it and Dave recognised the handwriting from the Avis forms.

'Bloody hell,' Ginger snapped, drawing back the curtain to reveal a few dead flies and a lot of fluff. 'I'll be having a word to the cleaners about this. They should pull the curtains back to vacuum. That's disgusting.'

Dave stared at the piece of paper, wondering what the numbers meant. They weren't in a telephone number format. 'Can I say I'm glad they didn't?' he asked.

Chapter 17

Chief barked, then snarled, his lips curling, showing his teeth.

'Steady there, mate. I'm friendly,' Tim heard a man's voice say. He gave a mirthless grunt. Wouldn't matter what you said to Chief, he wouldn't back down. Swinging around, he put a foot on the ladder and started up to the surface, wondering who was wanting him and how they knew he was down this shaft.

He looked out and saw a well-dressed man offering Chief a piece of meat and the dog staring at the man without taking his gift. Tim didn't like that. How did this bloke know he had a dog? Had he been here before? He squinted, trying to see whether he recognised the man. He didn't think so.

Before climbing the final steps, he checked his gun and wiped his brow.

'My dog is trained not to take food from strangers,' he said by way of a greeting.

'Just trying to be nice and not get bitten, mate. It's not like I'm going to poison him.'

Tim jerked his head at Chief. 'He doesn't know that and neither do I. What can I do for you?' he asked, his tone hard. He stood with his arms crossed and stared at the man.

'Are you Tim Tucker?'

'Who's asking?'

He brandished a small business card and tried to offer it to him, but Chief barked again and jumped up on his back legs, snapping at the man's arm.

'Fuck! Call your dog, off, will you?'

'He only does that to people he doesn't like,' Tim said calmly. 'I don't reckon he likes you. And if he doesn't, I won't either.' He snapped his fingers. Immediately, Chief came to sit next to his owner, still growling. Tim didn't say anything more, he just crossed his arms and waited.

The breeze cooled the sweat on his back a little. Didn't matter how cool it was underground, he always sweated and it was always musty. It was nice to get to the surface at the end of every day and breathe in the sweet air. He seemed to be sweating so much more than usual and he wondered if he should make an appointment with the doctor. No. The last time he'd been, he hadn't liked what the doctor had told him, so he wouldn't go back.

The man took a cautious step towards Tim and held out his card again. 'I'm Ross Pollard from HMA Mining.'

'And?'

'I've come to make an offer on your land.'

Tim stood still. He'd heard that one of the bigger mining companies had been trying to buy up some of the smaller leases, but it had always been on the other side of Barrabine. Not out this way. Why were they offering money for land out here?

There was only one answer to that question; they must believe there was still a lot of gold in the ground.

'What makes you think I'd want to sell?' He coughed a little, his throat dry.

'We're offering much more money than you'd ever make from what you've got here.' He named a figure and Tim had to admit he was impressed. It made him even more certain there was gold around.

'Thanks for the offer,' he said, turning away. 'But no thanks.'

'You haven't even heard me out!' the man protested.

'I don't need to. Not interested.' He leaned down and picked up the rope that was attached to a large piece of tin and pulled it over the shaft mouth. The clattering drowned out the man's next words.

After his children had died, Tim had taken to covering the mine shafts, but lately he'd become lax about it. Since he'd found the man's body, he'd made sure to start again. He wasn't going to be responsible for anyone else's death.

Killjoy had brought up a very good point in the pub the other week too. These days it was just as likely the dead man's family would sue him for not having the shaft covered, even though he'd been trespassing on Tim's land. It would be Tim who got into trouble, not the idiot who'd fallen in. Times were certainly changing—back when he'd first started out, people had taken responsibility for their own actions instead of trying to blame someone else.

Chief walked close to Tim, his eyes still on the man, as Tim gathered his tools and esky and placed them in the back of his ute.

'We've had others in this area sell their leases to us and we'd really like to put a nice package of land together,' Ross blustered on. 'It'll make your life very easy.'

'What makes you think my life isn't easy now? Or that I'd want to change it?'

'Ah, well, you know, you're, um, getting on a bit . . .'

Tim turned to face the man. 'How did you know where I was?' he stared at him, his eyes hard. 'See, from where I'm standing, you're trespassing on my land and must've driven over a fair bit of it looking for me.' The man began trying to explain but he talked over the top of him. 'Trespassing on land out here, mister, it's not a good thing to do. More than likely get a gun in your face for your trouble. So get in your car and get off my land. Now.' He didn't give the bloke any further chance to talk to him. He climbed into his ute, started it and whistled to Chief. The dog jumped in the back in a flash and Tim put the ute into gear and drove off.

'Damn intruders,' he muttered, checking his rear-view mirror to make sure his unwanted visitor was leaving. He reckoned the man would have followed his tracks from this morning and found him that way. These buggers would never give up. Nothing was sacred out here anymore.

Tim rested his hand on the side mirror as he drove, then reached around to pat Chief, who was smiling with his tongue hanging out, enjoying the breeze in his face. 'Pleased you were there, mate. You're an excellent deterrent.'

Half an hour later, he parked the ute under the weeping branches of the silver gimlet tree and got out. He looked at the ground and saw the unfamiliar tyre tracks. He was right.

Walking in through the doorway, he put his esky on the bench and reached into the fridge for a beer. 'Good thing I was just about to knock off, Mari,' he said quietly. 'If I'd had to leave before I was finished, I would've been really annoyed. Guess I'll need to make a trip to Oakamanda and phone Spencer. He'll be wanting to know about this fella.'

Marianne, as always, didn't answer.

Tim jiggled up and down on his toes. The visitor had sent thrills of agitation though him. He'd never liked unexpected surprises—and he liked them even less since finding the body.

He sighed and picked up the photo of his wedding day and thought about the dream he'd had last night. He always dreamed of Marianne, but recently he'd dreamed of her almost every night in vivid colour and detail and he always woke feeling hollow and empty and dripping in sweat. These were the mornings he asked himself what he had to live for. Like Dee had suggested, he had options. One which would see him live more comfortably than in a tin shed. Maybe he should take up the mining company's offer. He didn't have anyone to leave the lease to and he already had more than enough money to see him out to the end of his days. But what would he do with himself? With the endless empty days which would stretch out in front of him if he didn't have a job?

More importantly, how could he leave if there was even the remotest chance she might come back? She wouldn't know how to find him if he left . . . As the years had passed he had begun to assume she was dead but he could never be absolutely sure. His need to know where she was and why she'd left had not dwindled since that first devastating day he'd realised she'd gone. But he had learned to live with the gaping hole in his chest.

Tim hadn't realised she'd gone at first. Her clothes were untouched and there was dinner ready on the stove when he'd come home late that night. The bed had been empty and he'd called out to her a couple of times without reply. After eating his dinner, he'd gone to look further and found nothing. That was when the apprehension had begun to trickle through him. He'd stumbled back to the hut, calling her name; he'd heard the alarm in his own voice. Ripping open the small jewellery box which was hidden under a false floor, he stared inside. It was empty. And she never would have gone anywhere for a long period of time without the ivory and gold locket her father had made for her before he died. Seeing the box empty, he knew with certainly she'd gone. Left him.

Taking a swig of the beer, he went outside to watch the sun set and think about Marianne. And the body. It kept filtering into his thoughts at the most unexpected times, and every time it did he could smell the stench, hear the flies, and then his stomach would clench and he'd feel sick.

Needing to think about something else, he conjured up an image of Marianne. Exactly two weeks after he'd first heard the music across the dry and dusty road, he'd gone back to town and stood in front of the house again. He'd made sure it was at the exact same time. He didn't want to miss the beautiful sound again. And there it was, drifting across the street, light and floaty. The notes made him think of clouds hovering in a vivid blue sky. Then the pace picked up and the tone became bouncy. Like butterflies, or wattle birds, flitting through the air.

Sitting on the kerb, Tim listened, spellbound until the music stopped and the front door opened. The girl with the long black hair and silver-blue eyes let out a younger girl, bade her goodbye, then went back inside.

Tim never knew where his courage had come from but he was forever grateful for it. His feet carried him across the road, through the garden and to the front door, where he knocked. Jiggling from foot to foot as he waited for her to open the door, he tried to work out what he was going to say.

'Yes?' the girl asked when she opened the door.

'Um . . . I heard . . .' The words dried up in his throat when he saw how beautiful she was up close.

'You heard?' She looked at him seriously, those silver eyes curious.

He swallowed. 'I heard the music you were playing. It's beautiful.'

She smiled and he saw she had a dimple in her right cheek. 'It is the piano. I was playing Chopin to show my student how it should be performed. She likes to bang on the keys rather than skip lightly across them as she should.'

Tim now had no idea what to say.

'I don't know anything about music,' he admitted finally.

'Then your life will be much poorer than it should be. Come,' she waved him inside. 'Come and listen. Everyone should have music in their lives.'

Stuttering, he said he didn't think he should come in. 'It wouldn't look right.'

'My papa is inside. Come.'

He'd spent an hour listening to her play, watching mesmerised at the way her fingers had flown across the ivory and black keys. He hadn't known the name for any part of this new thing called a piano, but in that hour he'd decided he wanted to know everything about it and her.

A low grumble shook the ground and brought Tim out of his thoughts. It was dark now and the mozzies were beginning to bite.

Chief growled.

'Don't fret, my friend, it's just the mine blasting again. Though,' he frowned, 'usually they sound the siren first. I didn't hear it this time. Maybe I was too deep in thought.' He went back into the kitchen, putting the empty beer can in the bin.

Tim sat down on the edge of the single camp bed, made with nothing but a sleeping bag and mozzie net over the top. From under the grimy pillow he pulled a small notebook.

He looked at the cover, running his hand over it, trying to decide if he wanted to open it or not. Didn't need to because he knew every word written in Mari's hand. *Really,* he asked himself, *do you want to feel the raw grief all over again?*

Apparently he did, because without consciously opening the notebook he found himself looking at the beautiful cursive writing and reading her lyrical words.

Tonight the sun has kissed the leaves of the eucalypts as it has slowly sunk below the horizon. The fire is burning and I can hear the joyful laughter of the children as they duck and weave beneath the branches and bushes.

I asked the bush today about its secrets. But the land, it holds its mysteries close and you can be sure it will never tell. For a footprint which is once embedded in the soil disappears with a gust of wind and at once it was never there. You were never there.

The finches may flit from tree to tree and see every small thing that occurs, but they will never tell, neither will the broombushes even though they try. They rustle with the wind and try to talk, but are never understood.

This is why the land is the only one to confide in, for it will never tell.

Tim was never sure about this passage. What secrets did she think the bush knew? Was it her own or another's? Or perhaps she just understood so much good and bad happened out here and the only witness was nature.

He put the book down, refusing to let the melancholy get any worse.

In the kitchen he lit the fire in the bricked-up fireplace and waited until the pan was hot enough. He cracked two eggs and opened a can of beans. When they were nearly cooked, he took his fork and stuck it through a piece of bread, holding it up to the coals so it toasted.

Chief pretended he was asleep in the doorway, but Tim knew he was waiting for a titbit or for him to spill something.

He piled his dinner onto a tin plate, got himself another beer, then went outside and sat in his chair, this time to eat and watch the moon rise.

Chapter 18

Dave gathered the piece of paper he'd found in the motel room and the forms Glen had filled out at the Avis counter and sent them to forensics for fingerprinting.

He had woken in the middle of last night convinced the man down the mine was Glen Bartlett. He wasn't sure why, but he was absolutely convinced. One of the older detectives he'd worked with had always told him to trust his instincts. He'd always tried, but sometimes, without the evidence to back him up, it was hard. Especially when he had to put a case together with the prospect of going to court and a lawyer tearing his work to pieces.

If John Doe and Glen Bartlett were one and the same, it was Dave's job to link them with hard evidence, not his gut feeling.

Fingerprints seemed the obvious way, although Shannon had only managed to lift partials from the body. Claire had helped him print off two full facial images from the security video and he had faxed them through to Shannon to see if she could help with cranial or body recognition, but she had a backlog of post mortems to do and couldn't look at the case for at least two days.

That was the trouble with policing: relying on other departments to get the necessary information. Everyone always thought their case was more important than anyone else's and tried all sorts of tricks to get the information more quickly.

So much of investigative work was gathering evidence. Right now, all he had was a body, some small gold nuggets in a pocket and a missing hire car. From the outside, there was no reason for them to be linked. But in Dave's mind they had to be connected.

'Spencer,' Dave said, turning to his partner, 'just say the body we have down the mine is in fact Glen Bartlett. We need to match the two somehow. What would be your plan of attack?'

Spencer put down his pen and ran his fingers through his hair. 'I was thinking about this last night. That number you found on the piece of paper in the motel room, I'm sure there's something important about it. Maybe a numberplate from the eastern states or a bank account number . . .'

Dave got up and paced the length of the room before stopping in front of the map. He placed a finger on the pin where the body had been found. His eyes flicked from side to side, looking for places where a car could have been hidden. There was plenty of bush around but a cave or large hole marked on the map would be worth investigating.

Then he saw it.

Going back to his desk, he grabbed his jotter where he'd written down the number: 7008-0514. His heart began to pound. 'Yes,' he whispered, hurrying back to the map. 'Here. These numbers are the same as this lease. Are they an ID number like farms have location numbers? Is that it? Did he come to look at buying a lease?'

Spencer got up and came over. 'That's next to Tim's place,' he said. 'Fractured Hill, it's called. The old man who used to own it is dead. Need to get on to the Department of Mines to confirm who the owner is. I'll ring. I've got a contact there.'

Spencer picked up the phone while Dave bounced on his toes, the thrill of the chase running through him.

He looked again at the distance between Tim's place and Fractured Hill and wondered what the connection between Glen Bartlett and the lease would be. Why would he come all the way from Victoria to find 'someone' and why was the lease number in his room?

'Right, thanks very much,' Spencer said, finishing the phone call and hanging up. 'Damn, not much there. The owner is dead now and it's all caught up in probate, so they don't have the name of who the land was willed to yet. It's still in the hands of the lawyers.' He paused, frowning. 'You've run this Bartlett's DL, haven't you?'

'Yeah, didn't turn up anything. Just a speeding fine three years ago.'

Spencer changed tack. 'Now the interesting thing about this is there's a mining company getting around wanting to buy up small leases. I know they approached Tim Tucker. He gave me a call as a heads-up. When I went out to see China yesterday, he said the same thing. I think they're trying to put together a package of land big enough to start an open-cut. To do that, they must have clear evidence there's a lot more gold under the ground than the owners think.'

'So what's the next step?'

'Let's take a run out to Fractured Hill. Just to have a look around.'

❧

The bumpy track, which really wasn't wide enough to be called a road, wound in and out of large trees and bushes. It was a hilly area, different to the land Dave was familiar with around here.

'The land out here, it goes for miles being flat,' explained Spencer, 'then you turn a corner and there's a line of hills. The mining companies have created their own man-made hills as well. You see the smooth-sided ones with the young trees growing up? That's the mines trying to regenerate land they've used or have planted out in accordance with their environmental policies.'

Dave nodded. The man-made hills were clearly different to the natural ones.

'Hello, who've we got here?' Spencer muttered, seeing a cloud of dust coming towards them. 'Shouldn't be too many people on this road. It only leads to Fractured Hill and there's nothing out past that.' He pulled over to the edge of the road and Dave held on as the ute bumped over some deep corrugations. 'Well,' he corrected himself, 'there's lots of country out there, but no leases pegged as far as I know.'

As the vehicle came into sight, Dave realised something. 'It's red,' he said.

'So it is,' said Spencer. 'So it is. And,' he looked around to get his bearings, 'we're not that far from Oakamanda. There's a turn-off just down there,' he pointed, 'which will get you into Oakamanda the back way. Interesting.' He turned off the car and hauled himself out, planting himself in the middle of the road so the car had to stop.

The car pulled up and a man leaned out of window. 'You blokes all right?' he asked. He glanced at the four-wheel drive, which was unmarked, but his eyes widened. 'You the cops?' he asked.

'What makes you say that?' Spencer asked.

'Flashing lights in the windscreen there.' He nodded to the portable lights attached to the sun visor. 'Anything you need a hand with?'

'I was going to ask you the same thing,' said Spencer. 'This is not a road many people travel on. You looking for someone?'

The man frowned. 'Yeah, actually I am. I was supposed to meet a bloke out here yesterday but he never showed. Thought I'd head out again today and see if he was here, but I must've missed him. Hard to make appointment times when people don't have phones out here.' His frustration was evident in his tone.

'Oh yeah?' Spencer leaned against the door of the vehicle. 'I didn't think anyone lived at Fractured Hill?'

'Oh, I know no one lives there, but it's where he asked me to meet him. Far be it for me to question him when he's selling my company his land.'

Dave noticed Spencer's posture stiffen slightly. 'You're looking to buy land?'

'Not me. The mining company I work for.' He held out his hand. 'I'm Ross Pollard from HMA Mining.'

'And who were you meeting out here?'

'Well, I was *supposed* to meet Glen Bartlett. The deal was that he was going to sign the paperwork and I was going to give him a cheque. But he hasn't fronted. Been trying to track him down, but he's not at the hotel he's staying at. He seems to have disappeared into thin air.'

Dave felt his heart kick up a notch.

'Wait, wait, wait,' Spencer said before Dave could get words out of his mouth. 'Glen Bartlett owns Fractured Hill?'

'Well, yeah.' The man looked at him, puzzled.

'And how do you know that?'

'We were making enquiries, ringing and writing letters to owners and asking if they wanted to sell out. He contacted us and said he did.'

Dave narrowed his eyes. If the Department of Mines couldn't confirm who the owner was, how could this Ross Pollard?

'Now, that's a bit interesting. We were under the impression Fractured Hill was part of the previous owner's probate.

What was your name again?' Spencer questioned as he shooed a large buzzing blowfly away from his head.

'Ross Pollard. HMA Mining.' He handed over his card. 'And, yes, we know the land has been tied up. When Mr Bartlett rang us to accept our offer, he explained he was the executor for his late father's estate and he would be selling the land. Seemed very keen to sell. I can't work out why he hasn't turned up.'

'When did you see him last?'

'I haven't actually met him. All our negotiations have been done by phone and fax. He told me he had to come over to Barrabine for other reasons and he'd meet me here to sign everything.'

'Are you in town for a while?' Dave asked.

'Yeah, I'm still trying to get a few more of the blokes with the small leases in this area to sign with us. We're offering really good money, but they don't seem to want to give them up.'

'Had any other takers other than Glen Bartlett?'

'I can't tell you who, but there have been others.'

Spencer's eyebrows shot up. 'Tim Tucker?' he asked.

'Ah.' Ross looked around, and Dave could see he was trying to work out how to answer. 'Ah, no,' he finally said. 'No, he's one who seems to be a little against the idea.'

Spencer scoffed. 'I think "a little" might be an under-statement, knowing Tim the way I do.' He paused and looked around. 'We might keep going out to Fractured Hill. If you find Glen, can you give me a call?' He handed over his card.

'My number's there, but it's not much good to you since I'm not in the office very often.' He looked at them curiously. 'Are you looking for Glen too?'

'We'd certainly like to have a chat with him,' Spencer confirmed.

'I'll ring you as soon as I find him,' Ross promised.

'Great. Oh, tell me, where are you staying in town?'

'The hotel near the golf course. Jaffa's, I think it's called.'

'I know it. Cheers, good to meet you. By the way,' Dave said, 'have you been driving around in the early mornings at all?'

'Early mornings?'

'You know, three or four in the morning?'

Ross's face froze for a moment then cocked his head to the side. 'Why?'

'Just a question.'

'You wouldn't ask if there wasn't a reason.'

Dave and Spencer both looked at him steadily, not replying.

Finally Ross looked embarrassed. 'It was a few weeks ago now. I decided I was going to camp out, but early in the morning there was a dingo or something howling and it spooked me, so I packed up and left. Trouble was, I did it in the dark and left my GPS behind, so I had to go back for it. I reckon I was about half an hour past Oakamanda when I realised what I'd done. Had to go back and get it. Do you get many dingos out here? I swear this one was so close to my tent it could have come in.'

Spencer let out a loud laugh. 'They're all around here, mate. Usually all you see of them is tracks. It's a bit unusual to have them come so close. He must've thought you smelled good enough to eat!'

'Glad I hightailed it then. All right, I'll be off and I'll be sure to let you know when I find our man. I thought I might go to the hospital and see if he was in there. See you later.' Ross put his vehicle in gear and drove off.

Dave glanced at Spencer and yanked open the door. 'I'm even more sure now that our John Doe is Glen Bartlett. I don't believe in coincidences. And it sounds like this bloke is Dee's phantom vehicle. Nothing suspicious there.' He got in the car and waited for Spencer to get in.

'I think you're right,' Spencer answered as he started the car up again and followed the winding track. They didn't say anything else until they arrived at Fractured Hill. Dave was too busy sorting the information he had in his mind. He needed it straight and clear before he started talking.

The shack there was like the one at Tim's place. The walls were made of tin and there were four rooms: a kitchen, two bedrooms and a laundry. The cupboards were brittle, and a thick layer of dust covered the beds and table. Instead of having the homely feel to it like Tim's place, it was rundown and shabby.

'Doesn't look like anyone's lived here for a while.'

'Don't be fooled,' Spencer said. 'It only takes one dust storm to make a place look like this. You'd think no one had lived here for thirty years and yet someone could have walked out yesterday and it'd look like this after one of those mongrel storms.' He lifted up the sheet, which was still on the bed, and opened the door to the cupboard. Nothing.

Dusting his hands down he said, 'Don't think there's much here, though.'

Dave wandered out the other side of the hut and saw a crumbling wooden headframe rising out of the ground.

'Look at this,' Spencer called.

Dave looked around and saw he was being waved over to a grove of thick bushland. He jogged to Spencer and pushed his way in behind him, then pulled up quickly, eyes roving over the landscape.

There was a camp set up inside a small clearing. It looked like someone had gone to a lot of effort to cut down trees and make a spot for a camp. But not recently . . . years ago. A swag was rolled up next to a ring of stones, which clearly had had a fire burning in it. An esky was off to the side and a fold-up chair sat facing the campfire.

Dave flicked open the lid of the esky and dropped it again very quickly. 'Ugh,' he said. Rotten lamb chops were covered by melted ice and beer cans.

Dave unrolled the swag and unzipped it. Although it was covered in red dirt, it was obvious the swag was very new, as was the other equipment. Ginger had said Glen Bartlett had had a car full of camping gear when he'd checked out of the pub. With any luck there'd be a GPS in amongst it all, which would have a serial number they'd be able to match to confirm whose campsite this was.

'I reckon there's got to be a hire vehicle around here somewhere, don't you?' Spencer said.

'Totally agree. But why would he have decided to camp out in the bush when he had a perfectly good hotel to sleep in?' Dave wondered out loud.

'Another question we need to answer.'

Dave turned and walked back to the headframe to have a look into the mine. This one had a larger mouth than he'd seen before, certainly large enough to drive a car into, but it wouldn't be hidden. With his flashlight he searched for the bottom and saw only a rusty bucket about a metre and half down.

'No car,' he yelled back to Spencer.

'That's probably a good thing. If there was he might've been in it and that would've blown our theory. Cars at the bottom of mine shafts are a bit like bodies. Not supposed to be there.'

Dave sniggered. 'That's stating the obvious!'

They walked around a bit more, Dave going back into the humpy and opening drawers and cupboards. Everything, even the crockery and cutlery inside the cupboards, were layered with dust. In the second drawer he found some old papers and a diary. He drew them out and blew on them. He leaned against the wall, flicking through each of the fragile, yellowing pages. It told of days working the mines in unrelenting heat, of breakdowns and lack of gold. There wasn't anything helpful there. Finally he put the diary away and looked through the other documents, finding nothing useful to his investigation.

Spencer came into the house, puffing. 'I really wish people would die in winter when it's cooler. Come on, time to head back and get some search teams out here. And forensics. I doubt if Glen ever came inside here by the look of the dust. There haven't been any dust storms recently. It'd be easy to see if he'd shifted something 'cause it would leave a mark. I'm convinced the camp must be his. We know he left the Federal Hotel with a carful of camping equipment and all this is new. Now all we gotta find is his car.'

Chapter 19

'Little Maddie has been having trouble feeding,' Melinda said to Patti. 'Last week I recommended Janelle apply lanoline to her nipples after feeding and make sure the baby's latching on properly. She's in the waiting room now—have you got anything else I should suggest?'

'Why don't you ask her to try to feed her in front of you and then you can help her get Maddie into the right position and make sure she's latching on properly. Sometimes mums think they are, but the bub isn't quite in the right spot.'

'Oh yeah, good idea. I'll do that.'

'How's Janelle coping otherwise? She's very young and I don't think she has much support at home.'

'Seventeen, poor love. The father didn't stick around and her mother has told her she's on her own in looking after the baby. She's still living at home, but certainly without other support from any adults. I'll check again today but I'm sure there are some problems. I've had her coming in every week for the last three weeks.'

'Righto, sounds like you've got it all under control so I'll leave you to it.'

Out in the waiting room, Melinda smiled and called Janelle and Maddie into her office.

She liked her office now. After the first week she had added a few of her own touches to the room—some bright soft toys, a CD player which played nursery rhymes for the older children coming in, and a jigsaw puzzle she'd seen in the toy store. It was in the shape of a dump truck and she reasoned, this being a mining town, the toddlers and young children would relate to it.

'How are you today, Janelle?' she asked once they were settled. 'Had a good week?'

'Nah, it's been shit. She's still not feeding properly and I'm really sore.'

Melinda assessed the mother and saw she had dark rings under her eyes and looked extremely tired. 'How often are you getting up to her?' she asked.

'Probably every hour.'

Melinda took Maddie out of the pram and walked over to the scales with her. 'Well, let's pop her on here and see what she's done over the week. Is she taking a bottle?'

Janelle shook her head and stayed where she was. 'I can't get her to suck a dummy or a bottle. I even put honey on her dummy to try to get her to take it. And on my nipples. I remember Mum told me ages ago that's what she used to do with me, but that didn't work either. Why do they do this? I thought feeding them would be the easy part. They're only supposed to sleep, eat and shit, aren't they?' Her voice broke and tears streamed down her face.

'Oh, sweetheart,' Melinda said and put one hand on her arm while holding a fussing Maddie with the other. 'It's not as easy as that, unfortunately. I wish it was. Have you been to see the doctor? Got her all checked out? Got yourself checked out?'

'Yeah, we went last week. She was crying all the time and I didn't know what to do. He said it was nothing to worry about. Just settling into her skin.'

'Who's your doctor?'

Janelle named one of the local GPs and Melinda jotted it down. 'Did he ask about you?'

'Nah. Didn't need to.'

Melinda thought otherwise. Maybe there were indications Janelle was experiencing postnatal depression, or maybe she was just struggling with the adjustment of having a difficult baby. Either way, she needed a bit of extra help and support.

Melinda stripped off the jumpsuit and Maddie started to scream loudly as if she were in pain.

'Hey, hey,' she cooed, but doubted that Maddie would have even heard her over the crying. 'What's up, little one?' Gently, she laid her on the scales and watched as the numbers changed until they came to a stop. She frowned and took her off the scales, made sure they were on zero and checked the record book. It looked like the baby had lost two hundred grams. That couldn't be right. Placing her back down, Melinda saw the result was the same.

'Do you think you still have any milk?'

Janelle shrugged. 'How do you tell?'

'Are your breasts firm and tight? Do you leak milk? Have you tried to express and not had anything come out?'

Janelle glanced down at her chest. 'They feel a bit soft and soggy to me.'

'Maybe we'll try a bottle. I'm going to grab one from the kitchen and see if I can get her to take some formula. I just want to see what her sucking action is like, okay?'

Janelle nodded and sat down again, her hands over her face. 'I don't think I can do this any more.'

'You can and I'll help you,' Melinda promised.

She took Maddie, still crying, out into the kitchen and mixed up some of the formula they kept on hand. All the while she jiggled and talked to the baby, trying to settle her. Patti came in to see what the noise was.

'Och, you've got an upset one there,' she said and took over making the formula.

'Yeah, she's lost two hundred grams,' Melinda said. 'Like I said earlier, mum says she's not sucking well.'

Patti screwed the lid on and handed her the bottle. Maddie pounced on the teat and started to suck. Within a couple of minutes the bottle was empty and Melinda was staring at it in surprise.

'What?' Patti asked as she started to mix up some more.

'Janelle said she couldn't get her to suck. Not a dummy or a bottle. Looks like she knows how to do it to me.'

'Sometimes babies won't take a bottle if they can smell milk on the mother. Take this back in and get mum to try to feed and see what happens.'

Back in the consultation room, Melinda handed Maddie to Janelle and explained what had happened. 'So,' she continued, 'try with this bottle and see how you go.'

Janelle tapped the teat on Maddie's lips and again the baby grabbed hold of it with her lips and sucked hard.

'There you go. Maybe you're not producing enough milk for her. That happens, milk dries up and sometimes it takes us a while to realise. Sometimes the only reason we work it out is because they're unsettled and crying all the time.'

'But how come she wouldn't take a dummy or a bottle at home?'

'I wish these little cutie-pies could tell us what they wanted! Unfortunately, I'm not sure I can answer that and Maddie can't tell you either. But she's drinking now. I tell you what, why don't you take this bottle home because you know she'll suck using this teat and I'll give you half a tin of the formula we use here. That way you can go and get the exact same from the supermarket. This is a proven formula!' she quipped.

'Thank you,' Janelle said softly.

Melinda saw Maddie's eyelids start to shut and the teat popped out of her mouth as she fell asleep.

'Look what you've just done,' Melinda whispered delightedly to Janelle. 'You've fed her a bottle and put her to sleep. Aren't you a clever thing?' She smiled at the young mum who, for the first time since they'd met, smiled back at her.

❧

Melinda left the office with a sense of satisfaction. She knew she'd made a big difference to Janelle's world, which was why she'd become a nurse in the first place—to help people.

Walking to her car, she wanted to skip, but restrained herself. That wasn't becoming of a professional!

'Melinda! Hey, Mel!'

She turned and saw Kathy walking towards her.

'Hi, Melinda! How's the new job?'

'Kathy, hello! I'm loving it—I can't thank you enough for encouraging me to apply for this role. And now I'm busy during the day, I'm not as sad as I was. In fact, I'd almost say I'm beginning to settle!' She saw the delighted look on Kathy's face and rushed on. 'I mean, I still have to meet people outside of work, but I'm doing it gradually, and I love working with Patti.'

'Oh, isn't she just lovely? Heart of gold. Have you got time for a coffee now?'

Melinda hesitated, about to say no. Normally she would go straight home from work and call her parents, then her sister. They weren't the sad phone calls from before, but she liked to hear their voices every day. Still, she could call them tomorrow.

'I'd love to,' she said.

'Great. How about I meet you at the Mug? I just have to put these in the car.' She indicated to the shopping bags she had on her arm.

'Great, see you there.' She started to unlock the car but had a thought and called across the parking lot, 'Hey, Kathy?'

'Yeah?'

'You can call me Mel!'

Chapter 20

'We've got a match,' Dave said, adrenalin pumping through his body. 'Glen Bartlett and our John Doe are one and the same! I knew it!' He waved the report that had matched the fingerprints lifted from Bartlett's Avis forms with those taken from the body and felt the familiar thrill of energy rush through him. They were getting somewhere.

'No sign of his car yet. I bet it's in a mine somewhere and that's why we haven't found it. I would've thought if it was hidden in the bush, the vehicle would have been reported by now, or we would've found it. But you know what I don't understand?' Spencer said.

'What's that?' Dave was standing at the whiteboard, where he'd just pinned up the photo of Bartlett and written his name and birth date underneath it.

'What was he doing here? And why was he camping out rather than staying at the pub?' He pushed his chair back and swung his feet up onto the desk. 'More importantly, why was he murdered?'

'All very good questions. I'm going to ring the police station in Ballarat and find out if he has any family we need to notify.'

'Okay, you do that first and then we'll pull in Ross Pollard and have another chat with him.'

'Bartlett's mum is still alive, but there's no wife,' Dave told Spencer when they got into the car ten minutes later. 'Or children. Looks like he was on his own. The boys over there are going to do the inform. I wonder if she'll want to come over and collect the body.'

'Probably not, being elderly. God, I hate doing the informs. One time I had a lady hit me in the face and tell me I was lying. I'd had to break the news that her only daughter had been killed in a car accident on the Tonkin Highway.' He stared straight ahead, gripping the steering wheel tightly. 'It's a bastard of a job. Got to be done, but.'

'The first time I ever had to do it I was telling a husband his wife had drowned at the beach. She'd been caught in a rip. He didn't believe me until I took him to the morgue so he could identify her. Kept saying it couldn't be her because she swam there every day and knew the sea. Knew the area. Strange, isn't it? They always know why you're there but sometimes the mind won't let them accept what the heart knows.'

They both fell into silence, thinking about the other times they'd had to tell family their loved ones had died.

Eventually Spencer broke the silence. 'You know what's worse?'

'I don't think there is anything worse, is there?'

'Not knowing. Seeing the grief the family have to live with when they don't know. The son or daughter could be dead, but they might not be. If they're not dead, why did they leave? If they're dead, what happened to them and where is their body?'

'I had a case like that once,' Dave said, except it was the other way around: a body and no identification. 'It's one of those cases you can't let go, know what I mean?'

'Know exactly what you're saying. What happened?'

Dave sighed and looked out of the window. There was a group of kids kicking the footy on the road, but they scattered as the police car drove past.

'I worked a case where a body was found. A young boy's body. He'd been assaulted and dumped in the state forest. By the time campers came across him, foxes had eaten parts of him. He was in a bad way.' Dave took a breath. 'Tried everything I knew to identify him. DNA, dental records, fingerprints. We tried TV, radio, had the forensic artist come in and draw a composite picture. Never got a nibble.

'This kid didn't have a record—well, no fingerprints that matched any crimes we had on file. He'd obviously been the victim of assaults throughout his life because the X-rays showed broken bones—arms, cracked skull, that type of thing. There were no missing persons reports that matched and I never managed to ID him. He's buried without a name, without his family knowing.'

Silence filled the car.

'You know what probably happened there, don't you?' Spencer asked.

Dave nodded. 'I try not to think that he was a victim of his own family and one day something went wrong and they killed him. But it seems the only likely scenario, because what parent wouldn't report their child missing?'

'Exactly.'

Spencer drove without speaking until he turned into the hotel car park and pulled up. He turned to face Dave. 'There's a story just like that pinned onto the board in the kitchen to remind us what we're here for.'

'Haven't seen it.'

'It's a bit of legend around here. A man came in to report the death of a woman. He thought it was a suicide because she was hanging from a tree, and he was desperate to let her family know where she was buried. Trouble was, this was back in the forties. No forensics back then. The police didn't want to disturb the grave without reason and there was no ID, just a spot where there was a lonely grave, buried by someone she didn't know.' He sighed again, as if the weight of the world were on his shoulders. 'Back then, her family weren't found and even now her body is still in that grave. We don't know who she is, don't expect anyone knows who she is this far along, and because she's never been identified, her family has never been informed. Check it out sometime.' He took the keys from the ignition. 'It's important to remember these are real people and the families left behind are always going to be searching for answers . . . So we should too.'

Silence filled the car.

'You know, this Ross Pollard could be a suspect,' Dave said eventually, changing the subject.

'Yeah?'

'What if Glen changed his mind about selling the land?'

Spencer shrugged. 'Everyone's a suspect until proven otherwise.'

❧

'Morning, Mr Pollard,' Spencer said, striding into Jaffa's dining room and pulling up a chair at the table. Dave followed but didn't take a seat, standing next to the table instead.

For a moment the man looked confused, but then recognition filtered across his face.

'Have you found Glen Bartlett?' he asked hopefully.

'We have indeed,' Spencer said.

'Fan-bloody-tastic, I'll get my papers signed then.' Ross Pollard put his napkin on the table and pushed back his chair. 'Where can I find him?'

'I think you'll have a few problems doing that. Unfortunately, he's deceased.'

'What? . . . Oh my God! Dead?'

'Yes.'

Ross seemed at a loss as to what to say. Then realisation dawned and he asked, 'Is he the man down the mine shaft? I heard a few people talking about it at the pub last night. I never put two and two together.'

Dave would have said the look of shock on his face was genuine, but he'd also learned people were good actors. He stood back and kept watching.

'Yes, that's him. Can you tell us when you saw him last?' asked Spencer.

'I haven't seen him. Only spoken to him on the phone. I had organised to meet him at the Federal Hotel, first off, to get him to look over the paperwork. I thought he'd sign straightaway; he seemed eager to sell.

'Instead he asked me about the settlement date when I talked to him on the phone. I told him it was twenty-one days from signing. He wasn't happy. He wanted it earlier, so I had to go back to the finance department and make sure that was okay, then they had to redraw the papers. After that was done I organised to meet him at Fractured Hill to sign the paperwork. He said he was going to be out there by then; never said why though. But he never turned up.'

'Right, and he was in good spirits when you spoke to him? Hadn't changed his mind about selling?'

'No. Not at all. In fact, like I said, it seemed he was in a hurry. Having never met him, I couldn't say if he was in good spirits or not.' Ross lowered his voice and looked around, even though there wasn't anyone else in the dining room. 'I did get the impression he needed the money.'

'That's why he wanted a quick sale?'

Ross nodded. 'He said he had a large payment coming up. HMA Mining were offering him a substantial sum of money. They were more than happy to reduce the settlement period. They'd do anything to get the land they want.'

Dave was writing down notes but looked up at the word 'anything'.

'Really?' Spencer took the lead.

Ross realised what he'd said. 'Not *anything*, obviously. But they're keen.'

'Did Glen say what he needed the money for?'

Ross shook his head.

'Right.' Spencer paused. 'I need to clarify—he was the executor of his father's will and he had a right to sell this land?'

'He was bringing the required paperwork for me to sight.'

'I see,' Spencer glanced at Dave who wrote a reminder note to check this. 'Can you tell me—'

'Look, I understand the need for questions, but I'm beginning to feel—'

'I just need you to remind me,' Spencer interrupted him, 'you approached Mr Bartlett, not the other way around?'

'Yes! We'd written many letters to owners and he responded to me by phone.'

'And how do you find out the identities of the people who own the land?'

'We speak to Landgate, find out the owners' names and their details. We give them a call or send an email if they have an address. Or write a letter. Mostly we prefer to visit them face to face, which is why I'm in the area. I've spent the whole time I've been here trying to find humpies in the middle of the bush and offer these people a gold nugget they wouldn't otherwise find.'

'I would have thought that information was privileged.'

Ross looked uncomfortable. 'I'm not sure. I just do what I'm instructed to do with the information I'm given.'

'You spend a lot of time here in Barrabine?'

'I won't be going until I secure at least another three parcels of land. That's what HMA need.'

'And what if leaseholders just won't sell to you?'

Ross considered his answer. 'Oh, neither the company nor I are concerned about that. I think they'll be persuaded.'

'We appreciate your time, mate,' Spencer said, stretching his legs out and getting up. 'Sounds like there's a bit of urgency in getting hold of the land. What's that all about?'

Ross pursed his lips. 'I'll have to refer you to my supervisors if you want to know anything more than what I've told you because I don't know the answers.'

'But they must think there's a lot more gold in the ground to offer crazy money like they are?'

'My job is to get people to sell their land. I don't know what the company intends for it long-term.'

'One last question,' Dave said and the two men turned to him. 'Why did you decided to camp out the other night? I mean, the hotel is pretty comfortable.'

Ross shrugged. 'Just something I wanted to do. I'd seen so many great spots to roll out a swag. I did a lot of camping when I was a kid but none since, so I thought it was time to revisit. See if it was as good as I remember, you know?'

'Reliving childhood memories,' Spencer said.

'Yeah, that's about the sum of it. I borrowed an old swag and a few bits and pieces and went—' he frowned, trying to find the right words '—country? Bush? I've enjoyed being out in nature. Anyway, I was driving by a little creek and saw the perfect place for a camp.' He gave a bark of self-deprecating laughter. 'I got that wrong! Woke up while it was still dark, and everything, including me, was dripping wet! The tree I'd rolled the swag out under was dripping on my head. And I was freezing. So I thought, *Stuff it. The company's paying for a perfectly good bed back in the hotel, I might as well go back there, have a shower and warm up.* Then, as I was packing up, I was sure I heard a dingo.' Ross gave a shake of his head. 'Frightened the crap out of me, so I took off back to the hotel.'

Dave crinkled his brow slightly and wrote down what Ross had said.

'Time of the year,' Spencer said. 'Even though it's as hot as Hades during the day, the night-time is a different matter altogether. Often drops below zero. I can imagine how a first-time camper could get caught by that.'

Spencer nodded at Dave and the two men left Pollard to the remains of his breakfast.

Chapter 21

1945

The first thing Paddy registered as he woke was his cracking headache. He rolled over in his swag and reached for his water bag. His mouth was dry as cotton wool and the water didn't seem to make any difference. Blinking against the glare, he quickly assessed the time from the position of the sun: about nine in the morning. The hangover must be a good one; he didn't think he'd ever slept that late. The sun usually woke him.

He didn't remember getting the swag out of the car last night and he certainly didn't remember unrolling it right next to the front tyres. He wouldn't have normally slept in such a dangerous place. He was glad no one had thought to take his car for a joy ride.

'Geez, I feel crook,' came a voice from behind a thick bush.

'You're not on your own there, Rocco,' Paddy said. 'I think I need a Bex and a cup of tea. Maybe another good sleep. Where are the others?'

'Who knows? Who cares?'

Paddy saw Rocco's head rise above the bush. His friend certainly looked worse for wear.

He started to gather firewood so he could boil the billy.

'I think they fleeced us blind last night, the bludgers!' Rocco said as he staggered around the bush and took hold of Paddy's water bag. He drank greedily, water dribbling down his chin. 'I had five pounds when we came out here. Don't think I've got more than a bob left.'

Paddy checked his pockets for his roll of cash. His stomach unclenched when he found it was still there. 'I know a lost a bit. Maybe five quid too.'

'God, the missus is going to kill me.' Rocco looked around. 'I was supposed to go home last night!'

Paddy threw the firewood on some dry grass and used matches to light the fire. Small orange flames flicked through the grass and instantly bush smoke filled his nostrils. He piled a few more sticks on top, then went to the boot of his car to get the billy. The last of the water went into the blackened tin which he placed on top of the flames, pushing it down to make sure it wouldn't fall.

Rocco sat under the shade of the tree, holding his head in his hands. 'Need a Bex for sure,' he muttered.

When the billy was boiling, Paddy threw a handful of tea leaves into it before tapping the side with a stick and then pouring two cups.

'Come on, drink up. Then I'd better get you home.'

Rocco took the pannikin gratefully and took a long sip. 'Ah, that's good.' He turned to his friend. 'Do you reckon you'll come back from Victoria?'

Paddy shrugged. 'Dunno. See what it's like when I get over there. With any luck I'll find some gold and a lady who'll have me and I won't want to.'

'What are you going to do with your lease?'

Paddy sighed. 'There's not much gold left there, I'm sure. I reckon I'll lock it up and leave it.'

'What about all the freeloaders who'll have a crack at your mines?' Rocco sounded incredulous.

Paddy shrugged. 'I've been all over the lease; it's a dud piece of land. There's not enough quartz and ironstone. I think I've found five ounces in the ten years I've had it. More trouble than it's worth. Anyone who wants to have a go is welcome to it, but I'll keep the land. Never know, I might want to come back and set up camp on it. Spend the last of my days in the bush.' He drained the dregs of his tea and rinsed out the pannikin.

'Are you just saying that to put people off going onto it?' he asked with a quizzical look on his face. ''Cause from what you're telling me, I'd say you're mad. Been in the bush too long.'

Paddy laughed. 'I'm telling you the truth, my friend. Have you ever known me to lie?'

Rocco was quiet at that statement, for the truth was, in the ten years he'd know Paddy, his friend had never lied.

❦

Paddy left Rocco at the front gate of his house and drove away quickly. In the rear-view mirror he saw a dark-skinned woman come running out of the house and he could still hear her angry yells. He figured it might take Rocco a bit of explaining to calm her.

He was sad to say goodbye to his mate, thinking perhaps he'd never see him again. But life always seemed to move on and people came and went. Rocco was moving on and so was he.

Paddy stopped at the chemist and bought a packet of Bex, then went on to the police station.

'How can I help you, cobber?' asked the policeman behind the desk.

'I'm not sure, but . . .' He proceeded to tell the man what he'd found and what he'd done. 'I just want to make sure her family know what's happened to her,' he finished.

'Can you wait there a minute?'

Paddy nodded and leaned against the desk, wishing he had taken one of the painkillers before he'd come inside.

'Paddy?' a voice asked and a tall thin man walked through the door. 'I'm Detective Chris Pyke. Can you come and give me a statement?'

'Sure, no worries.' He followed the man into a cold interview room.

'How did you spot her?' Detective Pyke asked.

'I was driving and she caught my eye. The body was swinging and I thought it was a piece of bark at first. You know how the bark hangs on a salmon gum when it's shedding? She looked like that.'

'Bad business.'

Paddy found he couldn't talk for a moment. He swallowed. 'She wasn't in good shape. I couldn't leave her there to be eaten away at, so that's why I buried her.'

'Can you explain to me where?'

'Under the tree. I've marked it with my initials so you'll be able to tell which one, although the grave is mounded and I dragged heavy branches over it, so the dogs couldn't dig her up. Near the turn-off twenty miles to the north-west.'

'It's becoming more and more common, I'm afraid,' sighed the detective. 'I'm sure the heat sends some of them mad. I really believe that women shouldn't be allowed to live here. It's too harsh an environment. Why men would ask them to is beyond me.'

'I'm sure not all women would agree with you,' he said, thinking of the woman he'd seen a couple of days ago. She'd been wearing men's trousers and a shirt and had two buckets of water slung over her shoulders. On her face was a large smile as she walked along beside a man who was looking at her as if she were his fantasy.

'Perhaps not,' the detective backtracked. 'It's just such a waste of a life.'

'Lots of waste out here, mate. Not just women. Men and children too. It's a hard place to live, but the gold is worth it.'

'Spoken like a true miner.'

'Has anyone been reported missing?'

'No. If someone was missing her I'm sure I would've heard about it. Maybe they assumed she just walked away. That happens a lot.' He paused, thinking. 'Or maybe she's been widowed and doesn't have anyone to report her. Maybe . . . Ah hell, unless someone comes forward we'll never know. And that seems to be the way of the goldfields. Some things are meant to stay secrets of the bush.'

'Poetic,' Paddy commented, ignoring the dismay in his stomach. He got the feeling this copper wasn't going to do much to identify the woman.

'If I write up this statement, will you sign it?' Detective Pyke asked. 'I need a proper record of this.'

'I can wait.'

Putting a sheet of paper into a typewriter, Paddy watched as the man started to type with two fingers. It was going to take a while, so he tipped his head back and rested it against the wall. He'd slept in worse places.

❧

A couple of hours later Paddy walked into the offices of the local newspaper and asked to see a journalist.

'Got a story for you,' he said as way of greeting.

The journalist was young and green and his eyes rolled at the description of the body. 'You want me to put this in the paper?' he asked.

'You write the story and put in it what you want—you know what makes good reading, not me. All I'm doing is telling you what I've done so you can get it out there.'

'I'll get it written now,' he answered. 'Then you can check it.'

On the 23rd of February 1945, a local miner, who wants to remain anonymous, came across a gruesome discovery of the body of a woman, hanging from a tree.

'It appeared,' he said, 'she had committed suicide.'

Twenty miles north of the town site of Barrabine there is now a lonely, unmarked grave holding the body of a woman. Her identity is unknown and the miner is eager to make her family aware of where he has buried her.

'I came along too late to stop her from doing what she did, but I handled it the best I could once I found her. Everyone has a right to have a place to go to grieve,' the miner told me today. 'And everyone has a right to know what has happened to their family member. I want her family to know I took good care of her. That she had a Christian burial, as much as I could give her.'

This woman will be one of the many unnamed people buried in isolated graves in the Australian goldfields. The local miner said he couldn't find any evidence of a camp close by.

If you know of miners who were living out that way, or of anyone who is missing, please contact the local police.

Paddy nodded. 'Done me best, haven't I, lad?' he said when the journalist had finished reading it to him.

'Don't think you could do any more. Where you headed?'

'Victoria, mate. Try my luck over there.'

'Safe travels, then. If I hear she's ever identified I'll write and let you know.'

'Care of the Ballarat Post Office,' Paddy said, pushing his hat down tightly on his head. 'They'll know where to find me.'

Chapter 22

'Did you hear that?' Dave asked when he and Spencer were in the car.

'Hear what?'

'His story is different.'

'What?' Spencer put the key in the ignition and turned on the engine.

'When we saw him on the road, he told us he left camp because a dingo had frightened him and then he had to go back because he'd left his GPS behind. Now the dingo's an afterthought and he left because he got a little wet. I need to check my notes but I'm sure he camped in a tent during his first stay.' His tone was incredulous.

Spencer laughed. 'I reckon he's about that soft.'

'Wonder what he's up to.'

'Let's do a search on him . . .' Just then the radio crackled to life and the comms officer was calling their names.

'Roger that,' Dave said, picking up the receiver.

'Got a 3-4-0 at the Oakamanda Pub,' he said. 'Repeat, a 3-4-0.'

Spencer shoved the car into gear as Dave reported that they were on their way to check out the disturbance.

Even before they pulled up, Dave could see the front windows of the iconic old pub were smashed. Dee was sitting on the wooden bench outside, waiting for them.

'Bastards!' she said fiercely as they walked over to her.

'What's happened?'

'Thrown rocks through the window and got in that way. Knocked over the drinks fridge, taken beer and ciggies.'

There wasn't any cool air to greet them today as they went in through the front door. Dave looked around at the carnage and sighed heavily before snapping on his rubber gloves and picking his way through the glass shards and up-ended bar stools.

'When did you find it?' he asked.

Her usual bouncy, humorous way of speaking was gone. 'S'morning. Came to open at ten. You know, get set up for the day.'

'No alarms?'

The look Dee gave him made him wish he hadn't asked. 'Does it look like we have an alarm here?'

Dave looked down and walked around, seeing if he could spot anything that could be used as evidence but, really, all he could see was a hell of a mess.'

'Been any problems in here lately, Dee?' Spencer asked. 'Fights? Blokes you don't know causing trouble?'

'Nothing. Few tourists, some of the locals. Nothing out of the ordinary. Haven't had any fights here for ages.' She looked bewildered. 'Everyone comes in, has a drink. The tourists read about the history, I tell 'em a few tall tales and off they go. The locals sit and keep on drinking. Only people who were in last night were China and two other locals. They never cause any grief.'

'Here's the rock. Or one of them,' Dave pointed out. A large piece of quartz was sitting underneath the window.

Going back out to the car, Dave grabbed the camera and fingerprint kit.

While Spencer talked to Dee, he snapped shots of the window and stone in situ. Crunching over the broken glass, he dusted the inside of the windowsill, hoping that whoever had climbed in had left a print behind.

'It's a wonder Mary the ghost didn't scare them away,' Spencer said.

'I'd've scared them if I'd got hold of them,' Dee said bitterly. 'Why do people to do this? I've spent so much time getting this place lookin' spick and span, putting all the history together, and these mongrels come in and wreck it all in one night.'

'Seems pointless, doesn't it?' Spencer agreed.

Dee raised her hands. 'What benefit are they going to get out of it? A few smokes and drinks. I've got months of fixing up the joint again.'

Spencer walked to the bar and started to poke around. 'Have there been any kids out here recently? You know, ones who got all liquored up or looked like they were out to cause mischief?'

'Wait a moment,' Dee answered and went through the door to the kitchen. It only took a few moments before she was back, holding a large hardback book.

'My diary,' she said as way of explanation. 'I always write down if anything unusual has happened.' She started to flick through the pages.

Dave saw the beginnings of a fingerprint start to emerge and he held his breath, hoping it would be a workable one. He carefully lifted it and stored it in the evidence box before moving on to the next room.

'Three weeks ago five young blokes arrived in one car,' Dave heard Dee say. 'They stayed about two drinks too long, then got in the car and drove back towards Barrabine.'

'Cause any trouble?'

'Nah, just a bit rowdy, from my notes.' She flicked the page over. 'Oh, yeah, I remember now, there was a bloke who came in looking for someone called Glen Bartlett. Left his card—I've got it stapled here. He's from HMA Mining. Ross Pollard, his card says.'

At the sound of Glen's name, Dave came back into the room. Dee tore the card from the page where she'd stapled it and handed it to Spencer, who looked at it then passed it on to Dave.

'Do you know why he was looking for Glen?' asked Spencer, tapping his fingers against his lips.

'He didn't say. And I didn't ask. Less I know the better sometimes. Anyway, I haven't even clapped eyes on the man, so I wasn't sure how I was supposed to pass the message on. I assumed he had a lease somewhere, but the name is not one I've heard before. Still, people come and go easily enough.'

Spencer wrote a note in his notebook and looked up, squinting.

'What?' asked Dee. 'You're thinking, I can tell.'

'Just trying to put a few pieces together.'

'Do you know who Glen Bartlett is?'

'Yeah, he's the body down the mine shaft,' Spencer said. 'I thought you would've heard his name on the radio or TV since it was released yesterday.'

'Ha! As if I have time to take any notice of the TV,' Dee scoffed. Then she stopped. 'Wait, he's the dead guy?' Her voice held a note of fear.

'"The body" usually indicates someone is dead,' Spencer said, deadpan.

'Should we be worried? There're strange things going on out here right now. I know that bloke who was looking for Glen has been hitting up lease owners to sell their land—I heard Tim mention his name. I mean, how stupid! No one around here is going to sell to a big company. These guys are professional prospectors! This is how they make their living.

'China was saying someone drove onto his place in the middle of the night and shone their lights on his hut. He got up to have a look but they drove off. Then Jackie's been seeing footprints around his mine shaft—doesn't know whose they are or how they got there because his dog didn't bark. And Julie Goulde was saying she's had washing taken off the clothesline. And I've also heard that some of the bigger machinery the guys use—you know the loaders and dry blowers—have been moved during the night.'

Dave frowned. 'And no one has reported this?'

'I didn't think too much of it, but now I say it out loud, all in one hit, it sounds worse. People have only ever told me in dribs and drabs, you know? I'd hear one story from one person then it'd be a couple of days later before I'd hear something else. Didn't join the dots, I guess.'

'Yeah, I understand. Tell me, have you heard any more vehicles driving around in the early morning?'

'Not for a few nights. I heard something about eleven one night last week, I think it was, but it wasn't out of the ordinary. Not like the other ones I told you about.'

Dave thought about this. He wanted to get back to the station and write it all up on the whiteboard, to see the evidence set out neatly and in chronological order.

'You nearly finished up here?' Spencer asked.

'Give me twenty. I'll snap some more shots and then I'll be done.'

By the time they were ready to leave, Dave had a film roll full of photos and one fingerprint. He packed the camera into its case and replaced it in the back of the vehicle, while Spencer patted Dee on the shoulder.

'We'll do our best to find out what happened here, Dee. I promise you that.'

'Hope you do,' she said. 'Can I start cleaning up?'

'Sure can. Is there anything you'd like me to do for you?'

Dee shook her head. 'Nah, I'll get the daughter to come and help.'

'Right-oh. I'll be in contact as soon as I know anything.'

They said their goodbyes and Spencer hauled himself into the driver's seat, pulling his seatbelt on. 'Do you think we can get a decent photo of Glen Bartlett run off, show it around town?'

'Should be able to. I might need to see if Claire can help me lighten it a little, but the security camera footage should be okay for that.'

'Right. And do we have a photo of Ross Pollard? Or can we get one?'

That stumped Dave. 'I don't think we've got one—we've got no need to have one.'

Spencer drove without speaking. 'We need one,' he finally said. 'Without alerting him to the fact we're going to be asking about him.'

'Driver's licence,' Dave suggested.

'Yeah, that's it! Print off his driver's licence photo. It'll be on file. And maybe compare the security footage and DL photo for Glen. If there's not too much difference, use the DL for him too. It'll be clearer than the security footage. Right, when we get back to town I want you to go to the camping stores and see if anyone remembers selling Ross Pollard some camping equipment.'

'No worries,' Dave said. 'How many stores in town?'

'Four. Shouldn't take you too long to get around them. I'll run that print from the pub when we get back and see what it brings up.'

'You thinking kids?'

'Not sure. It looks like kids—it's a break and enter without a lot of thought or organisation. Mischief more than anything. But I'm wondering if there's an ulterior motive. Can't work out what it would be though.' He was frowning. 'There's something more, I'm sure of it. Too many odd things happening. I mean,' he searched for words to clarify his thoughts, 'this is the goldfields and strange things happen all the time. But I'm like you—I don't believe in coincidences. Look at this: we start with a body. Turns out it was murder. Then we find out the dead guy was selling the land of his late father. He's come to sign the papers and "find someone".' Spencer made quotation marks with his fingers.

'Then,' Dave continued, 'we have Ross Pollard, who is wanting Glen's signature, with two different stories about camping out in the bush, and a few smaller but equally odd things happening.'

They drove in silence and Dave watched the passing landscape. He'd fallen in love with this area—the country had seemed to seep into his veins quietly and now it felt like home. Last night, as he'd drifted off to sleep, he'd thought about buying a metal detector and an old ute. He could set it up as a camper and he and Melinda could go prospecting. Spend the weekends in amongst the trees and bushes. Make love under the stars and know they'd be unlikely to see anyone else the whole weekend. He'd fallen in love with the rich red dirt and open skies, the landscape and the locals. The people were friendly and he was enjoying his job. It looked like Melinda had settled in too. Maybe they could stay here a few more years.

'Check that out,' Spencer said, breaking into his thoughts and slowing down.

Under a large gimlet tree were three kangaroos. They were lying in the shade, propped up on their elbows watching the cars go by.

'They don't seem too worried,' Dave said.

'I guess they get used to their environment, don't they? The noise, or lack of. They know what's normal and what isn't. Same as anyone.'

'That's it!' Dave said, twisting around in his seat to look at Spencer. 'I've been trying to work out what's been niggling me about all these small incidents. You know, the lights, people going onto other people's leases . . . oh, and the machinery being moved . . . It reminds me of a case I had about three years ago. I was based out of a suburban cop shop and people were ringing up reporting small things—someone had their letterbox pushed over, another found their lawn had been sprayed with chemicals and it'd died. The community centre had a few windows smashed but nothing stolen. We couldn't work out what was going on, because none of it was particularly malicious. We thought it was probably kids.

'Then one night we were out cruising the streets, me and a mate. I was off duty and I came across an older bloke carrying a pile of washing in his arms. Didn't bother to hide it in any way, was just casually walking down the street with women's clothing.

'I started to talk to him—asked what he was up to, did he have a wife or a mother who these clothes belonged to. The answer was no.' He paused.

'What'd you do?' Spencer asked as he flicked on the blinker to turn onto the main highway into Barrabine.

'Got patrol to come and pick him up and put him in an interview room. Just to "help with our enquiries". Turned out he hated the suburb and was trying to create fear and unease.' Dave stopped. 'Could that be what's happening here? Creating enough fear that someone might be pushed into selling their land? Selling the pub . . .' His voice trailed off.

Spencer was quiet for a long time. As they pulled up at the police station, he said, 'You might just be right, you know. It could very well be something like that.'

Chapter 23

Dave walked down the wide streets of Barrabine, hands in pockets. Being the middle of the day and quite warm, there were few people out, but plenty of cars parked along the street.

He was on his way to the first camping shop when he heard his name called and turned to see Melinda walking towards him.

A smile broke out on his face and he stopped, waiting for her to catch up.

'Hey you,' he said, kissing her.

'Hey back,' she answered, slipping her arm around his waist.

'What're you up to?'

'Going to grab some lunch. I've got an hour to spare before my next appointment. Got time to eat with me?'

He glanced at his watch. 'Sure do. I could do with a cold drink. We got called out to Oakamanda today—Dee's pub was given an overhaul, and not one that was beneficial—and I'm a bit parched.'

'Oh no, that's terrible. Poor Dee!' Melinda exclaimed.

They walked hand in hand towards the Mug.

'How's your day been?' he asked as they sat down at a table close to the back of the café.

'I'm exhausted,' she said. 'Stupid because I slept well last night. I'm having trouble keeping my eyes open today.'

He reached out and took her hand. 'Are you doing too much, do you think?' he asked gently. 'You're putting in some long hours with the new job.'

'Not really. I'm just doing what's expected.' She glanced over at the door as the bell jangled and saw Janelle pushing Maddie into the café. 'That's one of my mums,' she said in a low voice, nudging Dave with her foot.

He turned around and caught a glimpse of a young girl with long, dull blonde hair and acne. Even with the quick glance he could see the pram was dirty and old, and the mother's clothes were either second-hand or had been dragged out of the rag bin.

Maddie was crying and Melinda frowned. 'Surely she's not still crying?' she muttered. They watched surreptitiously as the young mum order an iced chocolate and sat down, staring blankly at the wall in front of her. Maddie continued to cry and Janelle rocked the pram automatically.

From behind the counter the owner, Ruth, came out and started to fuss over Maddie, talking to her and Janelle, asking how everything was going.

'She's certainly got a good set of lungs on her,' Dave heard Ruth say. 'What's her name?'

'Maddie. She's hard work. Won't suck properly so I can't even get her to take a dummy to make her be quiet,' Janelle said above the noise. Ruth leaned into the pram and picked up Maddie, jiggling her up and down for a few moments.

'You poor thing,' she said to Janelle. 'It's hard when your baby is unsettled. Have you got anyone to help you at home?'

'Nope,' Janelle said. 'Mum says it's my own fault and I have to live with the consequences.'

A look of shock passed over Ruth's face. 'Oh, you poor love.' She jiggled Maddie even harder. 'Well, I tell you what, every time you need a little break, you pop in here for a free iced chocolate and I'll have a little cuddle with her while you have five minutes to yourself. What do you say?'

Janelle looked up at her with delight on her face. 'That would be awesome,' she answered.

Ruth looked down at the crying baby. 'Miss Maddie, I think you and I are going to be good friends.'

Dave put down his sandwich and said to Melinda, 'What's up?' He'd seen a strange look cross her face.

'I had her sucking out of a bottle last week. I'm not sure why Janelle is saying that, unless something's gone really wrong.' She shrugged. 'I guess I'll have to wait and see what's happened when she comes in for her appointment tomorrow.'

Dave knew she'd tried to brush off what she'd seen, but something had upset her. He changed the subject. 'How about we book in for a brothel tour this weekend?' He'd already run the idea past her. The brothels were an integral part of the town, almost like the supermarket. Even though there was a strong demand for their services, they weren't getting as much patronage as they used to and had started running tours to supplement their income. They'd never be locals until they understood the brothel culture.

'We might get some ideas, hey,' Melinda grinned. 'But I think I'd like to catch up on my sleep a bit too.' She picked at her salad half-heartedly.

Dave frowned. 'You're not getting sick, are you?'

'No, I don't think so. It's probably all the stress of moving, then starting this new job. I think I need a weekend of not doing very much.'

'That's what we'll do then. Sleep late, have breakfast in bed, laze in front of the TV and do a brothel tour . . .'

Melinda giggled. 'It's the words "brothel tour" that don't sound right in that sentence!'

Dave reached over and took her hand. 'I hadn't finished . . . Then we'll come home and go to bed. But maybe not just to sleep. What do you say?'

'Perfect!'

❧

The first camping shop was full of swags and sleeping bags, gas cookers and camp ovens. Dave saw a GPS display behind the counter and, enclosed in a glass cabinet, a selection of camping knives—small through to extremely large, Dave wasn't sure what they were made to cut. A camel maybe.

'How's it going?' asked the man behind the counter. 'Help you with anything?'

'Got a large selection here,' Dave said, putting his hands in his pockets. 'Been a busy month?'

'Nah, not really, mate. It's the wrong time of year. Best months are July and August when the tourists come through for the wildflowers and it's not so hot. You looking for anything in particular?'

Dave dug the photos out of his pocket and showed them to the man. 'Have you seen either of these men in the last couple of months?' he asked.

The man glanced at Dave then took a step back. 'You a cop?' he asked.

'Detective Dave Burrows,' he introduced himself and dug in his pocket for his ID. 'And you are?'

'Ah, Mick. Mick Smith. I own this store. What have these two done?'

Dave smiled. 'I can't answer that, but I'd really like to know if you've seen either of them around, or if you've sold them any camping gear recently.'

Mick studied the photos carefully. 'Nope, don't think so. There are another three camping shops in town you could try.'

Dave nodded and gave Mick his card. 'If you do remember them coming in, would you be able to give me a call?'

'Yeah, no worries.' He glanced quizzically at the card but didn't ask anything more. He was the sort of interviewee that Dave liked.

'Oh, one other thing. Do you have any security video cameras in here?'

'Nah, the bars on the windows mean nobody can get in and I'm always watching very carefully for shoplifting. I've worked out what type seems to do it more than others.'

Dave nodded and thanked him for his time. He didn't have any luck at the next two stores either, but the last one was different.

This time Dave introduced himself as soon as he walked through the door. The owner, Peter Campbell, recognised Glen Bartlett the minute Dave showed him the photo.

'Yeah, I remember him. Bought a stack of gear, which I thought was mad because he'd never been camping before.' He shrugged. 'Who am I to turn down a sale? Especially when things are a bit slow.'

'Did he buy up big then?'

'Sure did. Got a swag, sleeping bag, billy, chair—you name it, he bought it. Cost a motza!'

'Can you remember how much?'

'I can go back through the till if you want me to, but I reckon it would have to be close to a couple of grand.'

'Really? In one hit?' Dave was intrigued. He made a note to check on Glen's finances. That was a lot of money to spend, especially if he had a large payment coming up. Maybe he was counting on the sale of the lease and the money HMA Mining had enticed him with.

'Found it a bit difficult to believe myself. It was my payday, for sure.'

'Did he say where he was going to go camping?'

'Nah, just out north somewhere.'

Out north. Towards Oakamanda.

'And did he say why he was camping? Doesn't it seem strange someone would come in and spend that much when they've never been before?'

Peter gave a small laugh. 'Mate, I see all sorts in here. Let me tell you, humans are strange. Doesn't matter how normal they seem, they're still strange.'

Dave had to give him that one. He'd seen so many outlandish, weird and sad things people had done to each other, he was rarely surprised by human nature any more.

The owner continued. 'He did make a comment that I thought was peculiar, though. Said he was hoping to find an old mate. I suggested that camping probably wasn't the way to do that. Better to ask you lot if they know of him. Or enquire at the pub. Heading out and dropping into people's places unannounced out here isn't the done thing. Miners are suspicious by nature and are likely to pull a gun or set a dog onto you.'

'What'd he say to that?'

'Said he'd think about it, but the way he spoke, I knew he hadn't taken any notice, you know what I mean.'

Dave nodded. He certainly did. 'And you haven't seen him again since?'

'Nah, I helped him load everything into a hired four-wheel drive, then he took off.'

'And this bloke,' Dave tapped the photo of Ross Pollard. 'Have you seen him around?'

Peter took a moment to have another look before saying, 'He looks familiar but I can guarantee he hasn't bought anything from here.' He paused. 'I reckon he might have come in a couple of weeks ago, but I can't remember why.'

'And the camping gear that Glen Bartlett bought. Would you recognise it if it came from your shop?'

'Sure would. Even though we all stock similar brands, I remember what he bought.'

'We'll get you to come down to the station and identify the gear then. Is there a time suitable?'

Peter shrugged. 'When I shut up shop, I guess.'

Dave asked the well-worn question: 'Do you have security cameras?'

'Yeah, we do. But I won't have footage that goes back that far. Only a couple of days. Got it recording over the previous day, to cut down on costs.'

Dave nodded. 'Thanks for your time. Look forward to seeing you later.' He gave Peter a friendly salute and walked out.

Chapter 24

'I already told you I won't sell you my land,' Tim said to Ross Pollard. 'Now, I've asked you to leave. If you don't, I'll be calling the cops.'

'But, mate, you don't seem to understand the extent of the wealth we're offering you.'

'I don't care about wealth. I care about living here until I die.' Tim put his hand on his gun, which was sitting on his waist in the holster. He knew Spencer had said not to pull it out, but this bloke was going to need encouragement to leave and not come back. He swished away the flies that were gathering around his eyes and nose and glanced around to locate Chief. Sitting right behind him, like the loyal dog he was.

He realised his hands were shaking and he cursed the anxiety that had plagued him since he'd discovered the body.

'Mr Tucker, please understand that I'm doing my job here. There's no need to get nasty.'

'You got no idea what nasty is.' He brought the gun out and held it pressed to his side, trying to hide his shaking. Ross's eyes widened and Tim almost chuckled to himself. This boy—and that was what he was, a boy, not a man— had no idea how the goldfields worked. Most miners had unregistered guns, booby traps all over the place and ways to deal with trespassers the cops wouldn't agree with.

'There's no need for that. Fine, I'll go.'

Tim watched Ross trudge away and was surprised when he found himself feeling a little sorry for him. He holstered his gun. 'Going soft in your old age,' he muttered as he walked back inside the hut, yawning. He hadn't slept much last night. Haunted by dreams of Marianne turning into the body down the mine.

Ross Pollard's visit hadn't been unexpected. Dee had got a message to him saying Ross was doing the rounds again, trying to persuade people to sell.

The midday heat was taking its toll on Tim now. He'd used a lot of energy to get rid of Ross without showing any weakness.

He coughed and dabbed his mouth with hand. He needed to have a lie-down. He could dream of Marianne if he rested. And dream he did, flickers of memories flashing in front of his closed eyes like movie scenes.

❧

Marianne sat at the piano, her fingers pressing each note gently but with emotion. It seemed to Tim she was making the notes sing.

This was his fourth visit and she never ceased to amaze him.

She'd finished the song and she turned and smiled at him. 'What do you think?' she asked, her slight Italian accent making even her voice sound musical.

'It's beautiful,' he replied. It was more than that, but he didn't know what words he could use to express how he was feeling. Between the music and her beauty, he felt starstruck.

'Papa,' she looked over at her father, who was in the chair, a blanket tucked in around his thin frame.

Tim thought the man could only be days away from death, the way his eyes were sunk in the back of his skull. His teeth looked chalky when he smiled. Although it wasn't so much a smile as a grimace.

'Perfecto, my daughter. Perfecto,' Benito said, putting his fingers to his lips and kissing them before throwing his arm weakly into the air.

Tim saw how Marianne's face lit up at her father's words.

The three of them talked a little more and then Marianne went into the kitchen to make some tea.

Benito looked to make sure Marianne had gone before beckoning Tim over to him.

'You marry my girl, uh?' he said.

A feeling of butterflies exploded in Tim's stomach. 'Marry her?' he asked.

'Si, si. You marry her. I die soon. This, this . . .' He pointed to his chest and Tim knew it was the disease of

miners. The dust had got into his lungs and was slowly eating them away. 'She need a man.'

'I've got nothing but a humpy in the bush,' he said. 'I've got nothing to offer her.'

'This house, it is rented, but I have savings. Small, but they are there. They will go to her, to make her comfortable. She is good girl. Strong girl. She will adapt. You love her?'

Tim wanted to laugh out loud. Love? God, what was that? He'd never given it any thought. What he did know was he was fascinated by Marianne. He thought she was exotic, beautiful, accomplished . . . If that was love then, yes, he loved her.

'You ask her out. To eat maybe,' the sick man commanded. 'Or a walk. Something.'

Marianne came back into the room with a pot of tea and three cups. She poured the tea and handed the first cup to her father. 'What have you been planning?' she asked him. 'You look like you are being devious.' She looked across at Tim as if to ask for an answer.

'Not me,' Benito answered with a wink to Tim.

'I don't believe you, Papa,' she said gently, handing Tim his cup.

Then suddenly they were at the door and Marianne was bidding him good bye.

'Would you like to . . .' Tim spoke with a dry mouth. 'Would you like to come out to dinner with me?'

'Dinner?' Marianne answered, looking up at him with a smile. 'That would be lovely.'

'Tonight?'

'Are you not going back out into the fields later today?'

'If you say yes, I won't be.'

'Yes,' she answered.

The dream skipped forward a few weeks because next it was the day of their wedding.

A small do at the town hall in Barrabine. Marianne wore a rose-coloured dress which set off her dark hair, while Tim had paid one guinea for a suit from the second-hand store. It was a bit small for his tall frame and he kept tugging at the sleeves.

They'd walked in together, Marianne holding a small posy of wildflowers while the celebrant had taken them through their vows.

There were two guests at their wedding: Benito and an office worker, who acted as the second witness.

'You are husband and wife. You may kiss.'

Tim turned to Marianne and stared at her for a second, not sure what to do. Then he leaned forward and put his lips on hers for the first time. His thought was how soft they were and how she smelled of roses.

When he pulled away, he looked at her and saw she was smiling up at him, her eyes shining with what he hoped was love.

Benito clapped loudly and said with gasping breath that he'd like to sing but he really didn't have the voice.

The next scene was a funeral.

Marianne was standing at the side of a grave, crying, her hands clutching a handkerchief, while Tim stood beside her.

He didn't know what to do, didn't know how to comfort her. He felt physically ill as he watched her grieve, knowing there was nothing he could do to take away her pain.

As the coffin was lowered into the red dirt, Marianne let out a low, animal-like moan and Tim caught her as she fell.

'I've got you,' he whispered in her ear. 'I've got you. I'll always be here. I'll always look after you, I promise.'

The next day, with some of Benito's savings, he bought a little car and they drove out to Tim's hut to start their lives together.

Then there was a black hole.

Three children's coffins and a rotting body on top. A cloud of flies. The sound of falling . . .

∾

Tim woke with a start, his heart pounding. Breathing slowly through his nose, he tried to calm his heart by thinking of Marianne. He reached his arm out to touch the place she would have lain if she were next to him. Of course, she wasn't there. Hadn't been for many years. The hut was still the same, though. The wooden set of drawers and the piano they'd moved out of Benito's rental. She'd turned his little humpy into a home.

He burrowed his head into the pillow, feeling the embroidered flowers on the corner of the pillowcase. They were Marianne's handiwork. She'd made cushions with flowers embroidered in one corner and music notes in the other. She'd boiled water in the billy and scrubbed the encrusted dust away from the pieces of furniture he already had and then bought tablecloths and mats to brighten the place.

Smiling, he remembered the first big summer dust storm that had come through and how they'd sat inside with a sheet over them. It had been the first time Tim had seen her Italian temper, and what a rage it'd been!

When the wind had passed by and she'd seen the thick layer of dust on her piano, Tim had learned some new Italian swearwords.

'*Porca miseria!*' she cried, sweeping off the sheet which had been used to cover the precious instrument and finding there to be another layer underneath. 'Damn it! Damn it! *Il mio pianoforte!*'

He tried to calm her down, but she'd stalked the small room, muttering to herself in Italian and throwing her hands in the air. In the end Tim had left her to her anger and gone outside to the area he'd been digging out by hand. His tools and equipment were covered in dust too, but he guessed that wasn't as bad as the piano.

That was the day they'd started to become rich.

As he picked away the quartz from the soil, he had to look twice to believe what he was seeing: a reef of gold running through the rock. He chipped a bit further along and found the reef continued and in fact become thicker.

He ran his fingers along the rock, trying to understand what he was seeing. Surely he couldn't be so lucky? Could he?

Working long after dark, his miner's lamp glowing dimly in the pitch-black. By morning he'd opened up three metres of a gold reef. Running home, he roused Marianne from their bed and she started to yell at him for not coming home, but stopped when she saw how dirty he was.

'Come on,' he said, grabbing her hand. 'You need to see this.'

Together they ran through the bush, until finally he slowed to a walk and put his hands over her eyes. 'Trust me,' he said, and walked her carefully towards the entrance.

This part of the mine was open-cut and once he took his hands away she saw it. Tim rubbed tears away now as he remembered her standing there, her mouth open in disbelief, tears on her cheeks.

'I can buy you as many pianos as you desire now, sweetheart,' he said.

He could have promised to build her a big house, but no one did that out here and she never asked. Getting up off the bed, Tim rubbed his face again, and coughed. The sun had started to sink; he'd slept for longer than he'd intended.

In the still of the evening he could hear voices floating on the wind. Or was it just his memories coming to life again?

He stopped and listened. No, there were voices—someone was yelling. Tim couldn't make out the words.

Chief cocked his ears and growled softly.

'What is it, mate?' he asked. 'Or rather, who is it?'

Chapter 25

'Janelle, how are you?' Melinda asked as she ushered the young mum into her office. Maddie's wails had reached her as soon as the pair had arrived at the clinic and she wondered what on earth had gone wrong during the week.

'Maddie just won't stop crying,' Janelle said. 'I've had enough.' Tears trickled down her cheeks and she thrust the pram towards Melinda. 'She won't feed or sleep. Mum's being horrible and I . . .' She broke off, unable to say any more.

Melinda glanced in and saw the baby, her face red from crying, her little fists clenched tightly as she jerked around unhappily.

'When did you try to feed her last?' Melinda asked.

'Just before I came in here. I used the bottle and formula you gave to me but it hasn't been working.'

'Okay, well let's just pop her on the scales and see what's happened this week.' Melinda started to undress the baby and tried to shush her by putting a dummy in her mouth.

As Janelle had said, Maddie put her fists up to her mouth and pushed it away, but Melinda persevered and finally, after the fifth attempt, she managed to get it into her mouth and the crying stopped.

'That's much better,' Melinda said in her soft, cooing voice. She was sure the baby was hungry. Not wanting to alarm Janelle, she blocked the scales with her body and weighed the baby. Maddie had lost another three hundred grams.

'Tell me about trying to feed her at home,' Melinda said, at the same time thinking, *This is going to have to stop.*

'I do it how you do. Boil the water and mix it up. Sometimes she takes a little bit, other times she won't take anything.' Her voice became defensive. 'Mum always tells me I'm doing it wrong, but she won't help me and anyway I'm doing it the exact same way you showed me. It's not my fault she won't feed.'

At that statement Melinda felt a little tremor of apprehension. What if it was?

'I might just try to make up another bottle and see if I can get her to drink,' Melinda said calmly, all the while her mind was racing. 'Are you okay to wait here while I mix it up? I'll take Maddie with me.' She walked out of the room and straight into Patti's office.

'Got the same problem as last week, with Maddie and Janelle,' she said and told her about the weight loss. 'The baby's hungry, nothing short of it. And I don't believe the story that Maddie won't take a bottle. I bet if I gave her one, she'd drink it in two seconds flat. What do we do?'

Patti held out her hands for the baby. 'Let me have a look at her while you mix up the bottle.

In the kitchen Melinda boiled the kettle and added two heaped scoops of the powdered formula and mixed it enthusiastically. She wanted to think that Maddie was just a difficult baby, but there was something telling her things weren't quite right here. Dave had always talked about trusting his gut when he was investigating a crime. Well, this wasn't a crime, but she knew she needed to listen to her inner voice; and it was screaming to her there was more to this story than what she was being told.

Back in Patti's office, she handed her boss the bottle and watched as she squeezed a tiny bit of milk onto the baby's lips and then carefully put the teat in her mouth. Maddie started to suck instantly.

The women's eyes met over the hungry child, now oblivious to either of them. She was lost in a world of milk, warmth and comfort.

'I haven't seen any signs of Maddie being abused,' Melinda said softly, stroking the downy head. 'She's not got bruises anywhere and she's always freshly bathed and in clean clothes when she comes in.'

'Hmm,' Patti said, looking down as Maddie continued to suck.

'I can't even remember her having a nappy rash.'

'Let's go and have a chat with Janelle,' Patti said, taking the empty bottle out of Maddie's mouth. 'Do you want to make up another bottle before we do that? I think she'd take it.'

Back in her office, Melinda placed the sleeping baby into the pram. Janelle looked alarmed that both women had come back in, with serious looks on their faces.

'What's wrong?' she asked. 'Is there something wrong with Maddie? Is she sick?'

'She's hungry, Janelle,' Patti said softly. 'Very hungry. And because she's hungry, she's going to cry and not sleep but, also, she's losing weight and not growing the way she needs to.'

'She won't take a bottle!'

'I understand that seems to be a big problem. Janelle, we've had her feeding in here twice. She guzzles it.' Patti broke off when Janelle stood up and snatched at the pram as if to walk out the door. 'She's a very hungry baby and hungry babies feed.'

Patti subtly blocked the door.

'You saying I can't look after my own baby?' the teenager asked in a loud voice.

'No, Janelle, that's not—'

'You can get fucked. I know what I'm doing.'

'Janelle,' Melinda barked, needing to get the situation back in hand. 'Sit down. We are not saying you can't look after your own child. We're here to help you, not make life harder. Okay?'

'Why don't you believe me?' she pleaded. 'I *am* looking after my baby! It's not my fault she won't drink or take a bottle. It's not my fault I haven't got any milk!'

Melinda looked at the young girl, her tears wet on her cheeks, and remembered what she'd been like at seventeen. How could a girl who was little more than a baby herself be expected to raise a child? Especially without support from her family. It was no wonder she was crying out for help.

She squatted down in front of the girl and put her hands on Janelle's knees. 'Listen, Janelle, can I tell you what I think is happening here? It's you who's crying out for help here. You who needs some attention. Unfortunately, you're getting us to pay attention to you by hurting your baby, and as Maddie's nurse I can't let you do that.'

Janelle stared at her. 'I'm not hurting my own baby,' she said angrily. 'She's the one who won't drink. I'm trying to feed her but she won't . . . It's all her fault.'

Patti shook her head. 'Sweetheart, you're so young and I know you're not getting any help at home. In your situation it would be quite normal to need help. But you can't do it in this way. You're starving Maddie, while trying to get attention for yourself.' She spoke in a gentle tone. 'So, what we're going to do now is take you both across to the hospital. Maddie needs to be looked at by a doctor and you do too.'

'I'm not going nowhere,' Janelle said. 'You're both full of it. Got no idea about me or my life. Or Maddie. We're leaving.'

'You can't, Janelle. We're not going to let you. If you don't come willingly with us, I'll have to call social services to come over here and take you to the hospital.' Melinda didn't mention that the Department of Community Services would be called anyway. 'If you let us take you, it's going to be much better for you and your baby.'

Janelle didn't say anything, just stared at them with fire in her eyes. Suddenly she sagged and all the fight went out of her. She burst into tears and slumped back into the chair, her sobs breaking Melinda's heart.

Chapter 26

'I still haven't heard from the next of kin,' Dave said to Spencer when he came back in late on Thursday afternoon. 'But the coppers from Ballarat have called.'

'Took a while,' he said.

'They've done the inform. The mother is elderly and having a bit of trouble dealing with the news. Doesn't sound like she can get out much or has a lot of friends or support around her.'

'Tough.'

'Shannon has finished with the body so he can be sent back to his mother now,' Dave said.

'Okay, can you get hold of Shannon and organise it? Let her know that from our end she's right to release the body. I guess the funeral directors will do the rest.'

'No problems. Now, Peter from the camping shop has confirmed the items are from his store. He's also brought in a photocopy of the cheque that Glen used to pay for the goods. That camp was indeed Glen Bartlett's.' Dave drew in a breath, held it for a moment, then let it out in a whoosh. 'And there's something weird about his bank accounts.'

Spencer looked over at him, his eyes alert. 'Whose bank accounts?'

'Glen Bartlett's. They came on the fax this morning. His bank in Ballarat wasn't going to let me have any of the information I wanted without a warrant, so I got on to the judge on duty and told him what I needed. It was the fastest warrant I've ever got!'

'Judge Banrock is pretty easy to work with. So tell me, what did you find?'

Dave grabbed a sheaf of shiny fax paper and took it over to Spencer's desk and pointed to all the highlighted amounts.

'Looks to me like he was getting money from someone. Every two weeks there's been three hundred paid in. There's no reference to where it's come from other than a manual transfer notation and it's been happening for the past six months.'

Spencer flicked through the pages. 'Hmm. Did he have any other accounts? Credit card?'

'A credit card and another savings account. This one here is his running account. The credit card has a debit of five hundred dollars and the savings account has five grand in it. But you know the other thing which is weird? He doesn't have a lot of money, so this big payment he had coming up, what was it for? Did he have a gambling debt, trouble with drugs? Some kind of unsecured loan?'

'Better get onto it. Ask the bank to trace where the three hundred dollars is coming from.'

'Have already. It'll take a little time.' Dave looked at his notes. 'Okay, going back to my conversation with the Ballarat coppers—they don't know much about him and the mother was too shocked to give out any useful information. I'm getting the feeling he was a loner, didn't have a lot of friends. The mother, Carmen, wasn't aware he'd decided to sell the land, but she did say he was the executor, so she'd left it up to him. The money would then come into the estate and be given to the people it was supposed to be.'

'Why didn't the father leave the land to the mother?' asked Spencer.

'As far as I know they didn't ask that question, but I'll follow it up. Thought I'd leave it a few days before I give her a call. Give her a chance to get used to the news.'

'This is a murder enquiry, Dave. You can't waste time!'

'I know, but I've got other things to go on with—like finding the wagon.'

'Have you got any information about the land?'

'Nothing other than Carmen was happy for him to make decisions he wanted to . . . Just so long as the money ended up in all the right spots.'

'And was one of the right spots Glen's bank account?'

Dave looked at his notes. 'Yes. This is an assumption, and I know as detectives we should never make assumptions, but—' he took a deep breath '—from the information I've had from Ballarat, the parents are wealthy. Well, the mother is, since the father is dead. Made his money goldmining.

But looking at the son's bank accounts, he does have money issues. Like I told you, there isn't much in his accounts.'

'Ah, mummy and daddy don't hand out the dosh easily? Wonder why he didn't take over the finances for his mother if she's elderly. Does he work?'

'Doesn't appear that he does.'

'Well, no wonder he needs money. Alrighty then, I guess all we can do is wait until we hear back from the bank on the traces. I'm getting bloody frustrated. We keep hearing about this person Bartlett was looking for and we've got no idea who he is or how to find him!' Spencer stood, hoisted up his shorts and parked his ample bum on the edge of the desk.

'That's going to be like looking for a needle in a haystack.'

'Ring Ballarat back and see if they can search his house. Maybe there'll be something there.'

'It would be very helpful if we could find his car,' Dave pointed out.

'That too.'

The phone rang and Spencer picked it up. 'Brown,' he said.

Dave turned and went back to his desk, carrying the bundle of statements. As soon as Spencer had mentioned the person Glen was looking for, everything fell into place. Glen didn't need to come over here to sign the sale papers, Dave was sure. He'd have to check with a lawyer or real estate agent, but he was fairly certain they could've been signed over a fax or the papers mailed to Victoria and signed in front of a JP.

No, the sale was a cover.

Glen Bartlett had come over here to find someone.

Dave picked up the phone and called Ballarat.

❧

An hour later he was in his vehicle driving out towards Oakamanda and Fractured Hill. That was the last known place that Glen had been, so it seemed the best place to start looking.

He'd been to see Melinda to tell her he would be camping out tonight and tears had welled up in her eyes, taking him by surprise. He had to admit she was looking tired. A weekend of doing nothing was looking more and more appealing.

'Don't you worry, Mr Dave,' Ernie had said from over the fence as he was leaving. 'I watch out for missus, Dave.'

'Thanks, Ernie. You're a good neighbour.'

Spencer had helped him pack up a few camping things and sent him off with a clap on the shoulder and a good luck wish.

'We've got to find the car,' Dave had told him. 'That's going to hold a lot of information.'

'Only if it hasn't been done over by vandals,' Spencer had replied.

'The sooner we find it, the less likely that's going to be.'

Now, driving along the dirt tracks, he made sure the GPS tracker was on and he looked at the map sitting on the passenger seat. He planned to follow every little track he could find.

Ten minutes later Dave pulled up where a narrow trail veered off the road. He looked at his map and worked out which track it was before nosing his way down there. He didn't get too far before he found a large tree over the road; by the look of the track, no one had been down this way for ages. He turned around and drove out.

The next trail he came across was owned by a mine. TRESPASSERS WILL BE PROSECUTED, yelled at him in large black lettering. Dave was undecided. He guessed if there was an abandoned car on the road to the mine, someone would have reported it already, but again that was making assumptions.

He put a call out over the radio, hoping to get the station.

'Station receiving,' came the reply.

Dave grinned and asked for Spencer.

'Can you phone all the mines out here to see if there's been any suspicious activity by a white four-wheel drive?' he asked. He didn't want to explain why, even though the channel was supposed to be secure.

'Will get Claire and Tez onto it.'

From Spencer's tone, he knew what Dave was thinking. Excellent.

Back on the road, Dave found three more tracks before nightfall, but none of them held any of the secrets he was looking for.

Finally, before the sun set, he parked under a tree and started to collect firewood. Before long, cheery flames were licking up around the branches and Dave had unpacked his chair, swag and barbecue plate. He sat back with a beer in his hand and contemplated the bush as the stars began to appear in the salmon-coloured sky.

In the distance he could hear the hum of the closest mine but the noise didn't bother him. He mainly heard the crackle of the fire and call of the birds as they settled in the trees for the night.

He thought about his childhood and all the times he and his brothers had gone camping in the back paddock. And the time he and his cousin Kate had told their families they were going camping at one of their favourite spots. Taking the small Suzuki ute, they'd managed to get bogged in a creek. Not letting that small problem stop them, they'd carried what they needed to a dry spot, set up camp and spent the night as planned. They were good mates and they'd had great conversations around the campfire, cementing the friendship even more.

In the whole time they'd been together, Dave had never taken Melinda camping. He would have to rectify that now. He'd always been wary of suggesting it because she was a city girl through and through and he didn't think she'd like roughing it.

He remembered what Kate had said when he'd introduced her to Melinda. It had been at Kate's engagement party in the woolshed of their family farm. The dress code had been jeans and RM Williams boots. Melinda had worn black pants and court shoes. The drink of choice had been beer or rum. Melinda had sipped white wine.

Later in the evening Kate had dragged Dave away from the group and said to him, 'What the fuck?'

'Excuse me?' Dave had looked at her curiously. 'What's wrong?'

'Why Melinda?' she had asked. 'She is not your type. You need a country girl. Someone who's going to get down and dirty with you. Go camping, hiking, exploring. Not shopping in Myer or drinking lattes in Fremantle.'

Dave hadn't known what to say. Sure, Melinda came from a different world—and her parents, especially her father, weren't exactly his biggest fans—but he'd been certain then, as he was now, that Melinda was the right woman for him.

He'd take her camping, he promised himself, just as soon they found out who'd murdered Glen Bartlett.

Chapter 27

Dave woke to the breaking dawn and lay listening to the sounds of the bush.

Out here, north of Barrabine, the birds seemed to disappear during the heat of the day, leaving the flies as the only sign of life. But on dusk and dawn the birds came out with a cacophony of sweet-sounding songs. As he lay in his swag he tried to put names to the calls he could hear. There were finches and willie wagtails, and he thought he could hear a wattle bird, even though they were rare this far north, so he couldn't be sure.

The finches were darting in and out of the trees and knocking droplets of water from the leaves onto his swag. Rolling onto his stomach, he peered out to see if the fire had lasted through the night. It had, with red coals still glowing in the dull morning light. Wiggling out from underneath the heavy canvas, he put on his boots and did a few stretches to loosen his back before rolling up his swag and putting it in the back of the car. He'd learned to roll up his swag as soon as he got out of it on a camping trip with his brothers. A small python, completely harmless but a snake nonetheless, had crawled into his oldest brother's swag one morning when it had been left unrolled. It was only discovered as he got into it the next night. A nasty fright for boy and snake, but a good lesson.

Dave rekindled the fire with a few thin sticks and waited until there were enough coals to put on his billy. Soon it was boiling away and he threw in tea leaves as if he were an old swaggy getting ready to set off walking for the day.

He sat on a log and drank his tea and ate the bacon sandwich he'd cooked up, the ants racing around his feet claiming any crumbs he dropped.

Last night he'd scoured the map and found a couple of places he was keen to look at today—one was ten kilometres to the west of where he was camped, and the other was a track off the main road to Oakamanda. Camping out meant he'd been able to work later and could start earlier.

It took him half an hour to drive the ten kilometres—the road was very rough and Dave wondered if the corrugations might shake the car to pieces. He tried to angle one wheel off the road and out into the bush, but then he realised he might stake a tyre that way, so he had to stay on the road and drive carefully.

When he found the track, he was pleased it didn't seem to be used that much and therefore wasn't as rough. It twisted and turned through the bush and seemed to go on forever . . . until it didn't go any further. Dave drew in a breath and looked around. The road ended in a turnaround circle and it looked like someone had been here recently.

He shut off the engine and got out of the car, listening intently. He looked at the ground for tracks and saw a thin trail leading off into the scrub. Grabbing his GPS, water bag and camera, he followed the trail. It might be a kangaroo track and lead nowhere, but it was worth a look. Not that there'd be a car able to get through, but a look was a look.

Half an hour of hard walking and his legs were scratched from low spiky bushes and sharp sticks. He stepped over fallen trees, whose trunks were in the process of being turned into termite mounds, and pushed his way through thick bush, where the track was a little overgrown.

'Bugger,' Dave said as he felt another stick dig into his calf. He stopped and pushed hard on the spot with his finger to stop the bleeding. Grabbing the GPS off his belt, he looked to see how far away from the car he was: 3.3 kilometres.

As he looked around, a glint caught his eye. He swung back to have another look. There was something shiny to his left. Forgetting about his calf, he walked with a sense of urgency towards it.

Breaking out into a clearing, he saw what had caught his eye. It was a bunch of faded plastic flowers set on top of a wooden cross.

Dave's breath caught in his throat. Two graves were enclosed by a low rusted iron fence, about knee high. Goosebumps spread across his skin as he read the hand-carved plaque.

Our children lie in these graves. Victims of a life which has stolen ours. Twins Kenneth and Pammy Tucker lie together as they were born and died, aged four, taken in a mining accident.

Kelly Tucker, aged eighteen months, taken by a snakebite.

Tim and Marianne Tucker

Dave shivered and looked around. Three children, taken in tragic accidents, lying here in forgotten graves, watched over only by the birds and the wind.

∿

Back in the car, Dave thought about Tim, out in the middle of the bush, living a life by himself, after having lost his children. He wondered about Marianne and where she was. Surely if she were dead, she'd be buried with her children. Maybe the grief had got too much for her and she'd moved away. Gone to live in a town, or anywhere else, to get away from the life which had taken her kids.

He must have been on Tim Tucker's land while he was looking at the graves, so he got out his map and tried to work out where Tim's hut would be in relation to them. It must be about two and half kilometres away. A long way.

The sun was high in the sky now and Dave realised he didn't have much time left before he'd have to start heading back to Barrabine. He supposed he could always stay out another night, but he didn't have any way of letting Melinda know and he was a little concerned about how tired she'd been.

Driving as fast as the road allowed, he followed the last track he noticed, which looked like it led to a dead end. He was keen to check it out; it might be a good spot to dump a car. The track obviously hadn't been used a lot and there were tree branches growing over it. Some of the branches had been broken off, suggesting someone had driven a vehicle down here. Dave stopped and looked at the snapped branches, wondering how long ago they'd been broken. The leaves were beginning to wilt but weren't yet completely dead and dry, so it would have to be at least a couple of weeks. A simmering excitement started in his chest.

Grabbing the camera, he snapped a few shots of the broken branches then started to walk, following the track. About one hundred metres in, he turned to look back. He couldn't see his vehicle—it was if the bush had closed in around him and hidden him from the world.

He kept walking, taking in everything, stopping occasionally to take photos. The trail was easy to follow because the broken branches led him deeper into the bush like they were a Hansel and Gretel trail of crumbs.

Then suddenly there it was. The white four-wheel drive. Parked beneath a tree. The numberplate was the one he'd memorised and instantly Dave knew he'd found the secret world of Glen Bartlett.

❧

He took shots of the car in situ—complete with the leaves which had fallen onto the windscreen and now sat there, piled up. The birds had found it a useful perch, if the amount of shit on the roof was anything to go by, and there were clear dog tracks around the vehicle as if they'd circled it, trying to work out if it was prey or not.

With gloved hands, he opened the driver's side door and looked inside.

Nothing remarkable caught his eye. It looked like a hire car that had recently been picked up from the carpark. Clean and tidy. Dave noticed there were a few areas where dirt had been picked up on Glen's shoes and brought into the car. He snapped some pictures, wondering if the dirt could be analysed; it might help them track his movements, understand the places he'd been visiting.

He flicked open the glove box. Only the manual and copies of the hire agreement. Dave checked the starting kilometres against the kilometres on the speedo. Only three hundred. Nothing too substantial.

In the back of the car he noted a takeaway wrapper, *The West* newspaper and a map. He brought the map out and unfolded it on the bonnet, his heart in his mouth. Finding Barrabine, he looked for anything that might indicate where Glen had been visiting. Noting the worn crease lines, he folded the map back to them and looked at the section it showed, hoping for more clues as to where he'd been.

Oakamanda was in the middle of the square and around it were black dots, indicating all the different leases, but there was no handwriting, no markings to give a suggestion as to where he'd been.

Grabbing the newspaper, he looked at the date. Five months ago. That gave Dave pause. Why would he have a newspaper five months old? He flicked through the first few pages and couldn't see anything to do with either Barrabine or mining.

Frustrated, Dave let out a loud sigh and ran his hands over his head. Putting the map in an evidence bag, he left it on the front seat then went to the back. The two doors opened outwards revealing an empty area, which was carpeted. He stared at it carefully, checking to see if any of the edges had been folded back. He ran his fingers around just to make sure, but there didn't seem to be anything hidden under the carpet. The door trims hadn't been popped off either.

'Damn!' His voice was loud, causing a flutter of wings from above and a loud warning cry from a bird. Dave looked up. 'Sorry,' he said.

He checked under the seats, ran his fingers along the joins and even opened the spare-tyre well, to see if something had been hidden in there. It was clean too.

Finally, he turned to the outside surrounds. Carefully he looked through bushes and out past the clearing circumference, in case there were still footprints. He didn't see any.

One part of the clearing stood out to him, but he couldn't work out why. There was a slight mound underneath a tree, right next to the car. It looked as if someone had recently cleared away the leaves and bark in this area because the build-up was much thinner here than elsewhere. The top of the red earth was cracked slightly from being exposed—Dave thought it looked like the bottom of one of the dried-out dams on the farm—and a scorpion had made use of one of the cracks for its home. He took some photos just in case, then kept searching.

Dave was just about to head back to his car to call in the rest of the team when he saw something on the tree trunk. It looked like initials had been engraved into the wood.

Leaning in, he studied them—they were very old, and over time the tree had grown around them. He wasn't sure if the first letter was P or R and he couldn't make out the second letter at all.

He took photos of the initials as well—not that he thought they were related, but you could never be too careful.

Finally, gathering up the newspaper and map, he walked back to his car to call in the scene.

Chapter 28

1945

Paddy had been in Victoria for five months when he went to the post office to send a telegram to the police station and newspaper in Barrabine.

Have you found out who the woman I buried was? Stop.

Has anyone come forward since you wrote the article on the woman I buried? Stop.

He waited two weeks for a reply. The police didn't bother to answer and the newspaper's reply was one word. *No.*

Finding the woman had changed Paddy's life and not for the better. Often when he closed his eyes to sleep he would see her body, hanging from the tree. Or in the grave, her bloated face stared up at him as he shovelled dirt on top of her. He'd told no one of the nightmares, of how she haunted him, floating around his dreams, begging him to tell her family.

Twelve months later he was married and the dreams came less often. Carmen, his wife, sometimes asked why he tossed and turned in his sleep and occasionally cried out, but he was reluctant to tell her—he didn't want Carmen to live with the images too.

Then he found gold. Not just a small amount, a good solid discovery that would keep him and Carmen for the rest of their days.

He began to plan. He would buy the land the woman was buried on. Make sure she was safe and perhaps even mark her grave with a headstone. *To the unnamed woman who lies here, I hope you're at peace.* Or: *A woman who bore too much despair is buried here. She is unidentified.*

It took him eight years, but finally he went into a realty office and made the enquiry. Six months later he was handed the deed to Lease 7008-0514 and called it Fractured Hill.

Fractured because he was sure her family's life had been fractured by her death.

He placed a notice in the newspaper: *Searching for the family of a woman who died in the Barrabine region.* He listed the date, what had happened and his phone number, telling no one, not even Carmen, what he was doing.

Chapter 29

Dave deposited the evidence he'd gathered at the station and then checked in with Spencer. He'd handed over the GPS with the coordinates so forensics would be able to find their way out to the car and bring it back in.

'Has the search on the bank accounts turned up anything yet?' Dave asked Spencer after he'd finished telling him all the details of his expedition.

'Not yet. I've been following a couple of other leads, but nothing has come back on them yet either, so my advice is to go home and not think about this case until Monday. It'll probably take the blokes that long to finger-print everything out there and get the car back in anyway. Spend the weekend with Melinda.'

'Sounds like a great plan. We thought we might do one of the brothel tours.'

'What, you need some ideas to spice things up already?' Spencer gave a shout of laughter.

'Not yet!' Dave said, winking at him. 'Catch you Monday.'

～

When he got home, Dave found Melinda curled up on the couch, a glass of wine in her hand.

'You looked whacked,' he said, bending down to kiss her. 'Need a top-up?'

She shook her head and patted the spot next to her. 'I missed you last night. Grab a beer and come and sit next to me.'

He did as he was told. 'It's good to be home. You're still tired?' he asked, already knowing the answer.

'Mmm, I am. Feel a bit funny too, squeamish, but I think it's because I haven't eaten anything today. It's been full on. I think it's just all the emotion.'

'What happened?' He reached over to take her hand and waited.

He listened as she told him about Janelle and Maddie, remembering the girl, her dirty clothes and lacklustre hair and skin. The baby crying.

'We finally convinced her to go to the hospital. They're both admitted now—Janelle is in the mental health unit. The doctor thinks she has what's referred to as Munchausen by proxy syndrome. That's when mothers deliberately hurt their babies to gain attention.' She sighed. 'She's struggled ever since the baby was born, although there were glimmers when I thought, despite being young and not having any help, she was going to be okay. Clearly she wasn't. Apparently she's been going around telling anyone who would listen that Maddie wouldn't feed. I spoke to Ruth at the Mug and she told me that Janelle and Maddie were in there every day. Janelle would tell complete strangers how difficult Maddie was. Sometimes she got the sympathy she was looking for. Other times, when people ignored her, she'd get a little louder. Once, she was asked to leave.'

'Where's the father?' Dave asked.

'I don't think Janelle knows.'

'And the mother? Has she realised her daughter needs her?'

Melinda looked sad. 'Nope. When I went to see her this afternoon, she refused to come to the hospital. Said exactly what Janelle had been telling me: her problem, she needed to deal with it.'

'What the hell?' Dave said angrily. 'Who does that to their children? Their grandchildren? I hope she rots.'

'In a way, I'm cross with myself because Janelle was telling me exactly what was going on, except for the feeding side of things. That was her way of trying to make me notice.'

'What happens now? Has Maddie had any long-term damage done to her?'

'The doctor doesn't seem to think so. He was running liver function and full blood tests, just to check. She just needs to put on a little weight.'

'And Janelle?'

'I think she'll be on medication for a while. The hospital will call in welfare, get her set up in a small unit some-where and watch her closely. Now she's getting the help she needs, she should be okay. Or at least be able to heal.'

Dave squeezed her hand. 'You need to be congratulated, you know. It was you who picked that up. Patti didn't, no one else in the health centre did. You're incredible. Do you realise you've saved two lives?'

Melinda gave a wan smile. 'I know. It's pretty cool, isn't it? I'm glad I took the job.' She took another sip of wine and closed her eyes, her head flopping back against the couch.

'So am I. How about I get dinner?' he said, looking at her and realising she could fall asleep quite easily. 'But first, I really need a shower.'

Melinda opened her eyes and looked at him. 'Yeah, you're filthy! Do you need company?'

'Are you up to it?'

'Always.'

❧

The next afternoon at two o'clock they stood outside the Exotic Club and waited for the madam to open the door.

There were eight other couples, older than Dave and Melinda, and they all glanced at one another nervously.

'Ever done this before? Can't believe I'm on a brothel tour!' one man said to Dave.

'Never,' he answered with a grin.

One of the women giggled nervously. 'God, I wonder what we'll see.'

The door cracked open and a plain-looking middle-aged woman looked out at them. Dave stared, then glanced at Melinda and gave her a nudge with his hip. This was not the Narla he'd met the night they'd been called to the brothel.

That evening she'd been dressed in a short skirt and low-cut top, with heavy eye makeup. Today she wore grey slacks and a conservative white blouse. Her shoes were black sneakers and there was not one iota of sexiness about her.

'Please, come in,' she said in a honey tone. 'Welcome to the Exotic Club.' She waved them inside into a waiting room with seats lining the walls, and gestured for them to sit down.

The lights were dim and everywhere there were props: feather boas draped over the chairs, lingerie displayed on mannequins, and framed pictures of hand-drawn figures in many different sexual positions.

Dave grabbed hold of Melinda's hand and pulled her close, remembering their lovemaking the night before. A thrill of desire ran through him.

Once everyone was settled, the madam stood in front of them, her hands clasped. She gave off a calm, self-confident authority. It was clear she wasn't embarrassed by her profession one bit.

'Welcome to the Exotic Club, the oldest working brothel in Barrabine,' she began. 'My name is Narla and I am the madam here. I pride myself on running a good establishment, one which caters for a wide variety of needs and wants.' Her voice was like warm caramel flowing over ice cream—enough to make anyone melt, Dave decided. 'We get many men into this house—two are never the same. Some are quiet and shy, others are loud and flashy. Some arrive with bundles of cash, others with credit cards. But they all come here to have a need met. Today I will be showing you around my brothel. We have one bondage room and two standard rooms. So . . . the bondage room first. Follow me, please.'

They all filed in, single file, and Dave heard the gasps of the people in front of him.

'Oh my goodness,' Melinda said, stopping so suddenly he ran into the back of her. She was staring at the bed, which was covered in all sorts of toys and equipment.

'Check out those shoes,' she turned and whispered. 'How can spikes that long be classed as pleasurable?'

'Who knows? And check out the Bundy Bear—he's hand-cuffed to the bed!'

Melinda turned with a cheeky grin and looked up at him under her lashes. 'Did you bring your cuffs home from work, Mr Detective?'

Dave laughed out loud, then quickly stopped as everyone else fell silent.

'Many people ask to use this room,' Narla began in her smooth voice. 'The clients want to be whipped or chained to the bed. As you can see, there are chains on each corner of the bed and,' indicating the roof, 'clients may also be restrained standing up.'

Melinda raised her eyebrows and wiggled them at Dave. He knew she was wanting to ask which would be his preference.

Narla picked up a paddle and gently tapped the bum of the Bundy Bear, who was lying facedown on the bed. 'Bundy comes to us from Queensland during the off season.

Drop bears only work for a few months of the year, so he comes to us for a rest.

'Now if you'll follow me, I'll take you into the next room.'

❧

An hour later, Dave and Melinda were sitting in the pub, having a drink, laughing over what they'd seen.

'That was very illuminating,' Melinda said, her eyes alight. 'What about the story of the mayor who suggested a local madam ask the council to allow her to open a hatchery?'

Dave laughed loudly. '"Because she raised one thousand cocks a year!"' he quoted.

Melinda giggled. 'I wonder if the mayor was a frequent visitor!' She took a sip of wine and pushed her glass away. 'Why don't you drink up and we go home? I've got some ideas from the stories we heard today.'

At the smoky look she gave him, Dave felt himself start to harden. He swallowed the last of his beer and took her hand. 'I'd like to be your guinea pig,' he grinned.

Chapter 30

Dave went into work on Monday morning feeling refreshed. It had been the best weekend he and Melinda had had together since they'd arrived in Barrabine. For the first time there hadn't been any phone calls back to Bunbury—her parents had called three or four times but Melinda hadn't rung them back. The last message he'd heard from Mark was a biting 'Call me immediately'. It was clear he wasn't happy with the silence from his daughter.

'I just want to hang out with you,' she said by way of explanation, then ushered him back to bed. He wasn't about to complain, although he knew he'd cop it from Mark next time he answered the phone. The thought of a verbal barrage didn't bother him at all.

They hadn't even seen Ernie, and that was unusual.

'Look at you,' Spencer greeted him. 'A new man! Have a good weekend, did you?'

'Bloody brilliant,' he answered, setting his coffee cup down on the table. 'That Narla at the Exotic Club is pretty cool!'

Tez walked into the office, tucking in his shirt. 'Great, isn't she? So many stories and Narla is very matter-of-fact. She's running a business and that's all.'

'And the girls,' added Spencer, 'you wouldn't know they do what they do for a job—they're very quiet and don't cause us any trouble. If only the miners were as easy to deal with.'

'Forensics bring the car back in?' Dave asked, moving the focus back to police work.

'Yeah, got it out the back, all locked up. They've pulled prints and a few hairs, but nothing else. Certainly Glen Bartlett's though. We've matched them to the hairs we found in the swag on Fractured Hill,' Spencer answered. 'But they did find something else which was a bit interesting.'

'What was that?'

'They reckon there's an old grave out there.'

Dave jumped to his feet. 'Of course! Why didn't I realise that's what it was! Under the tree?'

'Yep. My guess is it's a pioneer's grave,' Spencer said. 'Trouble is, we find these things all over the place out here. Never sure if we should dig them up or leave them as they are.'

'Is there anything forensics can do to estimate how old the grave is?'

'God only knows, they said to leave it with them, so they might come back with something.' He slammed his hands down on the desk. 'Right, I'm going to go and have a chat with Mr Pollard again. Let's see what version of his camping story he tells this time. Are you coming or following up on the bank transfers?'

'Bank transfers, and then I'm going to give Glen's mother a call. See if she knows anything about who her son was wanting to find.'

Spencer gave him the thumbs up and left the room.

Dave called the bank and the manager told him the traces would be ready that afternoon or first thing in the morning. Satisfied with that, he prepared to ring Glen Bartlett's mother, writing down a few questions so he didn't forget anything. These types of interviews were difficult, particularly over the phone. He always felt like he was taking advantage of a horrible situation.

'Hello?' The voice that answered was frail and sad.

'Hello, my name is Detective Dave Burrows, from Barrabine, in Western Australia. I'm investigating your son's death.'

'Oh yes,' she said. 'Do you have some news?' The hope in Carmen Bartlett's voice tore at Dave and he wished he did have something to tell her.

'No, I'm sorry, but I was hoping I could ask you some questions about your son.'

'Of course. Anything I can do to help. I want to know why he was killed.' Her voice broke a little.

'And I can assure you we're doing everything we can to find that out.'

'Thank you,' she whispered. 'What do you need to know?'

'It seems Glen was over here looking for someone. Can you tell me who that might be?'

There was a short pause. 'His father probably sent him on a wild goose chase. If that's what got him killed, I'll be very angry.'

Dave raised his eyebrows and tapped his pen. 'Could you tell me a little about that?'

'Paddy and I got married about eighteen months after he came to Victoria,' she said. 'We met at the fruit and veggie shop. I was serving and he was buying.'

Dave listened with half an ear, knowing he was about to get the life story.

'After we were married I realised something was tormenting him. He had nightmares and would wake up sweating. I asked and asked what was wrong, but he didn't want to tell me.'

'I see,' Dave said, letting her know he was there. He wanted to hurry her up, get her to the crux of the story, but he couldn't force that. A detective's attention and patience were important to a victim's family, no matter the crime.

'It took some time but he finally told me. He'd come across a woman in the bush, in 1945 I think it was. She'd committed suicide and he buried her. Paddy was consumed with trying to find her family.' Her voice got stronger. 'I never really understood why. Everybody knows the gold-fields are harsh places and people die every day. I was brought up on them over here in Victoria. My parents were miners.

'But for some reason this woman haunted him, and until the day he died he tried to find out who she was so her family would know where he'd buried her. Every six months or so he'd send another letter off to the newspaper, trying to get people interested. He was toying with the idea of bringing in a private detective, but he died before he could do that. I suspect he told Glen the story and asked him to continue the search. Although why I wouldn't know. It's not like he's going to find the woman's family after all these years.'

'I'm sorry to hear about your husband's death,' said Dave. 'When did he pass away?'

'It's only been a couple of months,' she said, her voice wavering again. 'I didn't expect to lose Glen so soon afterwards.'

'I'm sure you didn't and, again, I'm very sorry for your loss.' Dave paused and looked at his notepad. He had comments and thoughts jotted down haphazardly.

'Was there ever any clue who this woman was?'

'Not that I'm aware.'

'Do you know if Glen had any leads on her?'

'If he did he never mentioned anything to me.'

'Do you think he would've stayed over here until he'd found out who she was?'

'I can't answer that because I'm not even sure this is the person he was trying to find.'

'I understand Glen was the executor of your husband's will?'

'Yes, he was.'

'Do you know what your husband's will instructed?'

'What he had was mostly to come to me. Glen spoke to me about selling the parcel of land in Barrabine—Paddy bought the land where he buried the woman, you see. He—Glen, I mean—didn't see the point in keeping it. It's a long way away.'

'And you agreed to this?'

'I wasn't bothered either way. I have more than enough to live my days out on. I guess it would have been hard to monitor from this distance.'

'We've been told that Glen was keen to finalise the sale of the mining lease because he had a large payment due.'

Carmen paused. 'Payment?' she said softly. 'Hmm. The thing you need to understand about my son is that he is . . . was easily led. He was very friendly and charming but easy to manipulate. He'd often get himself mixed up in harebrained schemes—the get-rich-quick type. Glen wanted to be rich but he wasn't prepared to put in the hard work that would involve. Of course, Paddy was a soft touch and indulged our son far more than he should have. How can a man learn to stand on his own two feet if his father is constantly bailing him out?' She sighed. 'If it wasn't shares, which were all the rage, it was greyhound racing, horseracing. You name it, Glen has been involved in it. And Paddy always came to the rescue when things went bad.' Even though her tone was soft, there was an edge of steel below it.

'When was the last time Paddy bailed him out?'

'Oh, maybe four years ago. Certainly not since Paddy died. I won't be involved doing that. He needs to learn to stand on his own two feet without his parents' help.'

'And could you tell me the last scheme he was involved in?'

'He got involved with deer farming. It was a high-cost set-up—you know, the fences are so high and there are limited markets for the meat. The people he went in with weren't good farmers either, and it only took a couple of years for the bank to ask for their money back.'

'And you put up his share?'

'Not all of it, but a substantial amount. He finished paying that back a couple of years ago. But I can tell you, sir, he has always had a weakness for gambling. If he had a big payment, maybe he'd bought a share in a dog. Or even a horse. People involved in horseracing never have any money.'

'Can I be clear then, Glen would have inherited the money from the sale of Fractured Hill?'

'As the executor, no, but as part beneficiary, yes, and he was both.'

Dave couldn't think of any more questions, so he thanked her and hung up.

Grabbing the bank statements, he went back through them to see if he'd missed anything. A thought popped into his head: could the three hundred dollars a fortnight be a return on some investment?

With his ruler and pen, he read every line on the statement again and looked at every transaction. There was one debit that might match what he was looking for, but that was only for twenty dollars. Dave suspected that the fee for such a service would be much more than twenty dollars per month.

There had to be something in these statements that pointed to what new venture Glen was involved in.

He picked up the phone and called the bank again. 'It's Dave Burrows,' he said when the manager picked up. 'I'm looking at Glen Bartlett's statements again and I'm wondering if there are any transactions here which could be attributed to any gambling agencies? Or something out of the ordinary. I know that sounds vague.'

'Very. What type of out of the ordinary are you talking about?'

'Get-rich-quick schemes. Racehorse or dog ownership. Regular payments or income from that type of person or business. I'm assuming the reference name for gambling wouldn't be so obvious as TAB, would it?'

'Ah, yes. Yeah, the TAB always has their business name on the statement. This would be a hard one to track unless you knew the business name. I can't tell you from his statement what type of business is making a payment or debit to his account. I can have my staff look into any transaction you want, but you'll have to tell us which ones.'

'Hmm, thought that might be the case. No worries, I'll keep looking.' He said his thanks and decided he needed a coffee before he tackled anything else.

His walk was brisk and he realised that since he'd gone into the police station a great mountain of cloud had started to build up to the north and the air was slightly humid.

At the Mug, Layla was working the coffee machine and Ruth was in the kitchen. He gave them both a smile and wave, knowing Layla would make his coffee without being asked. He leaned against the wall and looked around. There was a couple he didn't know at the back of the shop, reading the newspapers. The women looked up suddenly, her hands across her mouth. She said something to her husband and he reached for the paper, swinging it around to read. A look of shock crossed his face and they got up and quickly headed outside. Dave frowned as he watched them go, wondering what had upset them so much.

He walked over to their table and looked at the paper. It was open to the death notices. Someone they knew must have died.

Dave straightened. Of course! Why hadn't he thought of it before?

He walked quickly back to the counter and said to Layla, 'Don't worry about my coffee.'

She stared at him. 'It's nearly ready.'

'Haven't got time, sorry. I'll pay for it tomorrow!' He was out the door before she could reply.

He ran all the way back to the station and pushed open the door to the detectives' office with force, causing Tez and Claire to jump.

'You right, mate?'

'All good.' He opened the evidence room and grabbed the box containing everything that had come in from Glen Bartlett's car. Throwing himself into his chair, he pulled on gloves before picking up the newspaper. He took it out of the evidence bag and carefully turned the pages until he came to the death notices. He ran his finger down the columns, looking for a name he recognised. There was no one. Then he turned to the personals. He read each one, dismissing the women offering sex for money and women looking for men.

It took three pages of ads before he found it.

I'm looking for the family of a woman who has been missing since 1945. Very little is known of the circumstances surrounding her disappearance, but it was from twenty miles north of Barrabine, Western Australia. If your family has had someone missing since that year and don't know what happened to her, please contact Glen Bartlett.

Chapter 31

'He was certainly chasing this woman's relatives,' Dave said to Spencer, a tremor of excitement running him. 'Could there be any link between where he parked the car and the grave?'

'There must be. His father must have given him a mud map and he's gone straight there.'

Dave started to pace. Walking helped him think.

'Who is he linking this woman to? Who is still out in the field from back in the 1940s? In particular '45?'

Spencer rubbed his chin. 'There's China and Tim, a couple of blokes over on the southern parts, and that's about it. There's no saying that the family is still even out here, Dave.'

'I know, but these blokes might remember the story, mightn't they?'

'We can go and talk to them, sure, but . . .' He broke off. 'Let's go and give it a shot. Who knows, if we ID the woman, we might have a better understanding of why Glen Bartlett was murdered.'

'Exactly!'

❧

Dave drove and he drove fast. Excitement always gave him a lead foot. Spencer had to grab hold of the door handle a couple of times as they swung around corners on their way to Tim Tucker's.

'Steady up there, lad. This woman's been dead nigh on fifty years. A few more minutes isn't going to make much difference to her.'

'Sorry. I just can feel we're on the edge of a breakthrough.'

'Good,' Spencer said dryly. 'But let's live to tell the tale, all right?'

Dave grinned and tapped his fingers on the steering wheel. 'Hey, that reminds me—when I was camped out the other night, I went down a track not too far from here and found two graves. They were Tim's kids. A set of twins and a little girl. All died within a short time of each other. He ever talk about that?'

Spencer shook his head. 'I had no idea. God.' They fell into silence. 'What happened to them?'

'Mining accident and snakebite, according to the plaque.'

'Bloody hell, imagine living through that. I know my kids give me the shits often enough, but I'd never be without them.'

'Do you know what happened to Tim's wife?'

'She died. Tim's never talked about it much. I think it still cuts him to the bone. He loved her very much and he only told me one night over a few beers when I asked what the significance of the piano was. The piano in the humpy is hers. He said she could play like a dream.'

'I guessed it must've been 'cause I was pretty sure Tim didn't play it!'

Spencer looked across at him. 'What makes you say that? He could be the best pianist in the district.'

'His hands are a miner's hands; they're like a farmer's—thick and beaten up a bit. I wouldn't have thought he'd be able to hit the right notes.'

'Do you think I can do the cha-cha?'

Dave looked at his heavy-set partner, puzzled. 'Um . . .'

'Well?'

'I guess it's not the first dance I'd think you'd have a go at,' he hedged.

'You're going to be very surprised to find out I'm the best cha-cha dancer in Barrabine. So don't you be making assumptions about people.' He raised his eyebrows and pointed a finger at Dave.

Dave looked at Spencer out of the corner of his eye, then back at the road. 'The cha-cha? Are you sure?' He cast him another glance and said, 'Still, I don't suppose there are too many people in Barrabine!'

'Yeah, yeah, you wait until you see me.'

Dave grinned and flicked the blinker on and pulled to a stop in Tim's driveway. Spencer jumped out and started doing the steps of the cha-cha in the middle of the road.

Dave had to admit, for a heavy man, he was very light on his feet. The bloke, however, looked ridiculous, but Dave wasn't going to tell him that!

Spencer, smiling broadly, cha-cha-ed around to the driver's side and beeped the horn, hoping to get Tim to come out from wherever he was.

He didn't appear and Chief didn't start barking.

'God knows where he is,' Spencer said, looking around, 'but if there's no word from Chief, Tim's not around here.'

Dave stuck his head into the hut and called out, but there was no answer. He took a step inside and looked at the piano.

'Gee, it's a beauty, isn't it?' he said to Spencer, who'd followed him in.

'Just because there isn't a front door,' Spencer said, 'doesn't mean we can just go in.'

Dave ran his hands over the piano and lifted the lid. 'I know, but it really is a nice piece.' He went to shut it again. 'Okay, let's go . . .'

An old yellowing newspaper clipping fluttered down into the dust and Dave leaned over to pick it up. There was a black and white photo at the top of a column and underneath were the words: *Wanted: information on the whereabouts of Marianne Tucker. Missing since Thursday, 7 March 1945.* The contact details were via the Oakamanda Pub. He reread twice, then flicked it over. In scrawly, faded handwriting he made out a dollar sign and the number three hundred.

Wordlessly, he handed it over to Spencer.

Back at the station, Dave worked overtime to get a warrant to pull Tim's financial records. He didn't really have enough to go on—only one statement with one withdrawal, but they'd matched it back to a deposit in Glen's bank account. A good lawyer would argue that until the bank could confirm who had made the deposit, it was only circumstantial evidence. Dave didn't agree. He was convinced that for some reason Tim was putting money into Glen Bartlett's bank account. Spencer helped him embellish a little and within twenty-four hours they had the paperwork needed.

Together they walked to the bank and asked to see the manager.

'Can we have the last six months of statements for Timothy Tucker,' Spencer asked, putting the warrant on his desk.

Immediately the bank manager straightened. 'What are you wanting with Tim?' he asked. 'He's my best client.'

'I'm sure he is, but we still need access to his accounts please.' He held out the paper and the manager flicked through it before throwing it heavily on the table. 'What's going on?'

'We'll be able to tell you in time, but not now. If we could get the information stated on the warrant, please.'

It didn't take long before they had everything they needed.

Spencer was the colour of chalk as they drove to Tim's place.

Again the humpy was empty, but this time Chief was roaming around outside and let out a ferocious round of barking.

'Better stay in the car,' Spencer said. 'I'd say if Chief is here by himself, then Tim's at the pub.'

❧

Tim and China were sitting next to each other at the bar of the Oakamanda Pub and Dee was behind the counter talking to them.

Glancing up, she smiled and motioned Dave and Spencer inside.

'Come in, come in. Look, I've got it almost like new again,' she said with a throaty laugh.

'Looks great, Dee,' Dave agreed. 'G'day, fellas,' he said, pulling up a stool on one side of Tim and China, while Spencer sat on the other side. 'How's tricks?'

Both men answered 'Good' and they all shook hands.

'Everything seems to have gone very quiet,' Dee said with a relieved look on her face. 'No nightly visitors. It's great.'

'The trespassers seem to have dropped off too,' China said.

'Great news. Hopefully I won't get any reports of anyone putting a gun in anyone's face,' Spencer said. 'I get a bit edgy when things like that happen.'

China turned to him. 'Has that happened recently?'

'Hmm, I had a report from a bloke who's been trying to buy up land around here for a mining company. Said there was some old codger who pulled a pistol on him. Neither of you know anything about that, do you?'

Dave held his surprise in check—he didn't know anything about this report.

'Not me,' said China. 'But he's been to my joint. I just told him to fuck off. Said if he came back I'd push him into a mine shaft.'

Dave gave a mirthless chuckle. 'I wouldn't be saying stuff like that, China. You'll get yourself into trouble. We're looking for a murderer, you know.'

'Well, I ain't the bloke you're looking for. Just thought it might frighten him off.'

'It should've,' Spencer agreed. 'After all, it's not long happened to someone.'

Tim took a pull on his beer. 'It was me who pulled the gun,' he said.

Spencer shifted his attention to him. 'That right, old mate? Now what did you go doing that for? I've told you, ring me and I'll come out.'

'He'd been around three or four times and wouldn't leave. I just encouraged him a little.'

'Mate, you're lucky he didn't want to press charges. He would've had every right to.'

'But he didn't.'

Dave leaned back and looked at Spencer. They'd agreed on the way out here that Dave would take the lead—he wasn't local and could ask questions he wouldn't know the answer to.

'Ever married, China?' Dave asked.

'What? Me? Nope. What woman'd have me? Or rather, who'd want to come and live out here?'

'Don't get lonely?'

'Like me own company. Women just nag, don't they?'

'Oi!' Dee flicked the tea towel, which as ever was in handy reach on her shoulder, in his direction.

'Go on then, I'll have another one if you insist, Dee,' China said cheekily.

'What about you, Tim? Anyone ever caught your heart?'

'Oh, yeah,' Tim answered. 'My girl was the best. Beautiful and hot-headed. She was part Italian, you know.'

'Fiery then?'

'I used to call it passionate,' he said with a faraway smile.

'Did you have any kids?'

'We did, but they died. They're buried out on my plot. I go and talk to them occasionally, but it's years and years ago. You get used to living without them, and living with the pain instead.'

There was a pause and Dave wasn't sure how to frame his next question. As it turned out, he didn't have to.

'Gee, in all my time here I never knew that. What happened to your wife?' Dee asked, leaning on the bench with a sympathetic look.

'Don't like to talk about it, so I don't usually. She died.' Tim put his beer down and looked at her.

'Ah, shit, Tim, I had no idea. I'm really sorry.' Dee looked horrified at her own question. 'I'd never even thought about you having a woman—you, China and Killjoy have just always been here by yourselves. Assumed it had always been that way.'

'Not for me,' Tim said quietly.

Dave knew it was time to throw his hat in the ring.

'Do either of you know a bloke called Glen Bartlett?'

China was shaking his head before he'd finished saying the name. 'Don't know anyone called Glen, do you, Tim? What's he do?'

'He's the body down the mine,' Spencer said and held Tim's gaze.

Tim looked down at the table and pressed his lips together. 'I know him.'

The silence stretched out and Spencer dropped his head. 'You silly old bugger,' he muttered to himself.

Dave wasn't sure if he was talking to himself or Tim.

'How do you know him, Tim?' Dave asked.

Dee and China were looking from one person to the other, trying to figure out what the hell was going on.

'I answered his ad.'

'What ad?'

'I saw an ad saying he was looking for the family of a woman who'd gone missing in 1945 from the Barrabine area. I've been trying to find Marianne since the day she walked out of our camp and never came back. I saw his ad and answered it, hoping he'd have the answers I've been needing for fifty-two years.' He looked down at the bar.

'Trying to find . . . I thought you said she died?' Dee said.

Silence again.

'Want to tell me about it?' Spencer asked

'Not really, but I guess I don't have a choice. I figure you know everything already.'

Spencer paused before answering. Finally, as if it hurt him, he said: 'We know enough, Tim, but you can fill in the gaps for us.'

Dee leaned forward to say something but Dave shook his head.

'Marianne didn't die,' Tim said eventually. 'I've always told everyone she did because I didn't want to think she could just walk away. But she did. One morning she was at camp, smiling and cooking breakfast. Although her smile was never the same after the children died. Kenneth, Pammy and Kelly—they were her world. More than me, but I could live with that because I knew she loved me too, just not as much.

'I'd wanted a good breakfast because I had a big day underground. Mari cooked me bacon, eggs and beans with damper. I told her I didn't know when I'd be home, but it would be after dark. She kissed me goodbye and when I came home she was nowhere to be found.'

Dave stole a look at Dee, whose mouth was beginning to tremble.

'How did the children die, Tim?' Dave asked.

A look of pain crossed his features. 'Kenneth and Pammy fell down a mine shaft. One I hadn't covered. They weren't supposed to stray far from camp and they didn't usually. I don't know what happened that day, why they went outside their boundaries and why Mari didn't realise. She always kept such an eagle eye on the kids. You have to out here. So many things can kill them. Her screams were enough to bring me home. I found them about half an hour later. They must've died on impact.' He blinked.

'Kelly, that was another matter. I still to this day don't know how a brown snake got into her cot. By the time we found her, she was cold.' He looked up and stared at Spencer. 'She had three puncture wounds to her body.'

Tears were streaming down Dee's face and Dave decided he'd better put the closed sign up on the door. He didn't want anyone coming in and interrupting.

'Six weeks after we buried Kelly, Mari went missing.' His voice became loud. 'I couldn't believe she'd walk out on me. I was grieving too—I wanted us to do it together, but she turned away from me every time I went to comfort her. It was like she blamed me for their deaths.' His fists clenched in and out, then he let out a deep breath and seemed to shrink into himself.

'I supposed in a way I was to blame. I wanted to be out here. Wanted to find gold. I didn't have the fever as bad as some, but I had it. I'll admit it. It was my fault.'

'Tim, I need to ask,' Dave said, 'you answered an ad in the paper because you thought she walked away from you?'

'I think the pain she had to bear was amplified every day she woke up and looked at the country, our mines, their graves! I never believed she killed herself but I did think she moved away because she couldn't be here.' He sat ramrod straight and shook his head. Then his voice dropped. 'And because she couldn't look at me anymore. Marianne didn't want to be around me because she blamed me for the children's deaths and the torment she was enduring.'

There was a pain-filled silence, broken only by the fridge's motor kicking in and out.

'So how did you meet Glen?' Dave asked, his voice sounding loud.

'I saw his ad, so I wrote to him, telling him all about the circumstances in which Marianne disappeared. He answered, via the pub here, and said he had information on Marianne. I think his exact words were: 'I have information on the woman you are wanting to know about. If you send me three hundred dollars I'll give you the information.''

Dave couldn't help it, he groaned out loud. 'You gave him all the information he needed to extort money from you, Tim!'

Tim continued to talk as if he hadn't heard. 'And three hundred dollars turned into three hundred every fortnight. You've got to understand I *needed* to know . . . I had to know what happened to her. He would send back photos of a woman who looked like Mari—the first photo, I couldn't hold it I was shaking so much. I have it at the hut. She was in a garden, cutting back some rose bushes. It wasn't a very clear photo, but it was enough for me to believe—hope—it was her. She was old and her hair was tied up in a bun, just like she used to do after she had the kids.' He gave a mirthless harrumph. 'Looking back now, I was stupid. The woman looked nothing like my Mari would've at seventy-eight. I saw what I wanted to see. A black and white photo taken from a distance. He could have put a blonde woman in the picture and I probably would've believe it was my wife.' He pounded his fist lightly on the bar.

'When the request came for another three hundred, I paid it without thinking.'

'How long did this go on for?' Spencer asked.

'Five months.'

'And then he turned up here?'

'Yes.'

'What happened then?'

'He came out and saw me, introduced himself. He was such a nice bloke. Friendly, interested in me. Asked me loads of questions. I felt comfortable with him. And Chief liked him. That was the big thing for me. After we'd spent a bit of time talking, he told me he was here to show me where Marianne was. For another ten thousand dollars.

'Money doesn't matter to me,' Tim explained. 'I've got more than I need and no one to leave it to. I wrote him a cheque on the spot, thinking he must have brought her over with him and she was waiting in Barrabine. I told him if he took me to her now, I'd give him the three small nuggets I'd found earlier that day. I had them in my pocket. I would have given him my fortune if I'd thought I was going to see her again.' Tim shook his head. 'When you want something so badly, you'll do anything for it. Anything.

'But when I followed him in my ute, he took me to a clearing and pointed to an old grave. Of course, I knew it was there—I know this country like the back of my hand and I'd heard the story of the nameless woman who'd been buried here.' He sighed. 'Maybe I was naive, but I never once entertained the idea of her being my Mari. Like I said, she needed to get away from me, not life. I thought he was joking.' He looked down at the bar mat and started to rub it between his fingers. 'He wasn't.'

China was staring incredulously at his friend and Dee just looked sad.

'He told me how his father had buried a woman with long black hair. He told me about an ivory and gold locket around her neck. His father hadn't seen it at first because her neck was . . . swollen.' Tim bit out the word. 'Apparently it caught his eye as he was burying her. It had to be her. No one else would have had a necklace like that.' His voice trailed off. 'She'd been here all the time.' Pause. 'Close to me.' Pause. 'Within reach.' His head snapped up. 'I couldn't believe how angry I was. I'd never felt anything like it in all my life. I suddenly knew I wanted to kill him.' He shrugged. 'I told him there was something I wanted him to have and got him to jump in my ute. I drove him back to the mine shaft. I think he thought I was going to give him more gold nuggets to thank him. I led him over to the shaft, my shovel in my hand. When he was nearly there, I hit him hard and he fell. And that was it.'

The silence was only broken by Dee, crying again. China looked ill.

'Where's the cheque you wrote him, Tim?' Spencer asked quietly.

'He'd put it in the glove box of his car and I took it out.'

'Your fingerprints aren't in there.'

'Gloves.'

'So you went back out there?'

'Yes. I cleaned it of anything that would lead to me. There wasn't much, just the cheque.'

'And a newspaper with the ad in it,' Dave said softly.

Tim looked up at him in surprise, then he shrugged with a half-smile. 'Well then,' he said, resigned.

Spencer looked sad as he stood up. 'I wish you'd talked to me, old friend,' he said. 'Tim Tucker, I'm arresting you for the murder of Glen Bartlett.'

'No!' Dee cried out.

'Mate.' China looked stricken.

'I did it,' Tim said quietly. 'You gotta let me go.'

Chapter 32

'I've finally got the bastard!' Spencer let out a whoop.

Dave looked up, surprised. 'What are you working on?' he asked. 'I thought everything was wrapped up.'

'Come with me,' was all Spencer said.

They pulled up in front of Jaffa's and walked into the hotel reception. 'I need to see Ross Pollard, please.'

'I'll ring through to his room.'

Dave took Spencer aside. 'What's this all about?'

'Just watch.'

Ross came through the door, a large smile on his face. 'Detectives! Great to see you again. To what do I owe the pleasure?'

Spencer reached out and yanked his hands behind his back.

'Ross Pollard, I'm arresting you for harassing lease owners, damage to the Oakamanda Pub and for causing fear with intent.'

The girl behind reception screamed and stumbled back into the office, shutting the door quickly.

Dave only just had time to react to the charge when Ross twisted away and broke into a run.

'Fucker,' yelled Spencer.

Dave took off on foot and chased him down the street. People scattered every which way until finally Ross started to slow and Dave, whose pace hadn't changed, grabbed his arm and shoved him against the wall.

Out of nowhere Ernie appeared and helped hold him still while Dave got out his cuffs.

'Bad move, dickhead,' he puffed and slapped the cuffs on his wrist. 'Cheers, Ernie. You make a great neighbour and helper. Glad I got to know you.'

❧

'And it turns out,' Spencer yelled delightedly from across the bar, 'Ross Pollard was paid on commission from HMA Mining. No sales, no money. I looked into his bank records and found that he's in a bucketload of debt. Gambling, prostitutes. Turns out he was the one Narla spoke to us about the night we got called to the brothel; the one who was getting a bit rough with the girls. He would go in with a bundle of money and offer them extra to do perverted things.'

'What the hell?' Dave said.

'Long and the short of it, he needed money. So he tried to scare people into selling.' Spencer raised his beer. 'He won't be doing that again in a hurry!'

'Here's to Spencer,' Dave raised his beer, and a cheer went around the room.

Everyone broke off into smaller groups and started talking loudly.

Dave went to Melinda and put his arm around her. 'Who would've thought the case was going to end with a chase through the streets of Barrabine, hey? Just like the movies,' he grinned. 'Have you heard any more on Janelle?'

'She moved into her unit today. I went and saw her before I came here, but she's doing so much better. Maddie, oh my God, she's a pudgy, healthy little thing who just loves to laugh. She's gorgeous.'

'Good news all round,' Dave said. Then he noticed she didn't have a drink. 'Do you want a drink?'

'Well, actually, no,' she said. She pulled his ear down to her mouth and whispered in it.

Dave blinked. 'Sorry, what?'

'I'm pregnant.' Melinda was grinning from ear to ear. 'I'm pregnant!'

'Pregnant?'

She nodded. 'That's why I've been feeling so tired and squirmy.' She squeezed his arm. 'We're going to have a baby.'

Dave took her face between his hands and kissed her. 'Wow,' he muttered against her lips. His hands found their way to her belly and he touched her gently, his mouth still on hers.

'Come on, you two,' Kathy's voice filtered through the haze. 'I'll have to book you a room if you don't stop that.'

Dave pulled away and put his arm around Melinda.

'I'm going to be a dad,' he muttered. 'A dad?' Then he let out a whoop. 'I'm going to be a dad!'

Acknowledgements

Researching *Fool's Gold* was illuminating to say the least. The brothel tour, museums and mine tours were incredible fun. It's hard to visit the area and not to fall in love (as Detective Dave has done) with the landscape and dirt. And even though I find it hard to understand the drive of individual miners, searching for the elusive gold, I appreciate the need to keep prospecting until they find that life-changing nugget. It's a hard and harsh landscape in the goldfields—hellishly hot, wild and untamed, a law unto itself—and these people continue to prospect, walking over hundreds of kilometres of land in the quest for gold. I've tried it and it's certainly like looking for a needle in a haystack, or rather a five-millimetre piece of gold amongst millions of hectares. To all the prospectors who have inspired this book, I wish you luck.

'A head full of fears has no room to dream.' Lisa Bevere wrote that and it's the truth. Writing and creativity is all about dreaming and scheming and coming up with ideas, so it can be quite annoying when fear crowds in and there is a deadline looming!

Special thanks to Gaby Naher, Tom Gilliatt, Annette Barlow, Christa Munns and Julia Stiles, who not only help me overcome those fears but polish a rusty piece of work into something shiny.

Carolyn and Heather do the same, but usually with a bit more 'no nonsense' attitude! (To translate: 'Fleur, sit your arse down and write.') S'okay girls, I know you love me!

I've said before, pulling a book together involves a whole publishing house, so massive thanks to all those behind the scenes: Klara, Matt, Tami, Andrew and anyone who I've missed.

To Kiri, from the Ora Banda Pub, and Tim—your generosity to the stranger who walked in through the door without any warning and asked for some stories, thank you. I hope you can recognise some of them in here, with a lot of poetic licence!

To Mick Dowie from the Major Organised and Crime Squad (Rural) in Queensland, thanks for the three incredible, informative and fun days I had with you and your team. Detective Dave is a lot more equipped to handle anything crime throws at him now!

Again, massive love and appreciation to all my 'family who are not': Carolyn and Aaron, Emma and Pete, Garry, Heather, Jan and Pete, Robyn and Scottish. I wouldn't be who I am without your love and support. And to my canine support team—Jack-the-kelpie, Rocket and Beardog—love the way you keep my feet warm and don't answer me back!

Rochelle and Hayden, love you long time. Follow your dreams, work hard and never give up.

To all who love Detective Dave: there is no possible way I could have known when I first created him back in *Red Dust* how much of a beloved character he was going to become. I hope you now enjoy his journey from 1997 to the present day—all of his good times, achievements and heartaches—I'm about to hit him with as many as I can!

AN ORIGINAL STORY

The Farmer's Choice

It's 1990 and twenty-three-year-old Dave Burrows has
returned from agricultural college full of ideas and plans
to improve the family's farm. But his father sees only extra-
vagance in his son's innovations and Dave is pushed to the
outer while his older brothers, Dean and Adam, find their
father's favour. Dean's approaching wedding has everyone
on edge and the tensions erupt, causing Dave's life to veer
in an unexpected direction.

Chapter 1

1990

The motorbike pulled up with a spray of gravel in front of the large, lush garden.

Struggling to her feet, Carlene pulled off her gloves and stood up from the garden bed she was tending. She put her hands on her hips, drawing her brow into a deep frown and wagging her finger in a no-no fashion.

The rider had a large grin, even though his face was covered with a helmet. Her twenty-three-year-old youngest son always had a smile on his face for her, which matched his easy-going personality and she was so glad to have him home after four years of ag college. He brought a sunniness to the farm which hadn't been here before he arrived home.

'If you spray anymore gravel towards my garden, David Burrows, I swear you'll be out there raking it all back by hand. Your brother's wedding is only days away!' Carlene doubted he heard her words over the roar of the engine, but she felt compelled to remind him—even though she said it almost every day.

The farmyard was stunned into silence as Dave killed the engine and pulled off his helmet, still sitting astride the bike. 'Hi, Mum. Back making everything look perfect again?'

'The garden won't take care of itself, you know, and Mandy and Dean will be walking down the path in four days! The countdown is on, Dave.'

'I know, I know. But it has to be fifty degrees out here. Surely you could wait until it is cooler. Or at least get the groom-to-be to help you. Come on inside and I'll pour you a drink.'

Carlene smiled and watched as Dave got off the motorbike, dressed in shorts and a tank top. His short brown hair was slicked with sweat from where the helmet had sat. She reached out and patted his arm. 'I think you're exaggerating about the temperature. That's very kind of you, darling, but I need to keep on. Have you seen your father?'

'Not since yesterday.' He kicked the stand of the motorbike down. 'I'll bring you out something cold, then,' he said and bounded up the stone steps into the old homestead.

Adjusting her wide-brimmed hat, Carlene pulled her gloves on and turned back to the agapanthus she'd been deadheading before Dave had arrived. Thinking about her three boys, she knew that Dave was the most thoughtful out of all of them. And perhaps the most sensitive. Dean, her eldest, was serious and quiet, whereas Adam used his charm and good looks to draw people to him. They were all so different, her boys, but the one thing which linked them together was their vivid blue eyes—that was the one feature she recognised from her side of the family. Their broad foreheads and high cheekbones came from their father, Sam.

As she thought of her husband, her brow furrowed again and she turned to look out over the paddocks, hoping to see dust rising in the distance. All she saw was a shimmering mirage over the line of hills that bordered their property. The wheat paddocks had all been harvested, and the grain carted to the nearby silos at Northam. Now, the paddocks of golden stalks had ewes grazing in them, instead of large machines, which just days ago had seemed to eat up the wheat as they'd been driven in endless straight lines.

Dave had made sure the ewes were drenched and ready to put out into these stubbles as soon as the paddocks were harvested, so they wouldn't need hand-feeding unless the break of the season was late.

Turning towards the main road, where the cattle should have been camped on the dam in the midday sun, Carlene looked carefully but couldn't see any dust or cattle chasing the tractor to grab their first sweet mouthful of hay.

'Where are you?' she whispered to herself, slowly turning in circles, hoping to catch a glint of a vehicle or a cloud of dust.

Sam hadn't come home for lunch, which was unusual. Usually she'd hear his heavy footsteps pounding up the garden path at 11.56 am on the dot. That gave him four minutes to get inside, wash his hands and be sitting at the table when the ABC's Country Hour came onto the wireless. Today, his place at the table had been empty. When she'd walked up to the shearing shed, it had been silent and unoccupied. Further investigation had found his ute was missing too. Perhaps he was out checking waters, or stock. Carlene hoped he wasn't checking Dave's work. And, even if he was, it was unlike him to miss lunch.

She sighed, her secateurs automatically snipping at the long, dry stems of the flowers and piling them up next to her on the lawn. Her instincts told her he was still smarting from last night's disagreement.

With all three boys now living and working together at Wind Valley Farm, it was like pups fighting for food, except they were arguing about who should do what and how it should be done. Sam was used to being the boss and didn't like it when his authority was challenged. All the boys had gone to agricultural college and embraced new ideas for the farm—not necessarily in agreement with each other. Dean was certainly interested in all the innovative new cropping systems, which were now coming into play—things she'd never heard of before like tram lines, nil-till and raised beds. He'd taken a trip to New Zealand with the college and learned about them, bringing the ideas home. Sam had shot his ideas down in flames at first, but gradually, somehow, Dean had been able to talk him around.

Adam was more interested in the financial side. He'd brought home a new financial program called Agrimaster. No matter how much Adam tried, Sam wouldn't have anything to do with the large computer, which sat on top of the bench in the kitchen—he certainly wouldn't allow it in his office.

The interesting thing Carlene had noticed was that Adam wasn't at all keen on some of the technology which Dean had brought home. She'd heard him say the raised beds were short-sided and what did they need them in Northam for anyway? It didn't rain as much as it did in the southern part of Western Australia. Dean had responded that it might help harvest the water and Adam had scoffed.

Her youngest son Dave seemed to have other ideas—about fixing the place up, making sure that every part of it was operational, then he wanted to research what was best for Wind Valley Farm.

What was becoming clear was that Sam was stuck in his ways, and didn't want to change the way he farmed now. What was also apparent was that he would listen, if only half-heartedly, to the two older boys, but he considered that whatever poor Dave had to say wasn't worth listening to. Why the three boys couldn't sit down with a beer and talk about what they wanted to achieve was beyond her. The whole situation worried her.

'Here, Mum.'

Carlene looked up to see Dave carrying two large glasses of lemon cordial. It looked like he'd emptied the ice container into the glass!

'Thanks, darling.' She swiped the sweat from her forehead as she straightened up. 'I do think I need that drink after all.'

'Come and sit on the verandah for a couple of minutes,' Dave said. 'Two minutes break won't hurt you!'

'Probably not.'

Together they climbed the stairs and sat on a wooden bench seat. 'Do you remember helping me paint this chair?' Carlene asked Dave as she sat down heavily. She didn't want to admit it, but the heat really was getting to her today.

'Yeah. I think I started it without you knowing and then we had no choice but to finish it.'

Carlene nodded, a small smile playing at her lips. 'Yeah, you were always the one who could find trouble.'

'I'm not sure it was completely my fault. If Grandad hadn't left an open tin and a paintbrush at the door, it probably would've never crossed my mind to find something to paint.'

'Your grandfather was tidying up my front door and outside window frames. I'm almost sure he didn't invite you to paint the seat!'

'No, but I *have* always liked to help,' Dave answered, his blue eyes twinkling.

'Isn't that the truth?' she said, giving him a loving squeeze.

'Have you got much left to do here, Mum?' Dave asked, changing the subject. 'It's really too hot for you to be working in the middle of the day. It may not be fifty, but it's certainly over forty degrees.' He frowned, then muttered, 'Who'd get married in the middle of bloody summer in the wheat belt?'

Elbowing him, she answered, 'Your brother. And the house has to look beautiful for him and Mandy. Have you and Adam been back into town to try your suits on?'

'I've organised to go tomorrow. Haven't talked to Adam since last night.' He shrugged. 'His car's been gone all day, but I didn't hear him leave this morning.'

'Hmm, I suppose he's gone to see Tiffany.' An image of her middle son and his girlfriend came to her—they'd been in the shed with Adam shearing and Tiffany working the board. They'd seemed to work in fluid motion, knowing what each other was doing without having to look. She was sure that match was more suited than Dean and Mandy . . .

'Probably.' Dave interrupted her thoughts.

They silently looked across the large lawn and garden, which Carlene had lovingly planted from runners and seeds thirty years ago when she'd been a new bride and Sam had brought her to the farm which had been his parents'. He'd been the last-born child and his parents were elderly and not living on the farm by the time Carlene and Sam had married.

She looked up at the house, then across the garden with satisfaction. When she'd arrived the whole area had been run-down, paint peeling and no garden to speak of. Now the house was freshly painted and tidy. The garden, well, her friends in the CWA said it could go in the Open Garden scheme, but she didn't think so. There was still a lot to do before it was that good.

'Remember how you'd always have parts of the garden roped off when you were trying to get the lawn going?' Dave asked. 'If we were in there, woe betide us!'

'And more often than not, I'd catch you using the ropes for hurdle practice just before sports day,' Carlene remembered with a laugh.

Dave responded, 'That's why I always won the race.'

The multicoloured roses lined the edges of the large garden, with bushes and climbers covering the fence. Tall leafy trees blocked the midday sun from the kitchen and lounge areas of the house. It was a cool sanctuary in the middle of the burning summer heat and would be perfect for Dean's wedding, she thought.

'When do all of Mandy's family get here?' Dave wanted to know. 'I've mowed all the long grass over at the shearers' quarters, so they should be able to see if there are any snakes around. Can't wait to see what the city slickers do if they come across one.'

'Hopefully they won't. I'm not sure Anne would cope.' She thought back to the previous Christmas when Mandy's family had spent two days over the festive season with them. Anne had worn white pants and sandals. By morning smoko of the first day, the grey dirt had coated her outfit and she'd managed to get grass seeds under her toes. Since then, this would be their first visit back.

'Do you know what Dad was doing this morning?' Carlene asked casually. 'He didn't come in for lunch.'

Dave gave a disgruntled snort. 'He'd never bother to tell me what his plans were. You're better off asking the other two more important sons.'

Frustration shot through her. 'Dave,' she turned and looked at her son, a stern expression on her face, 'that's not how it is and you know it. You've all got the same importance in this family and are equal in the business.

I don't understand why you all can't get along.' *And that includes your father,* she thought.

Dave leaned back against the chair and crossed his arms. 'I get along with my brothers alright, you know that, Mum. Not as good as you'd like, I know, but we can talk to each other. But Dad? You can deny it all you want and smooth things over when the arguments start, but Dean and Adam are who Dad wants here, not me. He gets their opinions on all of the big decisions, never bothers to ask me. Not since . . .' He stopped, then looked over at Carlene. 'Still, it doesn't bother me too much. I'm farming here on Wind Valley and you know that's all I've ever wanted to do.'

Carlene looked across the paddocks, again, anxiety trickling through her. 'I know that, son.'

Chapter 2

Dave walked into his small bedroom in the shearers' quarters and slammed the door shut. Fiddling with the knobs on the portable air-conditioner, he used the bucket to pour water into the back of it, then switched it on. He bent down and let the breeze flow onto his face until all the sweat had dried and his body began to cool down.

Summer in Australia, he thought. *Heat, flies and endless sun.* Thinking about his mates from ag college, he wondered where they all were. Jimmy was probably still at home on the farm, working his way up the pecking order; and he'd heard Zappa had got a job managing a feedlot in the eastern states.

Maybe he should call Jimmy. It'd been a while since they'd spoken and he might be having the same problems at home as Dave was having here. Perhaps they could organise a weekend in Perth—head to the OBH and get a skinful. Soak up a bit of sun down at 'the Cott'. Dave liked

Cottesloe beach even though it was always crowded. The water was clear and cold and made for good swimming.

His eyes wandered across to the faded photo pinned to the wall next to his pillow. It was of Dave five years ago—a skinny, scrawny bloke of eighteen—with his arm around a girl with long curly hair and curves in all the right places. He wondered what Kim was up to now and wished again they hadn't finished their holiday romance that summer. She'd captivated him from the first time he'd seen her smile and heard her laugh—it had sounded like whiskey, dark chocolate and mischief all rolled into one and Dave wanted to be part of whatever she was involved with.

That summer had been a big adventure: he'd saved up the money to catch a bus all the way from Perth to Adelaide, where his aunty and uncle had picked him up and driven him two and a half hours north to their farm on the outskirts of Spalding. He and his cousin Kate had spent days riding horses and motorbikes, camping out and alternating between working and playing on the farm. Then the family had all packed up and gone to Wallaroo, on the coast, to their holiday shack. He'd met Kim on the beach.

Kim had been wearing a bikini, and although she had curves in all the right places, it'd been her hair and smile that he'd first noticed. Then once he'd heard her laugh, well, there was no going back.

Having become inseparable for the four weeks he'd been on the coast, his heart had been broken when they'd decided not to try a long-distance relationship. There didn't seem to be any point, she'd said. He was going to uni to study agriculture and Kim was going back to Barker, where her family lived. They could always write. And they had for a while. Then the letters had become fewer and, finally, they had stopped altogether.

He still missed Kim and, since that summer, no other girl had ever turned his head the way she had. Maybe he should write to her and see what she was up to. Or maybe not; finding out Kim had another boyfriend wasn't something Dave wanted to hear.

Pulling the chair away from the wall, he turned it around, before sitting down and resting his arms on the back. Dropping his chin down, and putting Kim out of his mind, he thought about last night's argument with Dad and his mother's desperate attempts to stop it. Her voice had been full of despair, as if she knew that nothing she said would make any difference.

'Sam, stop. You've got to listen to what all the boys have to say, not just the older two,' she'd said in a calming tone. 'Don't you want to keep this operation working well? Somehow you have to find a way to work together, but if you don't . . . God knows what will happen. Can't you see that? We're being torn apart.'

His father had slammed his fist on the table. 'Stay out of it, woman!' he'd roared. 'You don't know what you're talking about.'

Dave hadn't been able to stop the anger that had bubbled so violently to the surface. He'd pushed himself out of his chair and launched himself at Sam, stopping inches from his face. 'Don't speak to her like that!' he'd shouted at his father. Then he'd fallen quiet at the sound of his mother crying and begging him to stop. It wasn't until he'd felt her hand on his arm that he'd walked away.

Adam and Dean had sat still, not moving. Dean had finally got up and looked at them all, the disgust plain on his face. 'And to think I want to bring Mandy into a family who behaves like this,' he'd said, before walking out.

Dave had looked to Adam for support, but he'd been staring down at the table, his cheeks stained red. From anger or embarrassment, Dave hadn't been sure. Dave knew he hated the way his father spoke to his mum. Last time he'd tried to talk to Adam about it during the harvest after his father had yelled at Carlene for not having tea on the table at the allotted time, his brother hadn't responded. Perhaps it had been because he was tired. Or, after this latest confrontation, maybe not. Maybe he agreed, although how Dave couldn't fathom.

He hadn't been able to stay in the house another minute and Carlene had followed him out and said, 'Don't worry about it, Dave. He doesn't mean it.'

But Dave was worried. His sense of what was right and what wasn't had always been strong, even as a little boy. He'd never tolerated bullies or little boys pulling girls' pigtails. What his father had done that night was both bullying and mean. He'd done it before and Dave was sure he'd do it again.

His mother was right, however. If they didn't start pulling together it could mean that the business might be lost. They'd learned about succession planning at ag college and he knew how important it was, but it looked like Sam wasn't going to be entertaining that route anytime soon.

Dave had been home for two years now. He'd arrived back on Wind Valley Farm in the December after he'd finished ag college. Harvest had already started and both Dean and Adam were already working at home and being paid a meagre wage. Dean handled the seeding and Adam ran around behind him.

Dave hadn't been sure where he fitted in, so he did what he thought was right—improve the farm, which included the stock. Both brothers seemed happy to leave the sheep and cattle to Dave as they much preferred the cool air-conditioned cabs of the tractor and header. The yards weren't much fun in the middle of summer or in the winter when the freezing, dry wind howled around the hills and into the valley.

The animal work hadn't bothered Dave—he liked anything to do with farming. It didn't matter what job he was given or how hard or easy it was. As long as he was outside and had his hands in the soil, he was happy. It showed. He'd been awarded the Graduate of Excellence award at his graduation. Only his mum had been there to see that. Everyone else had been busy with the harvest.

By the time the harvest had finished in 1988, Dave had completed the drenching program, weaned the calves and started to change the water system so it was more reliable than waiting for water to siphon down from tank to tank to tank, and then into the troughs in the paddocks. More often than not, he'd been out checking the animals and paddocks and found troughs near empty and, in forty-plus heat, that wasn't an option.

Maybe he should have asked his dad's approval before buying a solar pump worth two thousand dollars, but they could afford it and it had been hard to track down. His dad had been keeping crazy hours, working sometimes eighteen hours a day to beat the summer storms, which usually arrived in January.

Peace of mind when it came to water, in Dave's opinion, was a no brainer.

He'd rerun the wires of the more rundown fences and cleaned out the sheep feeders ready for the hand-feeding, which would start once the sheep had finished on the stubbles. He'd spent hours walking the land of Wind Valley Farm, working out where soils changed and marking where soil tests would be best taken from. He'd revelled in the clear air, open spaces and creating a strong and viable farming enterprise. Flocks of galahs and white cockatoos had kept him company, as had his kelpie, Jip.

At first, when the harvest had finished, his father, Dean and Adam had been full of praise for him. His brothers could now have January off, which meant a potential holiday to the beach. All the stock work had already been finished. And Dave had done it all single-handedly. There was nothing left to do at all, other than normal stock checks.

But then his father had gone into the office and seen the invoices for the pumps and soil tests. 'You've made management decisions without speaking to me,' his father had said with suppressed anger. 'This is my farm. I'm in charge. Not you. Not your brothers. Me. I've worked hard to get here and just because you've got some fancy piece of paper saying you think you're shit hot doesn't give you any right to come in here and take over. You have to start at the bottom and work your way up.'

Dave didn't disagree with him—he knew a farmer needed to know how to do every job on a farm and, of course, the youngest son coming home from ag college wasn't going to be given the best jobs.

'Never ask a man to do a job you wouldn't do yourself,' his grandfather had told him.

But even understanding his father's way of thinking, surely Sam could see what he'd done, the improvements he'd made. Now there was never any chance of the stock running out of water. The fences were in tip-top condition and everyone knew what fertiliser was needed for the soil. These changes he'd made—small as they were—weren't they beneficial for everyone?

From then on, their relationship had never been the same and every time Sam was able to give out a crappy job, it was Dave who got it. At first, Dean and Adam had been supportive of Dave, offering to do some of the jobs and standing up to their father. Their help, however, had only made their lives difficult.

'Stay out of it,' Sam had told the two brothers. 'I'll get who I want to do what I want.'

As time had gone on, they'd liked not having to get under the shearing shed and shovel the shit out and, even though they'd both confessed to Dave over a beer that they felt uncomfortable seeing him get into silos and clean out rotten grain, they were pleased not to have to do it themselves. Over time, they'd started to see Dave as the 'shit-kicker', not their brother.

Sighing, Dave flopped on his bed and stared at the ceiling, his hands behind his head. He wondered if things would change much once Mandy moved out to Wind Valley into the cottage on the other side of the property that she and Dean had been gradually renovating and painting. In reality, he didn't think so. Perhaps her sunny nature might help lighten the atmosphere in the main house, as well as Dean's personality—which always seemed to be dark and brooding, like their father. Or maybe the Burrows family would rub off on Mandy. He hoped not.

Glancing outside, he realised the shadows were beginning to lengthen. The sheep would be out grazing now, so he knew he should go and muster the last paddock of ewes that hadn't been drenched. He could do them first thing in the morning, in the cool.

Pulling himself up, he turned off the air-conditioner and grabbed his helmet, before slamming the door behind him and calling to Jip.

Chapter 3

When Dave pushed open the door, the pub was noisy with roaring laughter and smelled like spilled beer and sweat.

It had only taken him thirty minutes to get the sheep in the yards, with the help of Jip, and he'd decided to reward himself with a beer and a Sunday evening feed at the local pub in Northam. Being only twenty minutes drive away, he thought he could use the company of the customers. He needed a break from Wind Valley Farm.

When he'd called in past the house to tell his mum he wouldn't be there for dinner, he'd seen his dad's ute parked outside. While he'd been there, Dave had asked his mum where Sam had been and why he'd missed lunch. She had just raised her shoulders in a shrug. Then he'd emptied two wheelbarrows full of cuttings into the rubbish bins and asked if there was anything more he could do before he left. She'd said no.

He hated seeing his mum slaving away in the house and the garden without any help and seeing her spoken to as if she were dirt, but he felt powerless to change anything.

'Davo, how goes?' asked Jack, one of the blokes on his cricket team. 'Harvest all done?'

'Yeah, mate. Finished a couple of weeks ago. What about you?'

'Done and dusted for another year. Good yields. Should help keep the wolf from door. Not like last year. Hope I never see another harvest like that again. Hardly got our seed back.' He took a long pull of his beer as if he were trying to wash away any memories of the drought which had hit hard, over three long years. Rain clouds had taunted them as they'd scurried over the sky, carried along by the strong, cold wind, but they hadn't dropped much rain. A few millimetres, every month or so, at best.

Selling stock had been the first thing his father had done—and Dave hadn't agreed with his decision. Sam had wanted to sell the core breeding ewes, rather than the lambs and wethers. Dave had argued with his father that it would cost too much to buy ewes back in and it would be best to keep them for as long as they could. Sam had ignored Dave's comments, and the other brothers had gone along with what their father had chosen to do.

Dave handed over a ten dollar note to the bartender and got a beer in return with some change. 'I hear you. Farming's easy when you get the rain and the sun at the right time.'

'And a shit of a profession to be in when it's not! Are you on the countdown to the big day?'

'Five days tomorrow. Things are mad. Mum is still snipping away at the garden and I think tomorrow is when all the people helping start turning up—caterers doing all the prep work and such.'

'Yeah, all the CWA ladies are going there first thing in the morning. Must be carting all the tables and so on out tomorrow. Anyways, Georgie wants to know if Mandy will join the CWA when she gets here. Can you make sure Mandy knows? Need to make her feel welcome, don't we?'

'I guess so. Still she's met a few of us over the past couple of years. She should fit in pretty easily.' Dave was about to ask if Jack had noticed any signs of worm burden in his sheep when his friend spoke again.

'Hoping to catch Dean for a beer before he ties the knot. Reckon we should organise a few with the team?'

'Probably wouldn't be a bad idea.' He glanced around and saw Adam was sitting in the dining room with Tiffany and her family. Unexpectedly, Dave felt a sense of loneliness envelope him. Life was changing quickly. Dean was about to be married and Adam seemed to be moving more towards his girlfriend's family. And with the harvest finished and all of the marriage arrangements happening, Dean hadn't been around much.

The three brothers had been close as kids but, somehow, as they'd got older and drifted in different directions, they'd grown apart. It saddened Dave; he missed the camaraderie he'd had with Dean and Adam. He was also positive that the breakdown in relations between the brothers and their father upset his mum more than she ever let on.

He shook himself out of his reverie. As his grandfather had often said to him, there was no use wallowing in self-pity as no one ever took any notice. He turned back and looked at Jack. 'We'd better get on with it if we're going to make this happen in time.'

'Leave it with me,' Jack answered. 'I'll be able to work something out.' He gave a wink and ordered another beer.

Dave took his drink into the restaurant and grabbed a seat at a table set for two. He half hoped Adam and Tiffany would invite him to join them, but they were sitting with their backs to him and hadn't seen Dave come in.

Listening as Adam laughed and talked, Dave took another sip of his beer. He really needed to be the one to pull them all together, he decided. They couldn't lose their family and Wind Valley Farm just because of in-house fighting. Or, rather, Sam fighting with Dave.

Grabbing the notepad and pen that he always kept in his pocket, he jotted some ideas down:

Weekly meetings.
Everyone able to speak without being interrupted.
Include Mum and Mandy so everyone feels involved.
Ownership.
Enterprise planning so everyone knows what is going on.
An enterprise each??? Dad—hay making, Dean—cropping,
Adam—cattle, Me—sheep??
Mediation????

He was sure his dad wouldn't agree to either the idea of an enterprise each or the mediation, but it was worth throwing out there. He thought about the time frames—Dean and Mandy would be back from their honeymoon by the middle of January, which was an ideal time for everyone to have this discussion. When they got back, the budgets would need to be done and planning completed for the twelve months ahead. The bank would be wanting to do a review of their finances and would need all this information.

'What can I get you, love?' Katrina, the waitress interrupted his note-taking. He moved his hand over the writing, not wanting her to see it. Katrina was the biggest gossip the town had known and she was friends with Tiffany's mother.

As he looked up, he could see by the expression on her face that she'd already read some of it.

'How are you, Katrina?' he asked, hoping if he engaged her, she might forget.

'Busy.' She looked over her shoulder at the filling restaurant. 'What can I get you?'

'Steak. Medium rare, chips and salad. Thanks.'

'Bring it out to you.' She nodded and gave him another hard stare before going back to the kitchen.

❧

'Hey Mum,' Dave said as he breezed through the kitchen the next morning. He stopped at the smell of chocolate cake and leaned over and put his finger in the bowl. 'Yum, raw mixture. My fav. Where's Dad?'

'Stop that or I'll give your knuckles a rap,' Carlene answered mildly. 'I need all the mixture I can get to feed the hordes arriving.'

'Everyone will be here tomorrow?' he asked.

'Yeah.'

Dave looked at the piles of sheets and blankets on the kitchen table and realised she was cooking and still had to make up beds for all the relatives. 'Do you want me to take any of these down to the rooms for you?' he offered. 'Have the extra beds been made up in the shearers' quarters?'

'Yep, they're all done. I did them while you were out last night.'

Carlene looked up and he saw the beads of sweat on her brow. She looked tired, too. 'Can I do anything for you, Mum?'

She shook her head. 'No, love. I've got everything under control. Your Aunty Peg will be here tomorrow and she'll be able to give me a hand. Once all the CWA ladies get here . . . well, you won't know the place.'

Dave paused. 'What about Mandy's family?'

'The morning of the wedding. I think she and Dean decided not to see each other the week leading up to it.'

Dave didn't respond to that. There were too many things he could say: how about a bit of help was the first one which came to mind.

'And the CWA ladies will be here tomorrow as well. We'll start setting the tables up on the lawn, but we won't put out any of the decorations until the morning of the ceremony. Don't want them getting dusty or faded.'

'Are you doing all of this by yourself?'

'No, no, like I said the CWA ladies and Aunty Peg will be here. I've got everything all organised. The tablecloths and decorations are in the other lounge room, which we never use. I've already got five beds made up, only another four to go. The caterers . . .'

'So, in other words you are doing this all by yourself, Mum. You've organised everything.' Frustration coursed through him. His brother was nowhere in sight. If it had been his own wedding, Dave would be around as much as he could, helping tidy the garden and lug tables and chairs around, not expecting his mother to do it all. Instead, it seemed Dean had disappeared not only from the farm work, but everything else.

'Where's Dean?' he asked.

'I guess he's still in the cottage. He has to get the painting finished so they can stay there on Saturday night. He's still got three rooms to go, from what he said last night.'

'Should dry pretty easily,' Dave commented. 'Maybe once he's finished, he can come and help here.'

His mum fixed him with a pleading stare, but didn't say anything.

He was thrown back to his grandfather's words, once again: 'Be aware of your actions and words, because someone is always watching.' He wondered what his maternal grandfather would've made of the way life was on Wind Valley Farm now? Having lived here very briefly before his death, he'd spent hours when Dave was younger, telling stories and wandering the paddocks together. Dave missed him and knew his mum did too.

Both Dean and Adam spoke to Carlene the way Sam did. They'd learned it from their father. He briefly wondered why he hadn't done the same. But that thought wasn't relevant because he was nothing like his dad and didn't want to be.

'Dave,' his mother put down the wooden spoon and looked at him, 'this is going to be such a special time. Dean's only going to get married once and I want to make sure it's perfect for him and Mandy.'

'They could have helped you.'

'They're busy. At least this way I can make sure everything is done properly. There are only thirty people coming to the wedding—it's not a big one. Hell! I've cooked for larger shearing teams than that in my time!'

'I can see you're tired.'

'I'm fine. Now what did you want with your father?'

Dave shook his head. His mother was stubborn and he knew he wasn't going to win with her. 'I had some ideas,' he said. 'Thought I'd run them past him.'

'Oh, Dave,' his mother groaned. 'Can it wait until after the wedding? I don't want any more issues. Please?'

'But I'm not going to cause any more issues,' he answered, frowning. 'I'm going to solve them.'

'That's what you think. Come on!'

'I'm joking, Mum! I promise.' He decided to file his ideas for the moment, not wanting to upset her. 'I've finished drenching all the sheep. I just wanted to know if he'd prefer me to put them into a different paddock.'

'We always need to change the paddock after they've been drenched. You know that.'

Mother's and son's eyes caught and they looked at each other for a moment.

'I know,' Dave finally said, turning towards the voice of his father. 'I just wasn't sure which one.'

'Where did they come from? The hill paddock?'

'No, these are the three-year-old yellow tags from the valley paddock.'

'Right. They can go into the one against the eastern boundary. I've got to go into town and pick up some oil, so wait until I go before moving them down the road, okay? Otherwise you'll hold me up.'

'Probably too hot to shift them now anyway. I'll wait until this evening.'

'Better to get them out and on water again,' Sam said, looking hard at Dave.

'Sure,' he answered amiably. 'I'll wait until you've gone then.' He tapped his fingers against his legs to keep himself from saying anything more.

'Do you need something in town, love?' Sam turned to his wife and gave her a smile.

'Not that I can think of.' She ran her hands through her short greying hair. 'Nope,' she said again. 'I think I'm organised. Thanks, though, darling.'

Dave noticed the beads of sweat were back on her brow and she looked pale. He looked across at his dad, wondering if he'd noticed. It didn't appear that he had.

'What've you been doing today?' Dave asked, wondering if he should mention that his mum looked unwell.

Sam picked up his wallet from the kitchen bench and put it in his shirt pocket. 'I've nearly finished the budget for next year,' he answered.

'Can I have a look?' Dave asked.

'We'll talk about it after the wedding,' he snapped, as if it were nothing to do with Dave.

'Right.' The silence in the room was heavy. Seeing his mum begin to look upset, he quickly said, 'We're going to organise a few beers with the cricket team boys if you want to come along, Dad. Jacko was keen to give Dean a bit of send-off into married life. Tonight at the club.'

'It's Tuesday.' Sam drew his heavy eyebrows together in his classic look of disapproval.

'We thought it'd be better than trying to do something on the Friday night before a Saturday wedding.'

'Whose we?'

'Jack Gatton has been organising it. Not a big do, just a couple of beers and snacks. Knowing Jacko, it'll be pies from the bakery!'

'I'll see if I can get away.'

Dave nodded, understanding his father would probably prefer to be sitting in his study, sipping whiskey and watching the cricket. 'I'll let you know the time when Jacko tells me. How long before I can head off with the sheep?'

'I'm leaving now. I won't need lunch today, love.' He strode out of the kitchen and, a few moments later, the ute door slammed and they heard the engine start.

'Mum are you okay? You're looking a bit pale.'

'Love, I'm fine,' she answered.

'Best go shift the sheep, then,' Dave said after a pause. Then, sticking his finger in the mixing bowl again and only just avoiding the wooden spoon coming down on his knuckles, he gave Carlene a mischievous grin and walked out.

Chapter 4

The beer glasses clinked in a 'cheers' gesture as Adam stood before the crowd of men. 'And we wish you all the best for your life to come,' he said, looking towards his older brother.

'Hear, hear!' the rest of the group bellowed, raising their glasses.

The club rooms were full of the cricket team and a few other farmers who didn't play, plus a couple of the farm businessmen around town.

Dave leaned back against the wall and watched Dean work the room, talking to everyone—he had his father's outward charm and could talk to anyone and make them laugh. But, inside their family situation, Dave knew how different he was, just like his father. He wondered if Dean would be the same with Mandy. Or did she just see the charisma?

His glance slid across to his father who was deep in conversation with Malcolm Nutt. He let out a loud laugh and slapped Malcolm on the back, nodding in agreement with whatever had just been said.

'G'day, Dave,' Mark Loxton said from next to him.

'Mark, how goes things?' Dave asked above the chatter.

The bank manager, who was also the team's main spin bowler, smiled and indicated towards the crowd. 'Great do. Jacko did a good job of organising it so quickly.'

'He's the man if you want anything social to happen! Busy at work?'

Mark took a sip of his drink. 'Yeah, you know what January is like. Gearing up for all the reviews. At least this year has been kind to most of you farmers. I don't like it when I have to put the hard word on people for repayments and, at the same time, I know there isn't any chance of them being able to make them.' He sighed deeply. 'That is the part I really hate about my job.'

'I can't see that being a lot of fun,' Dave agreed. 'Must be hard when you're so involved in the community.' He knew Mark was not only on the cricket team, but played tennis every Wednesday night and, during winter, was the goal umpire for the footy team.

'Mate, you wouldn't believe how difficult it is.' As he spoke, he looked over his shoulder. 'When I had to sell up the Grainger's farm, last year, it took me weeks to sleep properly again. The old man's face crumpled when I told him there was nothing more I could do for him. If I'd had my way, I would've given him another year, but the head office wouldn't have it. The problem with the big banks is they don't understand the variances of farming:

the seasons, the fluctuations in prices, all the things that can change in the blink of an eye.'

As Dave listened, he realised Mark had had a few too many drinks. The bank manager shouldn't be talking out of school; confidentiality was paramount in his business.

'How are you getting home?' Dave interrupted, thinking even though it was so early in the night, Mark should leave before he said too much more.

'Walking, probably.' He looked up at Dave and stared him straight in the eye, then glanced across to where Sam was still laughing with Malcolm. 'What are you going to do next year now, Dave?'

Pleased to be off sensitive topics, he waved his beer around before answering. 'Just what I've been doing this year. Working on Wind Valley. Trying to improve what I'm allowed to. Dad seems to resist my ideas.'

'Working on the farm still?' Mark's voice rose in surprise, then he seemed to gather himself. 'Well, you know, with the land you've got, I've got my reservations about how it's going to carry four families, Dave.'

'Why's that?' Dave felt the first stirring of apprehension in his stomach.

'Well, the forecast for grain prices isn't good. Now with Dean getting married it has to make a livelihood for both Sam and Carlene, as well as Dean and Mandy. Obviously, couples need more money than singles, but there'll be a time that both you and Adam want to marry. You should think about doing something else, I think. If you want my professional opinion.'

Gritting his teeth, Dave wondered where the hell that comment had come from. 'Thanks for that, Mark. I'll take it on board. Anyway, I'd better go and talk to some others . . .'

Mark grabbed his arm. 'Dave, I'm telling you. You need to think about what you're going to do next year because Wind Valley Farm isn't going to be your future.'

Butterflies rose in Dave's stomach as he thought back to his father's cagey answer about the budget, and his unexpected trip into town that morning and on the previous Monday when he didn't come home for lunch. 'What do you mean?' he asked.

'Look I've said too much already,' Mark answered. 'I just appreciate you've got so much potential as a farmer. You'll be wasted working with your family. Go see if you can make a name for yourself, Dave. Somewhere else. Away from here.' He swayed a little as he raised his glass. 'You'll be a leader somewhere, sometime, Dave. You've got the ability to go far.'

Dave revved his ute's engine and took off, gravel spraying the porch of the club rooms and the cars around him. He drove fast towards Wind Valley, taking the corners too close to the edge of the road. His heart was beating fast and he was sweating, feeling sick. He hoped he was jumping to conclusions, but he was sure Mark's warning had some kind of prior knowledge behind it. What he wanted to do was storm over to his father, in the middle of everyone, and demand to know what was going on. Make the whole community understand what kind of a man Sam really was. But he wouldn't. He would gather evidence first.

Before he'd left Dean's buck's party, he'd made sure his dad was still enjoying the drinks. Sam had gone from talking to Malcolm, to leaning on the bar, chatting to the football coach and acting out moves he thought they should try when the season started again.

Pulling up at the house, he heard the dogs barking, and felt the moisture of the cool night on his skin. Unexpectedly, tears pricked at his eyes; this farm was the only place he wanted to be. He didn't know what he'd do if he wasn't here. What if . . . Dave couldn't even think about the possibility of not being here.

Scratching at his face, he tried to get rid of any trace of tears, annoyed with his weakness.

Finally, composing himself, Dave checked to make sure the lounge light was out, meaning his mum was in bed, and quietly went up the front steps.

Sam's office was at the back of the house and it had been a fun place to be when he'd been younger. The sun filtered through in winter and warmed the room. All the brothers had enjoyed sitting under the window and reading farming magazines, once their dad had finished with them. Summer had seen the curtain drawn tightly to keep the heat out.

There was a photo on the wall of a pen of steers which had topped a sale in Sam's first year of farming and his desk was always neat and tidy. Against one wall there was a bar and on the floor a cattle skin. A TV was on top of a cabinet, so he could keep up to date with cricket and football scores.

Dave switched on the light and looked at the desk, wondering how had things gone so wrong. What had caused his dad to despise him so much?

Looking over his shoulder, he moved to the desk and flicked through the piles of bills to be paid and grain statements. He wasn't sure what he was looking for, but he thought perhaps the budget would hold a clue.

The heavy black cash-flow book was kept in the top drawer, and underneath it Dave found another book, one he hadn't seen before. Flicking it open, he saw it was a planner for the upcoming year and quickly made sense of the budget, which was on the first two pages.

It looked like they were going to be putting in more crop next year and scaling the sheep operation back. He drew in a sharp breath. His eyes followed the column down until he came to the wages section. Dean and Adam were listed there. They were getting two hundred dollars a week. Sam and Carlene were taking four hundred per week—that was understandable as it was their farm.

But Dave's name wasn't there.

He stared, unable to believe what he was seeing. Did his mum know about this or had Sam made the decision without talking to her? She wouldn't have ever agreed with him. His gut told him that she didn't know.

'Bastard!' he hissed.

'What?' Carlene stood at the door.

Unable to control his anger, Dave shot up. 'Did you know about this?' he asked in a low, measured voice. 'Did you?' He shook the book at her.

Carlene's eyes widened. 'What?' she asked, her fear obvious. 'Know about what?'

'That I'm not here next year? I'm not in the wages column and he's scaling the sheep operation back. He's chucking me out! Did you know, Mum?'

'No! I don't know anything. I don't know what you're talking about. Chucking you out? Maybe the budget isn't finished.'

'Oh, it's finished alright. And I'm not in it.'

'No,' Carlene whispered.

Dave saw as she swayed slightly and grabbed hold of the door, but was too angry to do anything.

'Yes,' Sam said, appearing next to her. Neither of them had heard him arrive.

Dave wanted to fly at him. 'You bastard,' he snarled. 'Why? Why after everything I've improved?'

'We can't afford you. Simple economic decision.'

'Sam!' Carlene's voice cut across them both.

'Stay out this,' Sam turned on her, his voice low and angry. 'Just shut up.'

'You're just going to kick me out? Out of the family business—with nothing.'

'Not nothing. You can take the ute and dog I bought you. But you need to be out of the shearers' quarters by the end of January. I can't afford to keep you here.'

'Sam!' Carlene gasped and grabbed at his arm. 'No, you can't . . .'

'I can. This is my farm. I warned you.' He pointed his finger at Dave. 'Warned you not to interfere and you've kept poking your nose where it shouldn't be. The quicker I'm rid of you, the better off we'll be.'

Carlene let out a high-pitched wail and slumped to the floor, still crying.

Dave stared at him, black dots covering his vision. Blindly he pushed past both his parents and ran out into the darkness. He heard his mum calling to him, but he kept going. Running. Running away to where his chest didn't hurt and he didn't feel betrayed.

❧

The wedding had gone ahead without him because, by morning, his ute had been packed and Jip clipped in the back. He didn't have many possessions, so it hadn't taken him long.

He'd driven aimlessly for three days, no idea where he was headed or what he was going to do.

When he eventually called his cousin Kate, Dave heard that his mother had fainted after he'd left. That was the only thing he regretted—not staying for her; not looking after her.

When he did stop, he wrote his mum a letter:

Dear Mum,
I hope you get this. I'm sending it via Georgie and Jack in case
Dad tries to hide it from you. I'm sorry to have worried you,

*but I'm okay. At this stage I'm in the south of WA, but I'm not
sure I'll stay here long.*

*In fact, I really have no idea what I'm going to do, but I
needed to write and say I love you and I'm sorry.*

I'll be in contact with an address later.

Love, Dave

He sealed the envelope and wrote his mother's name on
it and Georgie and Jack's address. As he sat in the ute, he
looked out across the vivid blue of the ocean from a beach
in a place called Esperance. He'd never heard of it before,
but it was pretty and he'd heard there was lots of work at
seeding time.

Maybe he'd stay here for a while, or maybe he'd move on.

Maybe one day he wouldn't be so angry and he'd be
able to go home. But not now.

Not for a long time.